A is for ABSTINENCE

KELLY ORAM

B
BLUEFIELDS

YA
891.

Published by Bluefields Creative

Copyright © 2014

Edited by Jennifer Henkes (www.literallyjen.com)

The characters and events portrayed in this book are fictitious. Any similarity to real persons, living or dead, is coincidental and not intended by the author.

ISBN 978-0-9914579-7-7

Also by Kelly Oram

Serial Hottie
The Avery Shaw Experiment
Cinder & Ella

The Jamie Baker Series:
Being Jamie Baker
More Than Jamie Baker

The V is for Virgin Series:
V is for Virgin

The Supernaturals Series:
Chameleon
Ungifted

For the fans!

1

B IS FOR BIRTHDAY

THE MUSIC IN THE CLUB STOPPED AND A SPOTLIGHT BLINKED on, momentarily blinding me as my eyes adjusted to the unexpected light. I wasn't surprised when I found myself staring down the world's biggest cake, but I acted the part anyway. Adrianna had gone to a lot of work to throw me this party. I wanted her to know I appreciated it.

"Happy birthday to you! Happy birthday to you! Happy birthday, dear Kyle! Happy birthday to you!"

I've spent my whole life performing for other people. It was nice to have them all sing to me for once.

"For he's a jolly good fellow! For he's a jolly good fellow! For he's a jolly good fellow, which nobody can deny!"

An arm slipped around my waist and Adrianna's soft lips brushed over my cheek. "Make a wish, birthday boy."

"Why would I need to do that?" I asked her. "I've already got everything I've ever wanted. Fame, money, a beautiful woman crazy enough to marry me…"

Adrianna gave me a look that sent shivers down my

spine. "If you don't make a wish, then how can I make it come true later tonight?"

The crowd of people around us laughed and jeered. I grinned at them. "I think my birthday wish list just became endless."

I swooped Adrianna into my arms and dipped her low. The kiss I planted on her hinted at exactly what I wanted from her for my birthday. After I set her back on her feet I finally blew out the candles—all twenty-five of them in one breath—and took a bow for the cheering crowd.

"Speech! Speech! Speech!"

"What can I say?" I asked, smirking for my friends. "It's good to be me!"

And that was the truth.

A lot of celebrities grumble about the inconvenience of fame—the lack of privacy, people only loving you for your money and connections, the constant hounding by fans and the paparazzi. I can't say I agree with them. If ever someone was meant to live the life of a celebrity, it was me.

I got my first taste of fame when I was eighteen and my band, Tralse, got our big break. Our song "Broken Passion" topped out at number one on the charts and our debut album went platinum. Our follow-up album, *S is for Sex*, went triple platinum, won six Grammys, and turned me into an international superstar.

For the last three years people have worshipped at my feet, and I've yet to tire of the attention. I'm never without friends or something to do, I always get everything I want, and I'm treated like a king wherever I go. I'm not ashamed to admit that I love it.

As someone started cutting the cake, the birthday guests

began chanting again. "Song! Song! Song! Song!"

Like with the money and attention, I never get tired of being asked to perform. I love being on stage, and now, ever since the band broke up, I don't get the chance to do it often enough.

Tralse got its start in my friend Reid's garage when he got a drum set for his birthday and called his four best friends to come have a jam session. We were all twelve years old. Shane and Dustin already played guitar, and I could sing. After that first night we forced Jeremy to learn the bass guitar so that we could be a complete band, and the rest was history.

About a year ago, Reid died of a drug overdose. The five of us were like brothers, and Reid's loss was devastating to all of us. The band didn't survive it. I stopped writing songs after that and haven't sung for an audience much since. But it was my birthday, and it was a great one so far, so I happily climbed up on stage.

The singer of the band Adrianna had hired for the night handed over the microphone with enthusiasm. "This is awesome, man," he said. "Tralse was our inspiration. We play a lot of covers, so the guys know all of your songs."

The thought of singing one of Tralse's songs without the guys to back me up felt sort of like someone trying to rip off a band-aid that had been fused to my skin for a year, but I saw the excitement in my fiancée's eyes and couldn't refuse.

Adrianna is, without a doubt, Tralse's biggest fan. I'd met her on the European leg of the *S is for Sex* tour. She and a group of her girlfriends followed us around the continent, sweet-talking their way backstage show after show. One night, I finally gave in and invited her to my tour bus after the show, and then I surprised everyone when I kept inviting her back. It took her six months to convince me to be exclusive, but we've been together ever since. For her, I could sing one of my old songs.

"The band says they know my stuff," I told the waiting audience. "What do you guys want to hear?"

As people started shouting out song titles, Adrianna took the microphone from me. "Oh no, you don't," she said to everyone. "He's *my* fiancé. This is *my* pick."

I laughed. "Anything for you, babe."

The look Adrianna gave me in response was a challenge. "I want to hear 'Cryin' Shame.'"

The "surprise" party hadn't been a surprise, but now I was shocked. She may as well have kicked me in the sac. The request was below the belt and she knew it. How could she ask me that? And in front of all of our friends?

The second I hesitated I knew I'd failed some kind of test. "Babe," I whispered, a sick feeling settling in my gut. "You know I don't sing that song anymore."

Everyone knew I didn't sing that song anymore. I'd written it for a girl, and, well, long story short: I didn't perform that song anymore. I hadn't since the first concert of the *S is for Sex* tour.

Taking my most popular song out of the set list had pissed off a lot people and disappointed a lot of fans, but I didn't care. I swore I'd never sing it again, and I intended to keep that promise. The guys were the only people who'd ever backed me up on that decision, until I'd met Adrianna. She'd always been supportive of me. I didn't understand why she was doing this now.

Adrianna put on her best pout for our audience and said, "Please, baby? It's my favorite. It was the first song of yours I ever heard, and the reason I fell in love with you. Won't you sing it for me just this once?"

I couldn't. She *knew* I couldn't. "Why are you doing this?" I whispered.

My heart physically hurt as I looked into her eyes and saw inexplicable anger there. I had no idea what I'd done to deserve this. "You love me, don't you?" she asked.

I wasn't sure why, but I started to feel panicked. "Of course I do."

Adrianna scoffed. "But you loved her more, didn't you? You can't sing that song for me because you never got over her. I'm just second best."

For the first time in my life, I wished I wasn't in front of a hundred curious people. The entire room was quiet, waiting to see what I would do. I could barely think, blindsided as I was by Adrianna's actions and the surprise resentment she held for my past.

When I looked back at Adrianna, her mouth curved into the tiniest smirk. It reeked of bitterness, but what pissed me off was the satisfaction in her expression. She was enjoying this ambush.

I pushed aside the hurt I felt and let anger take over. "I have always been faithful to you," I hissed, low enough that I hoped the whole room couldn't hear. "I've given you everything, including my heart. I don't deserve this. If you had a problem, you should have just talked to me about it."

I turned to the crowd and tried my best not to scowl at all my friends. "Thanks for the party, guys. Drinks are on me for the rest of the night."

I hopped off the stage and headed for the bar before everyone else in the club realized what I just said and made a mad rush for the booze. The only person in the club brave enough to approach me after that was Shane Leopard.

Shane used to be in Tralse with me and was my best friend. Shane, Reid, and I had been best friends since elementary school, and Reid's death hit us harder than the other guys. Since Reid's death, things were different between Shane and me. We barely spent any time together anymore. We were still best friends—brothers to the end, in a way—but hanging out was sometimes difficult now that our third amigo was missing.

"That was cold, man," Shane said as he slid into the chair next to mine and sipped a beer.

"No kidding."

A comfortable silence stretched out between us. Shane gave me fifteen minutes to drink in peace before he broke the silence. "So...maybe you should sing the song. I'll play for you, if it would help."

The offer was as huge as the request. I may have sung a song or two in the last year, but I don't think Shane had played for an audience even once since we buried our friend.

"You think I should just give her what she wants after that?"

Shane took another sip of his drink. "You love her, don't you?"

"Yeah, but—"

"Then you should do it." When I looked at my friend, he shrugged.

"I shouldn't have to. She has no reason to be jealous."

Shane laughed. "Women don't need a reason to be jealous. Hell, the only steady girlfriend I ever had besides Cara was Rebecca Carlisle back in high school. It only lasted about three months, but I lost my virginity to her and now Cara hates every woman in the world named 'Rebecca.' Her own niece is named Becca, and Cara got the whole family to start calling her by her middle name."

I smiled at that. Shane's fiancée Cara was a pistol of a woman. I couldn't imagine what she'd do if Shane even dared to look at another female. Which he never did, of course. Shane was the most pathetically whipped sucker on the planet.

"Women are always insecure about their boyfriends' past relationships," he said. "With one as notorious as yours, well…I can't blame Adrianna for being a little crazy about it. If you don't want to lose her, you're going to have to give her what she needs. Even if it means singing that song to prove you're really over it."

Singing that song again went against everything inside of me, but Shane was right.

"It's just a song, man. You can do it."

I sighed and then downed the rest of my drink. It wasn't just a song and Shane knew that better than anyone, but I appreciated the BS pep talk anyway. "Fine."

"That's my boy." Shane slapped me on the shoulder and got to his feet. "Let's go get this over with."

"Look, dude, this is my problem. I can handle it. You don't have to play for me."

"Don't worry about it. You know I've got your back."

I nodded, unable to tell Shane how grateful I was, but he didn't need to hear the words. He knew.

We waited until the band finished their set before we climbed up on stage. They were actually a pretty sweet group. "Hey, you guys are awesome," I said, shaking hands before I asked them to do me a favor.

"Especially you," Shane agreed, singling out their lead guitarist. "You kill it on that thing. What's your name?"

The guy's eyes lit up at the compliment. "Thanks. I'm Embry Jacobs," he answered, shaking both our hands with a little too much zeal. "I'm a big fan."

"You've got excellent taste in guitars, dude. You mind if I borrow that for a minute?"

Embry's eyes bulged. "You're going to play?"

Shane hid his distress better than I did. No one would know by the smirk on his face how hard this was for him. "Kyle's got a song to sing. Can't let him go it alone."

Embry happily handed the instrument over.

I took a deep breath as Shane pulled the strap over his head and slid his fingers over the strings. We looked at each other, our expressions identical: We were really about to do this.

Every member of Embry's band gaped at us. "You're really going to sing 'Cryin' Shame'?" Embry asked.

I glanced at him and then his bandmates. "You guys know it?"

They bobbed their heads, too stunned to reply vocally.

"Then I guess I'm going to sing it. Gotta give the woman what she wants."

I was sick to my stomach, but I felt a thrill of excitement as strong as my nerves as I stepped up to the mic. I loved this song as much as I hated it. "Hey, everyone!" I shouted, getting the attention of the entire club. I cleared my throat even though there was nothing stuck in it. "The lady asked for a song. I haven't sung this one in years, so, uh, bear with me if it's a bit rusty."

I waited for Adrianna to make her way to the stage but didn't see her.

"Adrianna, get up here. If I'm going to sing this for you, then I want you front and center."

The crowd fell silent when I got no response. "Adrianna? Babe?" A nervous laugh escaped me. "Has anyone seen my fiancée? I can't do this without her."

Heads twisted and turned, everyone searching for Adrianna, and I started to get a bad feeling. Shane must have felt the foreboding atmosphere too, because he stepped next to me just as we started hearing gasps.

The crowd parted like the Red Sea from the stage where I was to a booth in the back corner of the room where two people were locked in each other's arms. It was too dark to see anything other than their silhouettes, but the shock of the crowd told me enough.

The two dark outlines pulled apart, and though I couldn't make out her face, I could feel her stare burning into me. I knew I'd feel the sting of betrayal later, but right then I felt nothing. I was numb.

"Well, so much for that," I said into the mic. "Glad I didn't just make an ass of myself or anything."

I felt a hand come down on my shoulder. "Dude, let's just get out of here," Shane whispered.

I shrugged his hand off. "In a minute. I owe the woman a song first." I whirled around and looked at the nervous band behind me. "You guys know my song 'Giving You The Middle Finger'?"

Embry was the first to respond. His lips quirked into a smile and he took his guitar back from Shane. "Hell yeah, man."

2

C IS FOR CHEATERS

When I woke up, I knew I was in my own bed. Thousand-thread-count Egyptian cotton sheets don't lie. What I didn't know was the identity of the bombshell brunette sleeping in my arms.

I was seriously hungover. I'd been worse off before, but not by much and not often. I tried to think back to the previous night's activities, but things were a bit hazy. Something about a Lakers game and body shots with tequila.

Why I brought this woman home was beyond me. Don't get me wrong, I know exactly why I'd gone to bed with her—now that I think about it, I'm pretty sure she was a Lakers cheerleader, which, hello, yes, please—but why had we come back *here?* The rule was: always take women back to their place. It's easier to escape that way and seriously reduces the risk of psychotic stalkers breaking into your house.

Oh well, what was done, was done. Now I needed to figure out how to kick her out without seeming like a total douche. Maybe I'd offer to take her to breakfast before driving her home. First things first, though—coffee, Aspirin, and a nice, hot shower.

Gently, so as not to wake her up, I picked up her hand from my chest and slid away from her. My back bumped into something warm and solid. A soft moan sounded behind me and an arm slid around my waist. I wasn't alone in this bed. I mean, aside from the brunette.

I looked over my shoulder and was met with a sultry smile. Apparently, I had a hot blonde accessory to match the brunette. Two women at once wasn't a first for me, but it was rare.

"Morning, gorgeous," Blondie said, snuggling up to me.

Brunette stirred at the noise and snuggled in as well, placing a soft trail of kisses on my bare shoulder. One was bad enough. How the hell was I supposed to get rid of two of them?

"That was a wild night, huh?"

"Mmm," I agreed. It must have been, considering the significant lapse in memory. Maybe one or two less shots last night would have been better. "You two ladies sure know how to show a guy a great time."

"Just the two of them?" a third sleepy voice asked.

Three? Seriously?

A sexy redhead sat up and gave me a seductive pout.

Damn. That was new even for me. "I feel like I'm starring in my own personal joke. A blonde, a brunette, and a redhead wake up in your bed…"

The women all giggled, and the blonde tried to start a reenactment of whatever had happened last night, but I wasn't feeling it. My head hurt, I was cranky, I was pissed at myself for bringing them back home—and even with all three of them here, I couldn't shake the hurt from Adrianna. I just wanted these women to leave.

My prayers were answered in the most ironic way when my ex-fiancée burst into the room. "Playtime's over, sluts. You have thirty seconds to get out of my boyfriend's bed before I throw you out."

My guests weren't thrilled with the threat, and I really didn't want to indulge Adrianna's tantrum, but at least she'd solved my problem. "Sorry, ladies, it looks like the ex and I need to have a talk."

I got out of bed and pulled on a robe. As I tied it shut, I met Adrianna's heated glare with a bored look. "Apparently someone needs to go over proper breakup rules with her. For instance, not barging into my house uninvited, and minding her own damn business about my playtime."

I smiled at the women again and pointed to the master bathroom. "Shower's in there. Feel free to take your time. I'll get a pot of coffee going."

I followed Adrianna into the kitchen and started up the coffee machine. Adrianna waited until after I swallowed a handful of painkillers before she started in on me. "Three women at once, Kyle?"

It was hard to keep my temper in check. She shouldn't even be here, much less acting like a jilted lover. "Not just any women," I said, opening the fridge. "Professional cheer-leaders. Gymnasts."

Hmm…leftover Chinese takeout. Cold chow mien would do for now.

"How many women have you slept with this week?"

I shoved a forkful of noodles in my mouth and shrugged. "I haven't really kept count, why? How many men have you screwed? Aside from the one you left me for on my birthday, of course. I already know about him. *Celebrity Gossip* got a great money shot of you guys going back to his place after you broke my heart and humiliated me in front of half of L.A."

I pointed to the tabloid magazine cover of my fiancée cheating on me that I'd stuck to my fridge with magnets. I'm not sure why I'd displayed it like a Christmas card.

Adrianna looked at the picture and her face fell. Her big brown eyes misted over and her bottom lip quivered.

I had to look away. I hated her, but my love for her had been real. I was trying very hard to bury those feelings. If she cried, she was going to set me back.

The coffee was ready so I poured myself a steaming cup, dumped a little sugar in it, and took my breakfast out onto my back deck. I needed some air.

It was a beautiful Southern California day, and my Malibu estate was perched on the bluffs overlooking the Pacific Ocean. I took a deep breath, letting the smell of seawater, the cool ocean breeze, and the sound of the waves calm both my head and my nerves.

Adrianna joined me, cringing as she looked around. Her pain was as obvious as my own. Last week, sitting out on this deck together had been just part of our morning routine. We'd sip coffee, I'd update her on the Lakers or something I'd read in *SPIN* magazine, and she'd bore me to death with wedding details. Sounds dreadful, but I hadn't minded it. We were happy.

Adrianna broke the silence first. "I made a mistake."

Her voice shook as she wrestled with her emotions. It was a fight to control my own as well. "Vindictively ripping my heart out of my chest in front of all of our friends, and throwing away a two-and-a-half year long relationship because of a song was a *mistake*?"

"It wasn't about a *song*, Kyle!" Her eyes finally spilled over with tears. "It was about the fact that you couldn't sing it. It's been more than three years and you're still not over what happened."

"But *nothing* happened. You're jealous of a girl I never even dated."

Adrianna hit me with a hard stare. "You don't have to be in a relationship to be in love with someone."

"In *love* with…" I couldn't believe I was having this conversation. I'd buried every memory of the girl in question as deep as was possible. "Babe, how can you think I'm in love with her? I didn't even love her back then. Yeah, I hate singing the song, but I haven't thought about her in years."

"But you haven't let her go, have you?"

I turned my gaze back to the ocean and sipped my coffee in silence. What could I say? *Love* might have been overstating my feelings for Val, but she was the only girl in a very long string of women that ever got away. Because, like an ass, I'd let her go.

For months, Virgin Val Jensen had haunted my every thought day and night until I was forced to block her from my memory altogether. Once I was able to shut that Pandora's box, I made sure to lock it up tight and lose the key. But closure was something Val and I had never accomplished.

I pushed Val from my mind and focused on my current problem. "I loved *you*, Adrianna. Whatever condition my heart was in, *you* had it."

"I know," Adrianna whispered, dabbing at her eyes with

a tissue. "I can see that now. I can see how much I hurt you, and I'm sorry."

She was *sorry*? I scoffed into my coffee. She wasn't the only one who was sorry.

"I made a mistake, Kyle," she pleaded. "When you refused to sing that song, it hurt. Brian made me feel better in the moment, but he meant nothing. I was angry and upset and scared of having to compete with a memory forever. But I knew I was wrong when I realized what you were doing up on that stage."

"Yet, you still went home with him that night."

Adrianna threw her hands up in exasperation. "Well, you stomped out without talking to me! You sang that awful song and told me to have a nice life."

"Right. Which usually means the person saying it doesn't ever want to see the person they say it to ever again. So what are you doing here right now? Why storm into my bedroom and kick out my company like you have the right to do it?"

Adrianna reached across the small patio table and took my hand in hers. "Because I love you. We can get past this, Kyle. We both made some mistakes this week, so let's just agree to—"

"*You* made mistakes this week," I corrected, pulling my hand out of hers. "I did nothing wrong. I didn't go to bed with anyone until *after* that picture ended up on my fridge. My fiancée cheated on me. I'm entitled to cope with that however I want."

I got up from the table and leaned over the balcony railing. After taking a deep breath I faced her again. "I might have been able to forgive the kissing, but you went home with him. And don't say it was because I left. I kept my cell turned on all night. I waited for you to call. I would have sold my soul to the devil for one lousy text, I was that desperate for you to come back."

Adrianna joined me at the railing, desperation in her eyes. "I was hurt!" she said. "That song you sang—"

I'd tried so hard to keep a leash on my temper, but now I didn't want to. She had some nerve. "*You* were hurt?" I shouted. "How do you think *I* felt? At any time in the past *two and a half years*, you could have asked me about Valerie. Instead you chose to hurt and humiliate me in front of all of our friends. And the worst part is, you *enjoyed* it. I saw the look in your eyes when you realized I was falling apart inside."

I paused, giving her the chance to defend herself, but her guilt kept her silent.

I turned my head back to the view. "If you cared about me half as much as I cared about you, you would never have been able to treat me like that. Much less revel in your victory."

"Kyle…"

I heard the sob in the word, but I refused to look at her. She didn't deserve my compassion or forgiveness. "We're over, Adrianna. Leave your key and my ring on the counter on your way out."

She hesitated a minute but left without another word. I waited until I heard the front door slam before heading back inside. I was relieved when I found a note next to the empty coffee pot from the Laker Girl trio, and even more thankful to see Shane standing there raiding my fridge. He went for the carton of leftover takeout I hadn't eaten yet.

"A blonde, a brunette, and a redhead walk into a bar,"

he said as he turned around and leaned against the counter. "Which one do you take home?"

"Why settle for one when you can have all three?" I joked.

Shane shook his head and shoved a forkful of sweet and sour pork in his mouth.

"And I didn't pick them up in a bar." I stole the carton of food and the fork from his hands. I took a big bite and grinned at the man with cheer I didn't feel. "They were cheerleaders. Laker Girls, to be exact. I picked them up at the game."

Shane raised an eyebrow at me. He tried to hold a straight face but eventually broke down in laughter. "That's impressive, even for you."

"I guess it's nice to know I've still got it."

I sighed and plopped down at the kitchen table with my cold Chinese. Shane settled for a banana and a glass of milk and joined me. His tone sobered a little as he asked, "How'd Adrianna handle it?"

"About how you'd expect her to." I rubbed my hands over my face in an attempt to push away my headache. I was pretty sure the pounding had more to do with Adrianna than last night's tequila. "I'd say I felt sorry for her, but..."

"Yeah, I heard. Brutal. You okay?"

I glanced at Shane over the carton of pork. "I don't need to cry on your shoulder if that's what you're asking, you douche."

Shane snorted. "Well, could you at least tell my fiancée you need to? She sent me over here to make sure you're still planning to come to the wedding this weekend, but she only gave me permission to stay for twenty minutes. There was some sort of centerpiece catastrophe this morning and she's freaking out. I *really* don't want to deal with a centerpiece crisis."

Shane picked up the cheer squad's note and chuckled. It was covered with lipstick kisses and cell phone numbers. "Unless, of course, you'd rather hang me out to dry for a better offer."

I groaned. "Honestly, I think I've had my fill of all women for a while. Promise me a day of nothing but mindless action movies, video games, In-N-Out burger, and a case of beer, and I'll cry real tears for your psycho fiancée."

Shane gripped my shoulder and bore a solemn look into my eyes that made me laugh. "My hero."

3

W IS FOR WEDDING

THERE'S ONLY ONE THING WORSE THAN WEDDINGS, AND that's alcohol-free weddings. Cara's father was a sober alcoholic for eight years now, so they'd banned all alcohol from the reception. I respected their decision, but I seriously needed a drink.

At least the DJ was decent. Of course, this was *Cara's* wedding, so I wouldn't have expected otherwise. She's always had excellent taste in music, and I had no doubt she went bridezilla on the playlist.

Actually, as far as weddings go, this one was pretty amazing—lack of alcohol notwithstanding. The food was great, the music rocked, the guest list was small, Cara was a gorgeous bride—and hey, it was in Hawaii. If only I could get someone to bring me a damn glass of whiskey to help me forget the fact that two weeks ago I was cake testing with my own bridezilla.

"Why did I come to this thing?"

It was a rhetorical question, but my ex-bandmate Dustin

answered it anyway. "Because it's Shane." He took a swig of his soda and cringed. The poor guy didn't want to be sober right now any more than I did. Of course, he *never* wanted to be sober. He let out a burp and then added, "You know Cara would have thrown an epic hissy if you'd bailed."

That was true. Cara made a huge deal about having all of us here. It was the first time the guys had all gotten together since Reid's funeral. The whole band together was the only wedding gift she'd asked for from any of us. It was awkward as hell, but Cara was right: We needed to be here for Shane today. Plus, between you and me, I was afraid of the woman. If she said jump…

"Hey, man, at least you're going to get something out of it." Dustin nudged my shoulder and nodded across the room. "The maid of honor has been mentally screwing you since you showed up."

I followed his gaze out to the dance floor where the woman in question was engaged in the obligatory dance with the best man. Shane's younger brother was staring at her chest while she stared at me. When I met her eyes, her face heated up with desire. I knew that look well. I wouldn't even have to make conversation with her. I could just nod my head toward the exit and she'd follow me up to my hotel room.

She was hot. No question about it. She was an actress on that soap opera with Cara. I'm pretty sure she got the part for two reasons—the two reasons that her barely-not-a-teenager-anymore dance partner was still ogling.

"Maybe I should go save her from the twerp."

Dustin slid a curious glance at me but didn't say what was on his mind. Instead he shrugged and said, "If you don't,

I will."

I looked at Dustin again and saw something that pissed me off. Pity. The guy was pushing me toward the easy lay because he felt sorry for me. Suddenly determined to prove to the world—and especially to Dustin—that Kyle Hamilton is not a man to be pitied, I made my way out to the dance floor. Screw the fact that this was the "first dance," or whatever. I was cutting in.

"Excuse me. Would you mind if I—"

"I'd love to!"

The maid of honor was already in my arms before poor Ben even realized I was there. I shrugged off his glare and pulled the beautiful woman close. She smelled good and wore a dress that left almost nothing to the imagination.

She batted a pair of big brown eyes up at me and chewed on a very full, pouty, sexy bottom lip. "I was hoping you'd ask me to dance," she said.

I'd done this so many times in the past that my responses were automatic. "How could I resist the most beautiful woman in the room?"

"You'd better not let Cara hear you call me that today."

"It'll be our secret."

I winked and she gave me a sultry smile before she laid her head on my shoulder. The way her chest pressed against me was no accident. This woman was as familiar to the game as I was—a pro. Still, it was only polite to at least make some small talk before dragging her upstairs. "So you work with Cara?"

"Yeah." Maid of Honor looked around the room and then gave me another flirty smile. "What do you say we move this dance somewhere more private? I have a room upstairs."

I smirked. So much for politeness. "Don't you have some sort of wedding duties to uphold as the maid of honor?"

She shrugged. "It'll be at least forty-five minutes before they cut the cake and toss the bouquet."

My eyes fell to her chest. I know I was just bustin' on Ben for that, but I couldn't help it. It was such a nice chest—expensive, no doubt—and the rest of her was just as perfect. I tried to imagine all the things I could do with a body like hers, tried to get myself psyched for it.

I slid my hands low, enjoying a PG-13 sneak preview of events to come. Maid of Honor shivered with pleasure. She tilted her chin up, parting her lips slightly. It was a clear invitation, so I kissed her.

The kiss was pretty heated. She was in to it. She was *definitely* in to it. But I wasn't. There was nothing there for me. No fire. No spark. I was only going through the motions. I knew going up to her room with her would take the edge off, but for some reason it still didn't seem worth the hassle.

I stopped kissing her, surprised by my thoughts. Casual sex with a beautiful woman didn't seem worth the hassle? *What the hell?*

"Is there a problem?" she whispered as she swept her lips over my throat.

Was there a problem? I had no idea. I had no clue what was going on right now. I'd never experienced anything like this before.

Maid of Honor stopped her oral assault on my neck when someone cleared their throat. The bride and groom had twirled their way over and were watching us with amused looks on their faces.

"I see you've met Aphrodite," Cara teased.

Maid of Honor's name was Aphrodite? What kind of name was Aphrodite? A stage name. Because she's an actor. Like the jerk that banged my fiancée. I hate actors.

"We haven't met *properly*." Aphrodite giggled. "Would you guys mind holding off on the cake and bouquet and all that for a while? Promise we won't be gone long."

I waited for Cara to explode into a rage, but she didn't seem surprised by her friend's request. She rolled her eyes and said, "Thirty minutes or I'll throw it without you."

Aphrodite beamed and made air kisses at Cara. "Love you, babe. You're the best!"

She grabbed my hand but I pulled back before she could drag me out of the room. When she questioned me, I wasn't sure what to say to her. I wasn't sure what my problem was. But then I found myself saying, "Actually, I think I'll stay here."

I shocked Shane, Cara, and especially Aphrodite speechless. Aphrodite gaped up at me with those big blue eyes as if she couldn't quite comprehend what was happening. "Sorry," I told her. "You're a beautiful woman and all, but it's not going to happen. At least not with me." I pointed to my lonely bandmate and added, "Dustin would probably give you a go, though."

Aphrodite's eyes bugged and I knew what was coming. I didn't even try to avoid the slap when she raised her hand. I deserved it. She called me a very impressive string of curses and then stomped off to the ladies' room.

I turned to my two bewildered friends and gave them my most sheepish smile. "At least she didn't have a glass of champagne in her hand. I hear that stuff stings when it gets in your eyes."

They both continued to stare at me slack-jawed, waiting for an explanation I didn't have.

"What the hell was *that*?" Cara asked.

I cringed, realizing I might have really upset the bride on her big day. "Sorry if I just ruined your wedding or something. I didn't mean to insult your friend. I just wasn't feeling it."

I waited for the kind of emotional outburst that Adrianna would have definitely had if she were in Cara's position, but Cara burst into laughter. "I never, ever thought I'd see the day!" she cried, gasping through her giggle fit. "Kyle Hamilton getting slapped for refusing an offer instead of making one."

"Quick, call Guinness!" Shane chimed in. He was laughing so hard he had to grab onto my shoulder to keep from falling over. "This has to be some sort of record."

They didn't mean any harm, but I still got irritated. I knew it was ironic as hell, but I just couldn't share their humor. This wasn't funny to me. It was disturbing. What the hell was wrong with me?

I sighed and forced a smile on my face that I knew wouldn't fool anyone. "Congratulations, you guys. If you need me, I'll be in the hotel bar."

I WAS BUSY NURSING A GLASS OF SCOTCH WHEN CARA SAT down on the stool beside mine. "Skipping out on your own wedding reception?" I asked.

"Just taking a quick breather." She slapped her hand down on the counter. "Can someone get me a drink? Something strong."

"Mother-in-law?" the bartender guessed, chuckling as he slid a shot glass in front of her and filled it with vodka.

Cara pounded the shot back like a pro. She winced from the burn of the alcohol and groaned. "That woman drives me crazy."

This time I laughed, too.

Cara slung her arm over my shoulder. "Thanks for coming today. I know it couldn't have been easy so soon after…"

I was glad when her voice trailed off. "It's okay. I'm over it."

Cara raised an eyebrow at me, calling me out on the lie.

"No, I am," I insisted.

"Then what was all that back there?"

I shrugged, downed the rest of my drink, and then gestured for the bartender to refill my glass. "Hell if I know."

"Have you been with anyone since Adrianna?" she asked.

My shirt collar suddenly felt too tight. When tugging at it didn't help, I took my tie off and unbuttoned the top button of my shirt. "More than you want to know about in that first week," I said once I could breathe again. "But when it didn't make me feel any better I just…lost interest."

"You *lost interest?*"

I shrugged again. "I had something—*thought* I had something special with Adrianna. I guess the casual thing just seems…pointless now. Not worth the trouble."

"Wow." Cara blinked at me in surprise, but her reaction was still sincere.

I cursed when I realized what I'd just said. "She's ruined me, hasn't she? I'm broken now."

Cara stole a sip of my drink and then laughed a little. "Maybe," she agreed. "I guess it depends on how you look at it. I bet if you asked Val she'd say Adrianna fixed you."

Val. As in Cara's old best friend Valerie Jensen. As in the one and only Virgin Val. The girl my fiancée accused me of being in love with and cheated on me because of. What was it with everyone bringing up the past lately?

"Good old Virgin Val." I drew the name out in a long sigh. After a pause, I shook my head and took another drink. "How is she?" I asked slowly. Carefully. Grudgingly. My thoughts had turned to her more than once since my breakup with Adrianna. "Is she still a virgin, or did she actually find her perfect saint of a man?"

Cara swallowed hard. It took her a minute to respond. "I don't know," she whispered.

And then it hit me. "She's not here today." I knew Cara and Val had drifted apart after high school, but I couldn't believe Val would blow off Cara's wedding. "I'm sorry."

Cara shrugged. "I didn't invite her."

At my surprised look, she stole my drink again. "I wanted to, but in the end I couldn't do it. We haven't spoken since that night at the Tralse concert. I couldn't send her an invite because I was afraid she wouldn't come. I'm sad she's not here, but I'll get over it this way. Her blowing me off would have broken my heart."

In a blink, the hotel bar was gone and I was back on that stage from over three years ago. That moment at the concert with Val had been one of the best of my life. It had been Tralse's first-ever sold-out stadium show and we'd put on the greatest performance of our lives. The crowd had gone insane when I demanded Val join me onstage. She'd played along with me for once and had genuinely enjoyed herself.

Val and I reached a truce that night. She'd surprised me more than anyone ever had as she stood in front of me in that maddeningly sexy skirt and made me beg on my knees for her forgiveness. I'll never forget the look on her face as she struggled not to smile. That grin had been an unspoken acknowledgement of the friendship we'd developed that she'd never admitted existed.

"Kyle?"

"Huh?"

I shook myself from the memory and tried to focus on Cara. Her eyes had glossed over so I handed her a cocktail napkin. Guilt swelled up in me as she dabbed at her eyes. Cara and Val's friendship had been ruined because of me. I was the one who had come between them. "I'm sorry, Cara."

Cara squeezed my hand and shook her head. "It wasn't your fault. We all made mistakes back then."

"I made the most," I muttered.

We fell into silence, both lost in thought, each probably remembering that whole crazy affair and wondering how we could have done things differently. I had the added pleasure of comparing the one that got away with the one I should have thrown back.

"Hey, Cara, what's your biggest regret in life?"

Cara's response was quick. "Losing Val."

I smirked. Her and me both.

You would think my failed engagement was my biggest regret, but you'd be wrong. I'd spent the last two weeks looking back on my relationship with Adrianna and I realized now that I was better off without her. I'd hooked up with her to take my mind off of someone else and kept her around because it was easier.

I did grow to love Adrianna, but it had never been one of those life-altering, earth-shattering romances they make movies about. Three years from now there wouldn't be a song I still couldn't sing because I couldn't stand to think of her. I never even wrote her a song. Val was different. Even though we'd never had a real relationship, the girl got under my skin and messed with my head the way no one else ever had.

I felt Cara look at me, but I kept my gaze trained on my glass.

I never talked about the last time I saw Val—the night we said good-bye. I never told anyone but Shane about the kiss we'd shared that night. Only Shane knew that she'd offered her whole heart to me with only one condition—and that I'd been too scared, stubborn, and prideful to accept it.

Not knowing what else to say, I kicked back the rest of my drink in one shot. "Congrats on the marriage, Cara. It was a hell of a wedding."

Cara squeezed me in a tight hug. "Thanks for being here," she said again. "I know it was hard for you to come."

"Not at all," I lied. "Besides, this is your day. It's not about me."

Cara nudged my side with her elbow. "For once," she teased. "Come on, rock star. We'd better get back in there before Shane starts to think I finally fell for the great Cheerleader Seducer."

I laughed and tried not to look too proud. "Shane told you about that, huh?"

Cara gave me the sigh that made her so famous on her soap opera as she dragged me back into the reception hall. "My dear, sweet Kyle. Shane tells me *everything*."

4

M IS FOR MEMORIES

CARA NEVER CEASES TO AMAZE ME. SHE AND SHANE ONLY closed on their new house two weeks ago, and somehow she'd thrown together a housewarming party as glamorous as her wedding. The 3.5 million dollar spread up Laurel Canyon was almost as sweet as my place in Malibu, and tonight it was decked out with so many fresh flowers and twinkling lights you could both see and smell it from miles away. The potted orchid in my hands seemed rather ridiculous now.

"Kyle!" I hadn't been in the front door two seconds before Cara threw her arms around me and kissed my cheek. "You made it!"

"Congrats on the new house." I handed over the flower. "The guy told me it's supposed to be a symbol of wealth, beauty, love, and elegance."

"My kind of flower."

Cara grinned. Her happiness made her sparkle with radiance under the soft light. It could have been the glittery makeup causing her to sparkle, but the glow was definitely happiness.

"And for Shane...," I said, holding up a six-pack of Corona.

Cara gave me a look. "Beer?"

"Hey, this is the good stuff," I defended myself. "Plus, I thought you'd kill me if I showed up with the vintage pinball machine I wanted to get him."

Cara laughed. "You're right. Thank you. I think Shane's out back." She pointed to the beers in my hand. "Do *not* use those as an excuse for the two of you to sneak off and disappear all night. As I have warned him several times, he is a host this evening. He has to mingle. And as for *you*, I have someone I want you to meet."

Was it too late to get my keys back from the valet? I turned around and tried to walk back out the door.

Cara grabbed me by the collar of my leather jacket. "Oh no, you don't!" At my frown, she said, "Come on, Kyle. She's gorgeous and really fun. You'll like her. I promise."

"Like the last one?"

Cara rolled her eyes at me. Last time she'd tried to set me up with some woman she met in her yoga studio. I'd had to get a restraining order.

"No, not like the last one. Candy is a friend of mine," Cara insisted. "Prescreened and certified nonpsychotic."

"Candy?"

Cara waved a dismissive hand. "This is L.A. You know how it is."

Yes, I knew how it was all too well. "Maybe now would be a good time to tell you that I've had a change of heart. Jumped the fence. Swapped teams. Whatever you want to call it. Women no longer interest me, so there's no point in trying to introduce me to every single woman on the planet anymore."

Cara folded her arms over her chest and raised an eyebrow. "Gay? That's your excuse this time?"

"Yup. I've rediscovered my sexuality." I patted her shoulder. "I'm so sorry to disappoint you, Cara. Give my apologies to your friend."

"No worries." She flashed me a brilliant smile. "If it's men you seek now, then I have *two* people I'd like you to meet tonight. Edwin will be thrilled. He's a big fan of yours."

I turned and banged my head against the wall. "Cara, please. I came to the damn party. Can't that be enough?"

"I'm worried about you, Kyle."

I stopped abusing my forehead and turned back around. "I'm fine. I'm just sick of dating. All the women people have pushed at me since Adrianna are all the same. I want something real. I want what you and Shane have, and I'm not going to find it with Muffin or Lollypop, or whatever her name is."

"Candy." Cara sighed.

She looked up at me with a calculating expression that I found highly disconcerting. I loved the woman dearly, but she was a meddler, and her schemes had a tendency to end in disaster.

"Can I go find Shane now?"

"Promise the two of you won't disappear?"

"Cross my heart and hope to die."

Cara narrowed her eyes. "You *will* hope to die if you let my husband ditch this party. I will bring you so much pain I'll have you begging for mercy."

"Understood."

Cara gave me another warning look, then stepped aside. "Check out by the pool."

The backyard was even more spectacular than the house. The people who went crazy with the twinkle lights had not forgotten about the trees and bushes around the edge of the lawn. There was a fire ablaze in a pit on the deck, and the pool was lit up. Candles made the water lilies floating on top of the water glow and caused shadows to dance around the yard. And then there was the view. The house was perched on the side of the hill, and the entire city of Los Angeles spread out for miles below.

I found Shane standing near the gazebo, looking absolutely miserable as he nodded along to some conversation he wasn't paying the least bit of attention to. When I waved and held up the six-pack, his eyes lit up with relief and he practically ran across the yard to me.

"You're a saint! I thought for sure you'd bail."

I laughed. He was truly desperate. "Please tell me this place has a secret man cave somewhere."

Shane took one of the beers and snapped the top off on the deck railing. After he chugged half the bottle, he headed back in the house. "This way."

"We just can't get caught by your wife. She promised to make me suffer if I let you skip out."

Shane laughed, but he still stopped heading toward the living room and took me to a stairway on the other side of the house. "She knows I hate this crap. Her bark is worse than her bite, I promise."

"Says the man peeking his head around a corner to make sure the coast is clear."

Shane flipped me off, then pushed me up the stairs.

"Hurry. There're enough people here that she'll never miss us, but if she *sees* us leave, we're dead."

We made it safely to Shane's den. There was a pool table, a minibar, and a killer entertainment system. I smirked as I eyed the room. Should have gone with the pinball machine after all.

"Now this is more like it," I said, falling to the leather sofa.

Shane cracked open another beer and handed it to me.

"Hey, does that door lock?" I asked. "I really have to stay hidden. Your wife's trying to set me up again. Jolly Rancher or Snickers or something."

"Candy." Shane shuddered. "Run while you can, dude. That one is crazy."

A comfortable silence settled between us as we each sipped our beers.

"So, how's the married life treating you?" I asked.

Shane let out a breath and bobbed his head. "It's good. Not a lot different than the last three years we've been living together, but Cara seems happier."

I had to agree. "She did have a certain glow about her tonight."

Shane smiled. "The woman loves to entertain."

I finished my scope of the man cave and noticed that the far corner of the room was all devoted to Shane's music. Framed photos hung on the walls with some of our band's awards, and his instruments all stood on their stands, polished and shiny.

I emptied the last of my beer, then wandered over and picked up a bass guitar. My voice was my main instrument, but I played a little piano and could get by on bass, electric, and acoustic guitars.

My fingers curled around the neck of the guitar. I hadn't picked one up in months, but plucking at the strings was instinctive.

"Hey, remember this?" I asked, laughing a little to myself. I plugged the guitar into an amp and ripped out the bass line to Metallica's "Orion."

Shane laughed. He plugged his guitar in too and nodded at me. Before we knew it, we were jamming the way we used to back in high school. One song became two, became three. Metallica, Pink Floyd, The Beatles. Hell, we even got some Chili Peppers in there.

Then, suddenly, for no reason, I wailed out the intro to "Cryin' Shame." Shane didn't question me; he just followed along and I fell into a zone. When I opened my mouth, the words came out impassioned—filled with confusion, anger, and even desperation. I sang my heart out as I hadn't done in years.

> *She's smokin' hearts with a burnin' flame*
> *She's got a wild side without a name*
> *And when she's riled it's a cryin' shame*
> *Yeay! Yeah! Yeah! I've got it bad*
> *Yeah! Yeah! Yeah! I'm goin' mad*
>
> *'Cause in your head you've got it right*
> *Won't go to bed without a fight*
> *You think you're wise, you think it shows*
> *So show me wise without those clothes*
>
> *She's playin hardball and it's nothin' new*
> *Short skirts so enjoy the view*

She's a cold blooded tease baby through and through
Yeay! Yeah! Yeah! I've got it bad
Yeah! Yeah! Yeah! I'm goin' mad

'Cause in your head you've got it right
Won't go to bed without a fight
You think you're wise, you think it shows
So show me wise without those clothes

Come on legs don't go to waste
I could be your only savin' grace
Put those morals on the backburner
Something tells me you're a fast fast learner
Yeay! Yeah! Yeah! I've got it bad
Yeah! Yeah! Yeah! I'm goin' mad

'Cause in your head you've got it right
Won't go to bed without a fight
You think you're wise, you think it shows
So show me wise without those clothes

When it was over, I stood there: chest heaving, heart pounding, hands shaking. I wasn't sure where that had come from or why it chose that moment to burst out of me, but it had been a release I'd desperately needed.

"Feel better?"

Shane was watching me with a curious look.

I took a deep breath and attempted to pull myself back together. "A little," I admitted as I set the guitar back on its stand. "I don't know why that song haunts me so much."

"It's not the song that haunts you," said a soft voice, startling both Shane and me.

We whirled around at the intrusion to see Cara standing

in the doorway to the den, clutching some kind of book to her chest. Her eyes were misted over.

Shane panicked. "Babe! Hey! I was just giving Kyle the grand tour. I swear we were on our way back downstairs."

"I'm sure." Cara gave us a knowing smile and shook her head. "It's okay...this time."

She stepped in the room and shut the door behind her. Shane rushed to her side, whispering apologies and gratitude and other stuff I didn't need to hear that made Cara giggle and stick her tongue in his mouth. They've always been gross like that.

I cleared my throat, and Cara smiled at me. "It sounded good," she said.

I shrugged uncomfortably, having no idea what to say.

She held out the gigantic book in her arms. "I have something for you."

"What is it?"

She laid the book on the pool table and opened it to the first page. "This is the keepsake journal I made during the *S is for Sex* tour."

"You made a scrapbook?"

I slid up next to her and stared down at the pages as she slowly turned them. They were filled with pictures, magazine clippings, ticket stubs... Each page brought back a minefield of memories.

"It's not the song that haunts you, Kyle," she said again. "Remember this?"

She flipped to the last page in the book where a small, clear pencil bag was clasped into the book's rings.

Something twisted inside me at the sight of my old abstinence bracelet laying in the bag. I pulled the leather band out of the pencil bag and ran my fingers over the small silver *A* charm. "I thought I lost this."

"You almost did," Cara said. "I was backstage with Adrianna the night she found it. I barely stopped her from throwing it out. It was near the end of the tour and the bracelet was in the pocket of the pants you'd worn onstage that night. Adrianna was livid when she realized you'd been carrying it with you all that time—that you kept it on you while you performed, like it was some sort of lucky charm."

When I squirmed and started to back away, Cara grabbed my hand. "It's okay," she said, which only embarrassed me even more. "I kept my necklace, too. You weren't the only one who felt her loss."

"I don't know why I kept it." The confession came out in a whisper.

"Because you loved her, Kyle."

I'd been staring at the bracelet, but my head snapped up. Cara met my gaze with solemn determination. She was not about to let me deny it.

I dropped the bracelet and pushed away from the pool table. "Why does everyone keep saying that?" I asked, raking my hands through my hair as if that could solve the mystery. "Adrianna accused me of the same thing. Hell, it was the reason we broke up. But I *didn't* love her."

Cara gave me a look as if to say, "Yeah right."

She was crazy. I liked Val, sure. Wanted her? Hell yeah, more than anything. I'll even admit that I cared about her. But love? How can you fall in love with someone you never even dated?

"Maybe I was a little infatuated, but—"

"People get over infatuation. They don't take their

biggest hit out of the set list, even when their management team threatens to sue."

When she put it that way…

But that was crazy. It wasn't possible. Was it?

"Maybe you didn't know it," Cara said, breaking me from my thoughts, "but you loved her."

For reasons I couldn't explain, anger swept through me. "So what if I did?" I snapped. "What the hell does it matter? That was years ago. It's *over*."

"Is it?"

So now she was accusing me of still not being over Val, too? She was as bad as Adrianna. What the hell? Was the whole world conspiring against me? Why couldn't anyone just let it go? If I was still hung up on Val, I didn't see how people constantly throwing it in my face was supposed to help me.

I grabbed another beer from Shane's six-pack. Shane was ready and waiting with a bottle opener, a look of apology in his eyes.

I fell to the couch again and tried to drink away my frustration. Cara sat down beside me and placed her hand on my knee. "I haven't kept in touch with Val, but it seems Google still knows her pretty well."

I stopped drinking my beer and eyed Cara. I didn't know where she was going with this, but I was sure it was no place good.

"Word is she's single."

And now I understood. I buried my face in my hands and resisted the urge to yank fistfuls of my hair out.

"You said you want something real," Cara said. "I think you and I both know where you can find it."

I cursed Cara for even suggesting the idea, but at the same time the seed was planted. Hope exploded inside me. As much as I tried to push it down, I knew it wasn't going anywhere.

"Cara." I groaned. I didn't know what I felt right then other than an urge to strangle my best friend's wife.

"How long has it been since you've been with a woman?" Cara asked.

I glared at her, and she pinned me with a defiant look. I lost the battle of wills. "The cheer squad," I admitted with a sigh of defeat.

"That was two months ago, Kyle."

I glared again. "I don't need the reminder."

Cara's answering smile was full of mischief. Her face lit up and she grabbed my hand. My heart skipped a beat or two when she clasped the abstinence bracelet around my wrist. "Why don't you give your dry spell a purpose?" she said.

The bracelet felt heavy on my arm—its significance weighed me down. In all the months I'd carried the bracelet with me, all the shows that I'd kept it close, I'd never actually put it on. I couldn't do it, knowing what it stood for.

Cara kissed my cheek and left the room without another word. I continued to stare down at my wrist, my thoughts and feelings swirling out of control. This bracelet didn't just symbolize a conscious choice to abstain from sex. It represented the only thing that ever came between Val and me. This bracelet—and all it stood for—was the key to bridging the gap between us.

Could it really be possible? Could I do it? Did Val and I still have a chance? Did I even want to try and find out?

I knew the answer immediately. Hell yes, I wanted to find out. If there was even the slightest chance that a future with Val was possible, then you bet your ass I wanted it.

"Uh-oh."

Shane's chuckle startled me out of my epiphany. "What?"

"I know that look."

"What 'look'?"

Shane smirked. "That screw-the-world-I'm-about-to-write-a-chart-topper look."

I was startled again. I hadn't been thinking up lyrics just now, had I? I hadn't written a single song since Reid died and the band broke up. But now that he mentioned it, I recognized the familiar itch in the back of my brain.

Shane and I looked at each other for a long moment, and then he burst into laughter. "Well, I'll be damned. Virgin Val strikes again."

I stood up and punched Shane in the arm. "Shut up, jackass."

He punched me back. "You'd better let me hear it when you're finished. I doubt the guys will want to get back together without Reid, but if you go solo, you'll need a lead guitarist for your backup band and I'll kick your ass if it's anyone but me."

5

T IS FOR TALK SHOWS

SIX MONTHS LATER

THE LAST TIME I WROTE VAL A SONG, SHE LOATHED IT. CARA assured me things would be different this time, but I still couldn't shake the feeling that this plan was going to blow up in my face.

"Cara!" Shane hollered. "Get a move on it! You're going to be late!"

Seconds later, Cara came rushing down the stairs dressed in a different outfit than she'd been wearing when I arrived ten minutes ago. "What do you think? Conservative enough?"

She tugged at the hem of her jeans skirt with shaking hands. I'd never seen her such a nervous wreck. "Babe." Shane pulled her into his arms and planted a kiss on her forehead. "It's going to be fine."

Cara started searching through her gigantic purse for a

tube of lip gloss. Some people smoked cigarettes or chewed nails; Cara applied lip gloss. "I just can't believe she called me," she said, waving a wand over her lips with a shaking hand. "We haven't spoken in four years. I was sure she hated me."

"You guys were best friends forever," Shane reassured her. "You know she could never really hate you."

I would never have admitted it, but I was probably more nervous than she was. "Just play it cool, okay?" I said, giving her a hug. "Remember today is supposed to be a total surprise, so you can't let on that you know anything about it."

Some of Cara's nerves melted away and she gave me a cocky grin. "Have some faith in my ability," she said. "I am an award-winning actress, you know."

"Daytime," I teased, as if it were a lesser accomplishment. Ever since she won Best Supporting Actress for her role on that soap, I'd teased her mercilessly. She loved it. She knew how proud I was of her.

"Be nice, or I'll spill the beans," she threatened.

She gave Shane one last kiss and climbed into her car. Once the top was down and she'd wrapped a scarf around her head to keep her hair in place, she blew Shane and me each a kiss. "We're going to see Val!" she squealed as she drove off.

We watched the car disappear around the bend and Shane turned to me. "You ready for this?"

I felt myself grin. I was more ready for this than I'd ever been for anything in my life. Six months of hard work, and today would be my first payoff. I hoped.

Shane and I climbed into my car. Cara was having lunch with Val, but Shane and I had to be at the studio early for sound check. This was it. Today I was finally going to see Val again.

Shane said nothing about the way my knee bounced uncontrollably all the way to the studio. Then, he kept quiet about my nervous pacing once we were in a special guest lounge waiting to surprise Val. He did raise an eyebrow when I passed up the buffet table—crafty had gone all out for us today—but otherwise he let me keep pretending I was fine. It was Embry who finally called me out.

Once I'd written a few songs, Shane and I had to find a band to help us lay a demo track. We'd contacted the awesome cover band from my birthday party and we'd liked them so much we asked them to stay on as my official band for my solo album. They were psyched, and we killed it in the studio. Not to pat myself on the back or anything, but my new album was sick. I had more Grammys in my future.

"Relax, dude," Embry said, smirking at the way I was chewing my thumbnail, as he joined me on one of the sofas in the waiting lounge.

I tried to hold still, but the large TV screen mounted on the wall in front of me went from showing the standby screen to a live feed, kicking my anticipation up yet another notch. *Screw it,* I thought and went back to work gnawing my fingernails down to their beds. Better that than have my whole body start shaking, tipping the guys off as to exactly how messed up I was right now.

"Yeah. I'm cool."

Embry snorted with laughter. "No, you're pathetic. Doing all this to impress some chick whose not even going to sleep with you? And you're *afraid* of her, no less."

I rolled my eyes, but cracked a smile. Embry was cool. "Not helping, you douche."

Embry nodded at the television where the queen of daytime women's talk shows was now spouting stupid crap about some lame blog she'd discovered. "So what are you going to do if your woman's already spoken for?"

I let out a breath. At least I had that much going for me. "She's not married. Google said so."

Embry hit me with a suspicious look. "That doesn't mean she's not taken. What if she's madly in love with some boyfriend?"

I was worried about that myself, but I refused to let Embry know it. "That didn't stop me four years ago," I said with a hell of a lot more confidence than I felt. "If she's with someone, I'll show her that I'm better and wait out the prick just like I did last time. It won't take long."

Embry raised an eyebrow at me. When I didn't back down, he chuckled and shook his head. "Anyone ever tell you you're a cocky SOB?"

The insult made me grin proudly. "Not today."

I started to say something else, but then Val appeared on the television in front of me and my mouth went too dry to speak.

The woman on the screen was not the girl I remembered. Val was wearing a light purple pencil skirt and matching jacket with a white blouse underneath. The heels she had on made her long, toned legs look more delectable than ever—she must still play a lot of volleyball. Her hair was twisted up with just one or two ringlets escaping, and she still had that same damn *V* charm hanging from her neck.

She looked gorgeous in a sexy, smart, corporate-shark kind of way, and she walked with a self-assurance she hadn't had back when I knew her. She'd always been confident, but now it was more than that. It was as if she understood exactly who she was and what she wanted. She looked unstoppable. She was beautiful. Radiant. So much more stunning than the last time I'd seen her.

Embry cursed under his breath. I chuckled as he stared at the screen with wide, shocked eyes. "Not what you imagined?"

Embry shook his head, his eyes glued to Val. "No way," he said. "That woman is nothing like any woman I've ever seen you date. Not even close."

His comment made me smile. That was the whole point.

On the television Val sat primly on a couch, smiling as if she didn't have a care in the world while Connie Parker explained her story. She looked so…content.

Again, I felt a stab of fear that she had a boyfriend sitting in the audience who held her heart. I wasn't sure what I would do if that were the case. I wanted her to be happy, but I needed a second chance with her, and I'd spent the last six months telling myself I was going to get it.

The guys in my new band all knew the whole story of Virgin Val. They'd even seen the movie. But they still all laughed hysterically when Connie played Val's video—the one of her standing on a lunch table professing her virginity. I didn't laugh, but my face broke into a wide smile. I loved that stupid video.

After the video was over, Val fell into telling her story. She was completely captivating. With every second of her interview I became more and more anxious—more desperate to see her again. I needed to talk to her, touch her, have her in my life again.

The wait was killing me.

My stomach dropped in shock when Connie told Val she'd found her birth mom.

"Whoa," Shane muttered, falling to the couch on the other side of me.

I could only nod. If I was in shock, what was Val going through right now?

"Look at her. She's white as a ghost."

"Did you know they were bringing her mom on the show today?" Embry asked.

I shook my head.

"Do you think they told her that *you're* here?"

I pulled my eyes from the screen for the first time since the interview began and looked at Embry. "I know they didn't tell her. They wanted to surprise her and asked me not to say anything to anyone. Cara even had to lie to her at lunch and pretend like she didn't talk to me anymore so that Val wouldn't suspect anything."

Embry laughed and shook his head. "What are they trying to do, kill her? The poor woman. She's being completely ambushed."

I hadn't thought of that. Surprising her had sounded fun, but what if it was too much? What if she couldn't handle seeing me again after they'd just completely shaken her with her birth mom? Whatever relationship Val and I had was feeble at best—if we had one at all. What if stupid Connie Parker just ruined my chances?

"Dude, her mom's hot."

I didn't know which of my bandmates said that, but he was right. The original Valerie looked a lot like my Val, except my Val was better in every way. My Val was the New and Improved version of her mother. Val's mom was like a nice sporty Audi, but Val was the new Aston Martin Vanquish.

"Ugh," one of my bandmates groaned, frowning in disgust at the amount of emotions being displayed on the screen as Val and her mom bawled in each other's arms. "I hate these kinds of talk shows. At least on Jerry Springer they fight instead of cry."

All the guys agreed. I did too, but it was going to be worth the sob fest to see Val again.

Eventually the crying stopped and Connie Parker said, "So, Val, you recently graduated from Stanford with a double major in economics and political science, is that right?"

Val's smile was so proud. She beamed as she nodded. "Yes."

"Congratulations! That's quite an accomplishment in itself."

"Thank you. It's only a break, though. I start my master's program in the fall."

I smiled again. My little brainiac was still in school. Shane and I weren't surprised, but the rest of the guys were. They all laughed, and Embry elbowed me. "Stanford?" he asked. "A double major and a master's program? Politics? What the hell did she ever see in you?"

"Suck it, dude."

"I wouldn't put it past you, Val," Connie said on the screen, "to be the first female president."

"Has a nice ring to it, doesn't it?" Val joked back.

"I can see the appeal," Embry continued on, assessing Val with a critical eye. "But it's no wonder you're being such a wuss today. That chick is too much woman for any guy. Even the great Kyle Hamilton. Good luck, bro. You're gonna need it."

The guys all laughed again, but I didn't join them this time. Embry's taunt about not being good enough for Val stung more than I cared to admit. I'd accomplished a lot in my life, but I was on a completely different path than her. We were so different. We had different goals, were from different worlds. I already knew I didn't deserve her. Maybe I was only kidding myself that she would want someone like me.

Finally, Connie took the conversation in the direction I was dying for it to go. She said, "Okay, Val, I hate to ask, but you know I have to—are you still a virgin?"

Of course Val said yes. I knew she would. She wasn't married and I knew she'd have remained true to herself. It was the answer to the next question that had me holding my breath.

"Any special guy in your life?"

"Not at the moment."

I breathed out so loudly that the guys laughed at me. I ignored their jabs and watched Val.

"I've been so busy with school and starting F is for Families that I haven't had much time to date."

Single. Not just unmarried, but *single*. And from the sound of it she hadn't dated much at all. There hadn't been anything serious. How was it possible? Even *I* had managed to settle down once.

Whatever. The *how* didn't matter. She didn't have anyone important. That meant I had a shot.

"That's a shame," Connie said.

"Yeah, a *cryin'* shame," Shane teased, setting everyone howling again. He got an elbow in the ribs for the effort.

From the smile on Connie's face, I knew what was

coming next. I jumped up from the couch and started pacing the room. "What ever happened with that one guy?" she asked. "What was his name? Kyle something?"

I froze in place, holding my breath as I waited for Val's reaction.

The roar of applause that came from the small studio audience at the mention of my name took me by surprise. Not that fans didn't always cheer for me, but the way these people cheered was different. They weren't cheering for me; they were cheering for both of us—for Val and me together. Four years later, and the world was still just as in love with the idea of us as they used to be.

That cheer was my first much-needed burst of confidence. The second was the look on Val's face. There was a brief instant where a single flash of emotion lit her up before she smoothed her expression out. But what emotion was it? Fear? Surprise? Excitement? I couldn't tell.

"I suppose you can't interview Virgin Val without bringing up Kyle Hamilton," she said. She sounded playful, but she was nowhere near as collected as she'd been when she first walked out on that stage.

She was nervous, but was it a good nervous or a bad nervous?

"I suppose not," Connie said. "You're a good sport, Val. So, do the two of you keep in touch?"

Val shook her head. "He went on the *S is for Sex* tour and I left for Stanford long before he came home. We never spoke again."

Was that regret I heard in her voice? Or was I imagining it?

"I'm sure he's forgotten all about me."

That got me another round of teasing from my band-mates. Even I laughed that time. Forgetting Val was impossible. Sure, I'd managed to bury her for a few years, but I could never forget her entirely. No one could forget Val.

"I heard he was pretty serious with someone for a while. Got engaged, even."

Thank you, Connie! She was broaching the awkward topic so that I wouldn't have to, and she was letting me see Val's reaction to it. I'd never say another bad thing about chick talk shows and their gossip ever again.

Val swallowed hard. Why? What was she thinking?

"I heard that, too."

Her answer was too vague. I wanted more and Connie, bless her heart, delivered. "Then you heard it was a bad breakup?" she pressed. "Broke his heart, she did."

Val's smile fell from her face. "I did hear about that," she admitted, "but from my experience there's never much truth in those tabloid stories, so who knows?"

I had no freaking clue what was going through Val's mind as she shrugged for Connie, but she was definitely battling some kind of emotions. If I didn't talk to her soon, I was going to go crazy.

"He and I were kind of notorious for not getting along," Val said, "but I hope it wasn't as bad as it sounds. I hope he's well wherever he is."

My lips curled into a big grin. She cared about me. It was written all over her face. Virgin Val hadn't forgotten about me any more than I'd forgotten about her.

My missing confidence finally showed up. It surged through me like lightning, leaving me charged with excitement. It may have been four years, but Val was still Val. And

Virgin Val had always had a weakness for Kyle Hamilton.

Well, she was in for it now, because I wasn't the same Kyle Hamilton she'd known then. Like her, I'd done some growing up, too. I'd been around the block a few times, learned a few things. I was ready for her this time.

Game on, Virgin Val, I thought to myself just as Connie yelled, "Come on out here, Kyle!"

6

V IS FOR VALERIE

My entire body buzzed with energy as I walked out into that studio.

The screams from the fans helped me focus. They brought me back to myself. I was onstage now. I was in front of an audience. I was *home*. I smiled for the cheering women and blew them kisses, stalling as I braced myself to meet Val's gaze.

I strutted over to Connie, oozing as much confidence as possible. I knew I looked cocky, but I wouldn't show any fear. I was Kyle Hamilton. I was capable of handling one woman, even if it was the infamous Virgin Val.

After Connie shook my hand and welcomed me to her show, I pulled Val to her feet and wrapped her up in a hug before she had the chance to do or say anything. I crushed her to me so tightly I was sure she felt the erratic beat of my heart.

She trembled a little as she returned my hug with a gentle and hesitant embrace. I rubbed my hand across her back, hoping to soothe her, and she melted against me. She laid her head on my shoulder and released a soft sigh that I doubt she was even aware of.

I came undone. Every feeling I'd ever had for Val—and believe me, there had been a lot of them—rose to the surface of my skin. I felt alive again, the way I used to. Val ignited something in me that I couldn't ignore, couldn't control. She always had.

When Val and I broke apart, I forced myself to focus. It wasn't easy; she'd completely scrambled my brain.

I had to get a grip.

Her birth mother rose to her feet as well, staring at me a little starstruck. "It's an honor to meet you," I said, holding out a hand to her in greeting. "I have to say, thank you for bringing my favorite virgin into the world."

The woman burst into tears, but I figured they were happy tears because she was laughing while she was crying. "I don't know whether to thank you for your part in bringing my daughter back into my life," she said, "or smack you for the way you treated her."

I concentrated on smiling so that I wouldn't roll my eyes. I was often accused of being a jerk to Val back in the day, but, honestly, I didn't see what I'd ever done that was so wrong. Val always knew I was just messing with her. I think. She fell for me anyway, so I couldn't have been *that* horrible.

"Well, if I get the chance," I said, forcing a laugh, "I'd prefer the thank-you. I've been slapped on national television before and it's not all that fun."

Okay, maybe, on the *rare* occasion, I'd been a little bit of a jerk.

Whatever. She still liked me.

Val and her mom scooted down on the sofa, making room for me to sit on the end closest to Connie. Val scooted a little too far away for my taste, so when I sat down I pulled her over to me, closing all distance between us. She cast me a flustered glance, letting me know exactly how much I affected her.

I grinned and tucked her snuggly against my side. Val stiffened, as if I was making her nervous, but I didn't care. It felt right. It'd been years, but the chemistry between us was still there, still thick enough to choke on.

I kissed the side of her head and whispered, "It's been way too long, Val," not sure if I was trying to calm her down or rile her up.

My attention was pulled away from Val when Connie cleared her throat and said, "So, Kyle, Val was just telling us she was sure you'd forgotten all about her. Is that true?"

Connie smiled so big her face had to hurt. She looked ecstatic as her eyes bounced back and forth between Val and me, obviously proud to have reunited us.

I laughed. "Connie, there are some people that could never be forgotten."

"I have to agree," she said. "Tell us what you've been up to."

"Well, I've got a solo album coming out soon, but other than that I've just been taking it easy." I gave Val a meaningful squeeze and added, "Waiting for the right woman to come along and make an honest man out of me."

Connie nearly melted into a puddle of pleasure in her chair. Even the audience swooned. I tried to gauge Val's reaction and noticed little pink spots of color on her cheeks. She was blushing. That was a good sign.

"You're looking to settle down then, are you?" Connie asked, following my lead.

"Something like that." I smiled to myself. We were talking about settling down, but inside I was only getting worked up.

My gaze drifted to Val again. She was wearing the faintest trace of perfume. It was just barely enough to make me want to lean in and bury my nose in her neck, taste her skin. It was maddening.

Her lips looked so soft. If I didn't do something fast, I was going to kiss her. I couldn't let that happen. She'd been so mad the last time I'd done that in front of the cameras.

I reached across her lap and pulled her hand into mine. I needed the distraction. She gasped, but it wasn't the hand-holding that had her shocked—it was the bracelet tied around my wrist.

That's right, Virgin Val!

"What is this?" she asked, fingering the black leather strap with the small *A* dangling from it.

I grinned, loving her reaction. "You don't recognize it? You gave it to me once, a long time ago."

"Yeah, I recognize it."

Her eyes drifted out of focus, as if she were recalling a memory. I was sure she was thinking of the day she'd given me the bracelet at the Huntington High School Fall Festival. She'd handed it to me as a joke. It had been an attempt to put some space between us. I don't think she realized that I kept it.

The night she gave me the bracelet, she'd blown me off and missed my song. I was so pissed. The brush-off stung. That night I became determined to win her over. I decided I was going to seduce her, take her virginity, and rub my victory in her face as revenge for hurting my pride.

Somewhere along the way, my need for revenge turned into real feelings and the bracelet became priceless to me. I took it with me on the *S is for Sex* tour and wore it in my pocket for every performance until I'd lost it toward the end of the tour.

My mouth lifted into a smirk as we both stared at my bracelet. After everything Val and I had been through together—after I'd pushed her away and lost her because I refused to play her game—I ended up giving her what she wanted anyway.

Oh, the irony.

"Eight months, now," I admitted.

Val didn't get it at first. "Eight months, what?" she asked.

The idea of me abstaining from sex was so impossible to her she couldn't comprehend what I was saying. I had to spell it out for her. "Haven't you heard? The *A* stands for abstinence."

I stared down at her, waiting for her to understand, and I saw the exact moment it clicked into place. *"You?"* she gasped.

I laughed. The look on her face was worth the last eight months of celibacy.

My good mood died quickly as she sat there waiting for an explanation. The situation didn't seem all that funny anymore. I didn't want to explain it, but I knew I'd have to prove myself to Val if I was going to convince her I was sincere.

I gritted my teeth and shrugged as if it didn't matter. "It was my relationship with Adrianna. I loved her, you know? When we broke it off I realized I hadn't been with anyone else since I'd met her, and that I didn't want to be with anyone else. The woman ruined me because now I don't want to sleep with anybody I'm not in love with. Believe me, I tried. When she cheated on me I tried to sleep with a million girls just to get back at her, but I couldn't do it."

I couldn't believe I was admitting all this in front of the whole freaking world. Adrianna was probably going to see this interview and would laugh about how she broke my heart for the rest of her life.

I pushed Adrianna from my thoughts. I didn't care about her anymore. It didn't matter what she thought. "I figured since I wasn't doing it anymore anyway, I might as well wear the bracelet."

I forced myself to meet Val's gaze. She'd been waiting for me to look at her. When our eyes met, she stared at me as if she were trying to tell me something important. As if my life depended on whatever secret message she was about to convey.

"Good for you, Kyle," she whispered.

Her eyes misted over, and I realized what she was trying to get me to understand. She was proud of me. I'd surprised her—impressed her, even—and she was proud of me.

I'd been waiting *years* to see that look from her. I'd tried so hard to win her approval back in the day, but I'd never gained it. Yes, she'd grown feelings for me, but I'd never fully earned her respect. Until now.

My chest started to burn. I squeezed her to me again and brought my lips to her ear. "I've figured it out, Val."

Before I could explain myself, Connie interrupted us. "Are you going to perform something for us today?" she asked me.

Hell yes, I was going to sing something today.

My adrenaline spiked. I'd never been so anxious to sing a song in my life. Not even the first time I sang "Cryin' Shame."

"Uh, yeah," I said.

Unable to sit still another second, I jumped up and crossed the stage to where my band was set up.

Things were going to be different this time. Val wasn't going to hate this one. She was going to love it. The whole world was going to love it. Shane had been right that day. I had another chart topper on my hands. I was sure of it.

This was going to be just like "Cryin' Shame" all over again. I could feel it in my bones. This moment, right now, was the start of something epic. Kyle and Val: the Sequel.

I couldn't wait.

I adjusted my mic and gazed out at the anxious audience. I could feel their excitement as sure as I could feel my own. "I'll be singing the first single of my new album," I said, a wide grin spreading across my face, "and in grand Kyle Hamilton tradition, I've written it for a certain someone who I couldn't manage to get out of my head."

The audience went crazy at the confession and after smiling for them, my eyes found Val's. The expression on her face was classic—something akin to horror. Laughing, I winked at her and said, "It's called 'Worth Waiting For.'"

I know it sounds horribly cliché, but music is my life. I literally live and breathe for the moments I get to hold a microphone to my mouth and share all my innermost thoughts and feelings in song. Singing isn't just what I do; it's who I am. I love it.

As soon as the first chord of music sounded, everything

faded out and all was right in the world. All the nerves I'd been trying to shake all day melted away and I opened my mouth to sing, feeling as if I were on top of the world.

Thoughts of you runnin' through my head
Heart's pumpin' full speed ahead
Body's screaming to get you in bed
Need you, want you, baby gotta be mine
Come to me girl, I'm done wastin' time

You ask me to wait, don't know if I can
Too scared to lose, I'm only a man
But I can't let you go, can't shut the door
Heart's telling me you're worth waiting for

The feel of your lips, hot breath on my skin
Touching you, touching me, I'd relish the sin
Let's find a way for us both to win
Need you, want you, baby gotta be mine
Come to me girl, I'm done wastin' time

You ask me to wait, don't know if I can
Too scared to lose, I'm only a man
But I can't let you go, can't shut the door
Heart's telling me you're worth waiting for

Forever I'll wait, it's drivin' me mad
Driven by memories I've not yet had
Hangin' on a promise of you and me
Hope springs eternal for things that could be

You ask me to wait, don't know if I can
Too scared to lose, I'm only a man

But I can't let you go, can't shut the door
Heart's telling me you're worth waiting for

You ask me to wait, don't know if I can
Too scared to lose, I'm only a man
Bring on the torture, forever and more
'Cause girl it's true, you're worth waiting for

The music ended, the audience cheered, and I basked in the thrill of a performance well done.

Man, I'd missed this.

If nothing else came from today, at least I'd found my muse again. It'd been gone since Reid died, and for a while I'd given up all hope that I'd ever feel like my old self again. As I came down from my adrenaline high, I knew I was back. I was myself again. I was ready to let this solo album take me on my next great adventure. I had a purpose again, and it felt amazing.

It was all thanks to Val.

That thought had me crashing back into reality. Val. What did she think? I took a deep breath and looked in her direction. Her eyes were already on me. She sat there, completely motionless, as if she'd been frozen in place. Her eyes were wide, but otherwise her face was smooth. Either she was doing all in her power to hide her thoughts, or she was in so much shock she was unable to express them yet.

Good or bad? Good or bad? Good or bad?

I had no idea what was going through her head. We were caught in a crazy staring match and I couldn't tell *at all* what she was thinking. Not a freaking clue.

I had to do something. I had to move, or look away, or something. Anything besides just standing there staring at her. I lifted a finger in her direction and mouthed the words, "For you."

The spell holding us finally broke. Val turned her head away from me and discreetly dabbed a tissue to her eyes. She was crying. I'd made her cry. That *had* to be a good thing. Right? Or was it bad?

I moved exactly one step toward her and then Connie was there, hugging me and complimenting the song. My brain went to autopilot, unable to think of anything but Val, until I heard a roar of applause. I shook myself from my daze. Connie was thanking me for something. What had I just agreed to?

A signing. All of the audience members had received a copy of my new album, and I'd just agreed to stay and sign them. No, no, no! Val would be long gone before I was finished. That was unacceptable.

I held the microphone up to my face so that I'd be good and heard by everyone in the room as I answered her. "Sure, Connie. I'd be happy to stay behind for a while and sign a few CDs...as long as Virgin Val agrees to stay with me." I flashed the women in the audience my best smile. "I haven't seen her in four years. I can't give her the chance to sneak away from me too quickly."

This got the reaction I was hoping for, the reaction I knew it would get. No matter what, when it came to Val and me, the fans would always be on my side.

I waited out the screams and then turned my grin on Val. She was across the room, introducing her birth mom to her parents, and whirled around at the sound of her name. The incredulous look on her face made me burst into laughter. Just like old times.

"What do you say, Val?" I taunted. "Want to do the Virgin and the Rock Star thing with me again?" Time to bring out the irresistible sexy pout. "Just this once? For old times' sake?" I turned my puppy dog face on the audience and said, "It'd really make you guys happy, wouldn't it?"

Everyone in the audience went crazy again. Val had no choice but to throw her hands in the air. Groaning, she said, "All right, you win. I'll stay."

"Excellent." I grinned at her so big she laughed.

"But just this once!" she warned.

Not if I had anything to do with it. "Of course just this once. I swear."

As I crossed my heart for Val, I shook my head "no" at the audience, making them all laugh and cheer again. Oh, yeah. I definitely missed this.

7

R IS FOR REUNIONS

VAL ASKED FOR A TEN-MINUTE BREAK BEFORE THE SIGNING, so I used the time to say good-bye to my bandmates—all of whom wished me luck while making endless fun of me—and use the restroom. On my way back into the main studio, I stopped by the guest lounge for a bottle of water and some snacks that would get me through the next hour. I'd been too nervous and excited before the show to eat anything, but now that crafty table was practically luring me in like a siren's song. It's never a good idea to interact with fans on an empty stomach, or with Val, for that matter. Actually, it's never a good idea to have an empty stomach in general.

I stopped dead in my tracks, my quest for food forgotten when I entered the guest lounge and saw Val. She was standing there alone in the dark, leaning against one of the couches. Her back was to me and she was distracted enough that she didn't hear me come in the room. I opened my mouth to say something flippant about her trying to get me alone when she sucked in a big breath and her entire body started shaking. I realized she wasn't leaning against the couch, but gripping it as if it were the only thing keeping her on her feet at the moment.

I'd never seen Val so upset before. I'd flustered her on a regular basis back in the day. I'd always pushed her to her limits on purpose, trying to get her strong façade to crack, and she never once had. She was the strongest person I'd ever met. It said something about her emotional state of mind that she'd asked for a few moments to collect herself before having to do the signing with me.

I knew she probably wanted these few minutes alone, but I couldn't pull myself away. I couldn't leave her like this. I cleared my throat to gain her attention, and she jumped at the intrusion. She whirled around, hastily wiping away a tear or two as she forced her emotions down and reverted back into the calm, controlled woman I'd seen onstage.

She opened her mouth as if to explain herself but shut it again, realizing that there was no hiding what I'd just witnessed. Instead she decided to ignore it. "Kyle Hamilton." It was a warm greeting and a sigh at the same time.

Her smile was sincere, and her eyes held genuine pleasure, but there was a wariness about her that made me afraid to approach her. We stared at each other in silence, both cataloging the changes four years had brought. I wasn't sure what to do or how to break the silence between us, so Val took the initiative. "I didn't think I'd ever see you again," she said with a small shake of her head.

"Me, either." I finally broke from my stupor and managed a small smile. "Hug for an old friend?"

I held out my arms, still not taking any steps further into the room, letting her come to me on her terms. It took her a moment to decide, but eventually she pushed her smile up into her eyes and crossed the room to me.

We sank into the embrace and simply held each other as the tension left our bodies. Her arms were low around my waist and mine tight around her shoulders. Thanks to her heels she was only a few inches shorter than my six-foot-three inches, putting her at the perfect height to rest her head on my shoulder, which she did with the smallest sigh. My eyes drifted shut and I enjoyed the moment. It was a long time before I whispered, "Are you okay?"

She sucked in a sharp breath and pulled herself out of my arms. "I'm fine."

I didn't believe her. The words sounded too much like a personal pep talk. "Val, if you're not up for sticking around to sign autographs with me, I'll understand. I'll tell them you're not feeling well."

Val gaped up at me, stunned by the offer. She was shocked that I'd let her off the hook. Normally I wouldn't, but the image of her crumpling to pieces alone in this room was not one I was going to forget anytime soon.

"The thing about surviving fame," I told her, "is knowing when to say no. The public will always take everything you give them. They'll take and take and take, and it will never be enough. You have to remember that ultimately you come first. If there's ever something you need, you have to put your foot down."

For instance, not singing your most popular song again no matter how much it pisses people off and lets them down. I didn't voice the thought, but I wondered if she was thinking about that, too.

"If you're not up for it today, then go."

Val studied me for a moment, and her nerves melted away. Giving her the chance to say no had apparently been what she needed to say yes. "It's okay, Kyle, I don't mind staying."

She sounded much more confident, but I still asked, "You sure?"

"I'm sure," she promised. A smile crept over her face, reaching all the way up into her eyes. "I can't let you go out there alone. Who knows what kinds of rumors you'd start. I'd probably wake up tomorrow and learn that I'd been hospitalized after going into severe shock when you kissed me backstage."

Surprised, I burst into laughter. "That does sound like something you'd do," I teased.

She laughed with me and we headed back to the main studio and our waiting fans. "It may have been four years, Kyle, but that doesn't mean I don't remember how you operate."

I snatched her hand as she reached to open the door to the studio. I wasn't ready to end this moment alone with her. "You don't think I've learned a few things since then?"

She smirked and shook her head. "New tricks. Same dog."

It was impossible not to take her words as a challenge. I pushed her back until she was pinned against the door and leaned in close enough that our breaths mingled. Her eyes snapped wide the same way they always had whenever I'd invaded her personal space, and I watched, satisfied, as she sucked in a lung full of air and held it.

"That mentality will be your downfall this time around, Val." I leaned in, letting my lips linger at her jawline for a moment too long before bringing them to her ear. "Same old tricks," I whispered. "New man."

With that, I kissed her cheek and breezed past her into the studio, leaving her flustered and in need of another moment to collect herself all over again.

When I returned to the main studio the fans were already lined up, clutching their CDs to their chests. Their excitement was palpable.

I moseyed over to the table the stage crew had set up for the signing, picked up a Sharpie, and waved the first waiting fan forward. She bounced over, a blush in her cheeks, and shyly handed me her CD.

"What's your name, hon?"

"Laurel."

I took the lid off my marker and let it hover above the CD case. "You have a beautiful name, Laurel. What'd you think of the song?"

She sighed. "It was so romantic. Did you really write it for Val?"

I winked, causing her cheeks to turn red all over again.

"Speaking of my favorite virgin, you know I can't sign this CD until she's sitting in the seat next to me, right? I mean that *was* the deal."

"Oh, keep your pants on, Kyle. I'm right here."

The voice came from right behind me and sounded as irritated as ever. I felt my smile stretch to ridiculous proportions. "Did you hear that?" I asked Laurel. "We haven't even been reunited for two seconds and she's already reminding me that we're not going to have sex."

Heaving a dramatic sigh, I stood up, jiggled my belt buckle, and gave my jeans a good yank. They stayed put. "Yup. Everything's properly locked in place. My pants are not going anywhere. It is safe for The Virgin to sit next to me without fearing for the loss of her virtue."

"Cute," Val said with a roll of her eyes.

I gave her a grin that showed all my teeth. "I've missed you, Val. How did I ever live without all this verbal sparring for the last four years?"

"I don't know, but I lived rather peacefully. It was nice."

"Whatever. I know you missed me, too." I sat down again and pulled out the other chair for Val. "Sit with me already, so I can sign the lovely Laurel's CD."

After I grabbed Val's chair and pulled it so close to mine that we were practically touching, I finally started signing autographs.

It turned out Val was as popular as I was and most of the fans asked her to sign their CDs, too. I thought it was interesting that she signed her name "Virgin Val" and not "Val Jensen."

"What's with the signature?" I asked after the third time she'd done it.

She shrugged. "I guess it's like my stage name. That's who my fans want to meet, so that's what I write."

She scribbled "Virgin Val" on a CD and handed it to me.

"As much as I love 'Virgin Val,'" I said as I signed my name beneath hers, "I think it's time I get to know 'Valerie Jensen' better. Don't you?"

"I don't know. I find the idea of us getting more personal rather terrifying."

Sure she did. "Only because it excites you so much."

I looked at the CD in my hands with Val's signature and mine together and got the brilliant idea to draw a plus sign between the names and a 4-Ever beneath them. The cover of the CD now read: Virgin Val + Kyle Hamilton 4-Ever.

The woman standing in front of us gasped at the drawing. Val looked up to see what was wrong, and I held out my masterpiece. "What do you think? We look good together."

Val sighed, but her face broke into a smile as she shook her head at me. "You really haven't changed much, have you?"

It took me a minute to respond. I was too busy enjoying the smile I'd put on her face. I don't manage to make her laugh very often, so when I do, I have to relish in my success.

When I let my gaze linger a second too long, Val frowned and snatched the CD out of my hand. "If you're going to sign it like a middle-schooler, you forgot the most important part."

She drew a big heart around our names and held it up for me to see. "There. Now we've officially reverted back to the sixth grade."

She handed the CD back to the woman standing in front of us. "Here you go, Brenda. Take good care of it. I have a feeling Kyle's especially proud of this one."

I loved that Val was having fun with this. Not everyone could do it. Adrianna hated having to interact with my fans when we were out in public together. It wasn't like that for Val. She pretended not to like the attention, but she was so good with people. It helped that my fans were her fans, too.

They loved us both. Val would be the absolute perfect girl-friend for a guy like me.

"I will! Thank you so much!" Brenda replied, mooning at Val and me as if we were so cute it was painful to look at us. She started to turn away and then stopped, chewing nervously on her bottom lip. "I'm so glad you're finally back together. You guys are too perfect for each other."

"We're not—"

I threw my arm over Val's shoulder and cut her off before she could finish her sentence. "Thanks, Brenda. We're pretty excited about it, too. We'll try not to screw it up this time."

Val shot me a look that I could only laugh at. "What? You don't have to be absent for me to start rumors."

"All right, fine. If that's how you want to play."

The wicked gleam in her eyes sent a rush of excitement through me. The Val I remembered had always been feisty beneath her poised exterior. It was the reason I loved to get her so riled up. "Take your best shot."

She waited until after we'd signed a couple more auto-graphs. I'd almost forgotten about the whole incident when she leaned over between signings and said in a low voice, "Of course I don't think less of you. You're not the first man to have an impotence problem, Kyle. I think it's great that you've decided to abstain, no matter what the reason behind it is."

I wasn't sure what she was talking about until I glanced up and saw a woman gaping down at me with wide eyes. "She's kidding," I said as Val smiled at the woman and held out her hand for the CD.

The woman handed it over, but her eyes drifted back to me. Her cheeks turned pink and she shyly said, "A problem like that's nothing to be ashamed of. It doesn't make you any less of a man. I think it's romantic that it made you want to reconnect with Val."

My jaw fell open and I'll be damned if I didn't blush bright red. This woman *believed* Val! She thought I was abstaining because I was *impotent.*

"Oh, yes," Val said without missing a beat, "it was *so* romantic. He cried when he told me what was going on with him, and I was so touched. Knowing the truth has only brought us closer together."

I turned my shocked gaze on Val and she winked at me before smiling up at the lady and saying, "What's your name?"

"Melanie."

Before I could even try to dispel the rumor, Melanie moved the conversation along and made it impossible. "Could you sign it to Chloe, though, please?" she said to Val. "That's my daughter. She's in high school right now and is waiting also. She used to really struggle with it, but after she saw your movie she gained so much confidence in herself. I got her a Virgin necklace for her birthday and she wears it every day."

"That's so great!" Val said.

I was surprised by how sincere Val was. Her playful attitude had melted away upon hearing Melanie's story, and her eyes became shiny with actual tears. She honestly cared about this woman and her daughter. I think that's the reason she made as big an impact on the world as she did—because she genuinely cares. That's also why, as much as I disagreed with her cause, I'd always found her irresistible. I admired Val.

Val scribbled "For Chloe, Stay strong! Virgin Val" on the cover of Melanie's CD.

She handed me the CD with a stern look, but I didn't need the warning. I could see that this was important to the woman. I wasn't going to mock Melanie or her daughter. I took the CD and simply wrote, "For Chloe, We're in this together. Kyle 'A is for Abstinence' Hamilton."

Melanie sniffled. "It's going to mean so much to Chloe that you're doing the abstinence challenge, Kyle. Thank you so much for being so brave."

Ignoring the fact that this woman believed I had problems beneath the covers, I tried to sound just as sincere as Val had when I handed the CD back to the woman in front of me. "If it helps people, I'm glad to do it. Tell Chloe we're proud of her, and that she's not alone."

Chloe's mom swallowed hard and sniffled. "I will," she croaked. "Thank you so much."

After she walked away, I turned to Val, a grudging smile on my face. "Impotence?"

Val shrugged. "If you can't take it, don't dish it."

"You win. Lesson learned. Truce?"

Val smiled. "I'm having the strangest sense of déjà vu." She laughed. And shook her head. "I can't believe you handled that so maturely."

"Kind of hard not to when the woman was all teary-eyed."

"Still. I'm impressed."

Score one for me. "I *have* changed, Val," I promised, taking advantage of the situation and taking her hand into mine. "At least in the important ways." I glanced at the bracelet on my wrist and corrected myself. "In the *most* important way. I'm going to prove it to you eventually."

Val stared down at our hands for a long moment and I watched her entire countenance change. Her smile became strained and her eyes glossed over with moisture. "I'm glad," she said with a pained smile as she pulled her fingers from mine and turned her attention back to the fans.

The mood was much more somber as we finished signing autographs. Something had changed between us, but I didn't know what it was. I couldn't figure Val out. I'd never really been able to do that, though, which was always a big part of our problem.

As the last of the audience members got their autographs and left the building, Val and I sat there in silence, unsure what to do or say next. I decided to be the brave one and break the awkward tension. "Thanks for staying with me today. I think the fans really appreciated it."

Val's answering smile was small and sad. "I think you're right. Thank you for asking me to do it. I haven't had to be Virgin Val in so long; I forgot how much the campaign meant to people. The reminder was good for me."

I wasn't sure how to respond. Moments like this, where Val and I were real with each other instead of bantering or fighting, were rare. I didn't want to ruin it.

The silence dragged out between us until a stagehand asked if he could take down the table we were still sitting at. Val and I were the only guests still in the studio, so we headed for the door. As we reached the exit, I held out my arm. "Walk you to your car?"

I was surprised when I got no resistance. She looked at my offered elbow and smiled as she linked her hand through my arm. We walked the entire way to the parking lot without speaking, but this time the silence was comfortable. Once we stepped out into the late afternoon sunshine, and it was time to go our separate ways, we stopped and looked at each other. "It was good to see you again, Kyle," she said.

She had that pained expression back on her face. She was smiling, but it wasn't reaching her eyes. I wanted to know what she was upset about, but I didn't know how to ask.

I looked at her, wishing she would say something, and she watched me, waiting for the same thing. The moment felt almost identical to the last time we'd seen each other. It felt like this sort of hopeless, bittersweet farewell. Saying good-bye felt so inevitable four years ago, but now I couldn't accept it. I wasn't going to let her get away so easily this time.

"Val, have dinner with me tonight. Please?"

I heard the desperation in my request, but I couldn't calm myself. I was slightly panicked that she might turn me down.

She opened her mouth and nothing came out of it.

"I really have missed you," I said.

I took her hands in mine and squeezed them. She squeezed back and gave me another tragic smile. "I missed you, too." She glanced across the parking lot to where her parents and birth mom were waiting for her, trying—and failing—to look like they weren't watching us. "I think my parents and I are going to have dinner with my birth mom tonight." She paused, torn by indecision. "If you'd like to join us, I'm sure they wouldn't mind."

I almost accepted the offer. I wanted to more than any-thing. I was shocked she'd invited me, and touched that she was willing to include me even if she did seem unsure about it. But she needed privacy while getting to know her birth mom, so, as much as it killed me, I turned her down. "I don't want to interfere with that. That should be a family thing."

Val's tiny sigh of relief was bittersweet. "Thanks." She took a big breath. "I still can't really wrap my head around it. My *birth* mom." She closed her arms around herself as if the idea made her insecure. "She says I have a younger half-brother, too."

"Wow."

Val nodded. "Yeah. Wow. I mean I'm happy but…it's a lot to take in. I think I'm going to need some time to sort out my feelings about everything."

I didn't like seeing her so flustered. "I'm sorry they blindsided you like that. And I'm sorry they threw me into the mix on top of it. I couldn't have made it any easier dropping another song on you."

I was too nervous to smile. Did she like the song? She still hadn't said anything about it. Was she upset about seeing me again?

Val shook her head. "I'm glad you were here. It was good seeing you again. I'm sorry we don't have more time to catch up."

I finally realized what her sadness was about—she was saying good-bye. She wasn't planning to keep in touch after this. I had to do something.

"How long are you in town?"

Val's smile fell again. "I fly back early tomorrow morning. I've got work."

My gut twisted. She was leaving in the morning, and from the way she said it, she definitely considered this the end. *Hey, it was so good to see you again, Kyle. It's been fun, but my life doesn't include you anymore, so good-bye, Kyle.*

Not knowing what else to do, I pulled one of the remaining CDs out of my bag and scribbled a note on it. I signed it "For the world's greatest muse. Eternally in your debt, Kyle Hamilton." Then I wrote, "Call me!" and put my cell number below it. I underlined it several times.

"I mean it," I said as she read the inscription. "Call me."

Val nodded, but I had my doubts that she would call. She looked back toward her family and gave me one last miserable smile. "I should go."

When she turned to leave, my heart pretty much stopped. "Val, wait!"

I grabbed her and crushed her to me in a hug that was likely to suffocate her. I didn't know what was wrong with me, but I just couldn't let her go. I squeezed and squeezed as if that could somehow magically convince her not to walk away from me.

The second our bodies connected, my heart pounded in my chest and my entire body ached. I was alive again, tingling all over with reckless, passionate energy. Having her in my arms like this was right. It was what I needed. She was the part of me that had been missing for so long. I'd loved Adrianna and would have been happy with her, but she'd never made me feel like this. Like I could do anything. Like I deserved everything. Like I was complete, and life just couldn't get any better.

Val's chest heaved against mine, her heart pounding, too. I could feel it.

"Val." It came out a strangled whisper.

I didn't lose control. When I kissed her, it was deliberate. I wasn't letting her walk away from me without making sure she understood that things were not finished between us. I threw my mouth on hers as if both of our lives depended on it. And you know what? She. Kissed. Me. Back. Our lips touched and we exploded. We were gasoline and fire. We were years of suppressed desire finally being unleashed. We were hunger, passion, and need.

We were epic.

Val broke away first, gasping for breath. "I should go."

My arms tightened around her waist. "You should stay."

"I *have* to go."

She sounded tortured enough that I knew I'd gotten to her. Our kiss would stay with her long after she walked away from me. Good. She just needed one more for good measure. Okay, maybe it was me who needed one more.

I pushed a strand of her hair that had fallen from its twist behind her ear and lowered my lips to hers again. I kissed her gently this time, reveling in her sweetness now that the passion was out of the way. This kiss was different—more. It was an expression of all the quieter emotions in us; feelings neither of us would acknowledge that refused to stay silent any longer. It was soft and tender. I felt it all the way to my bones.

When I pulled back, her eyes fluttered open as if she were waking from a dream. It made me want to kiss her all over again. "Fine. You have to go," I said, running my fingertips across her cheek. "But this isn't good-bye. I'm not letting you walk away this time."

"Kyle…"

"No. I made that mistake once. I won't do it again. Good night, Val. Have a good time with your parents. I'll talk to you soon."

I walked away before she could argue.

8

P IS FOR PLANS

THE NOT EVERYBODY'S DOING IT FOUNDATION RENTED OUT an office the size of a Crackerjack box in a strip mall in Pasadena that had seen better days. I felt depressed just looking at the place, and that was *before* I worked up the nerve to go inside.

I still wasn't sure I was doing the right thing—my managers thought I was crazy—but I didn't know how else to get Val's attention.

It had been over a week since the Connie Parker Show taping, and she'd never called. I wasn't surprised. I'd been too caught up in the moment to recognize that kiss for what it was until hours later when I was unable to sleep. She'd kissed me all right, but I was pretty sure that for her that kiss had been something we'd never quite managed four years ago: closure.

At first, I was hurt when she didn't call. How could she want closure after that kiss? How could she stay away? Then I got angry. I didn't deserve to be blown off. Finally, I decided to just get determined. There was no way the connection I felt between us was one-sided. I've been with way too many women in my life not to know that chemistry like ours was real—a tangible, undeniable energy. Hell no. She felt it. I knew she did. And I was going to make her admit it.

Phase one of The Plan was on the other side of the dingy window I sat parked in front of. I tugged my baseball cap low over my eyes and headed inside before someone recognized me. I didn't need to get mobbed before I was ready to answer questions about what I was doing at an organization that promotes abstinence.

The office looked even smaller on the inside, packed, as it was, with boxes of leaflets and brochures on everything from STD awareness, to avoiding teen pregnancy, to celebrating virtue.

There was an entire table in the front window devoted to V is for Virgin and Val's abstinence challenge. There was a computer there so that people could browse the website and sign up for the challenge. Above the desk and all over the walls there were pictures of people with their name and their pledge to abstain from sex.

I sort of understood now—a little—why someone would make the choice to wait to have sex, but why did all these people look so damn happy about it? I might be abstaining from meaningless casual sex now, but I wasn't jumping for joy over my newfound celibacy. In fact, it pretty much sucked.

"Kyle Hamilton?"

I managed not to jump at the unexpected voice, but I still felt like an idiot just for being here. "Uh, yeah." I took my hat off and ran my fingers through my hair. "I guess I need to speak to the person in charge?"

"That would be Darla. She's already gone for the day. Is there anything I can help you with?"

I was about to say no and use this as an excuse to leave when I recognized the woman standing in front of me. "You were at the taping last week."

She nodded. "I was there."

The woman, whose belly looked as if it were ready to burst, looked me over with a mixture of wariness and amusement that could only mean she knew me. Well, knew me by reputation, and not just my celebrity status. I'd bet money that this woman knew Val personally, and therefore knew my history with Val.

"Have we met?" We probably had, and I felt stupid again for not knowing who she was.

The woman smirked. "I don't know that we've ever been formally introduced, but we've met on several occasions, yes." She held out a fat, swollen hand. "I'm Robin. I've known Val since high school."

A vague recollection of a younger, less pregnant girl with soft brown hair and a light smattering of freckles hunched over a computer jumped into my mind. "That's right. You were her friend who did all of her website stuff."

Shock washed over the woman, but she quickly smirked to cover it up. "I'm surprised you remember."

She might not be as feisty as Cara or Val, but I could see why she was her friend. "Contrary to what Val might have told you," I teased, "I *am* capable of paying attention to more than just myself."

She raised a questioning brow that made me laugh. Busted. "It happens on rare occasions," I admitted. "When it's important."

"If you say so." She still seemed skeptical.

She suddenly hunched over and grabbed her stomach as she forced out a long, slow breath.

When I realized what was happening, I panicked. "Are you having a *baby*?"

I don't know why she thought my question was so funny, but she laughed, waving off my concern as I helped her into a nearby chair. "Should I call an ambulance or something?"

She laughed again. "It's fine, Kyle, just a mild contraction. I've been on my feet too much today."

"Don't contractions mean it's time to have a baby? I can drive you to the hospital, if you need. Is there, like, a baby daddy you need me to call?"

"You mean my husband?" She kicked off her shoes and rubbed her feet—which looked twice the size they should have. "Relax," she said. "This baby's not coming for almost two months, I promise. Mild contractions are completely normal once you're in the third trimester."

I pointed to her ankles. "*That* doesn't look normal. I really think I should take you to a doctor."

She laughed at my horrified gaze and finally loosened up. The edge of wariness she'd had since I walked in dissolved into something I could almost mistake for affection. "I can understand what she sees in you," she said suddenly.

The burst of pride I felt at her praise was unexpected. I generally didn't care what anyone thought of me, but this woman was a friend of Val's. Her approval meant something. And maybe if I could win her over, she would help me with Val.

"So what can the Not Everybody's Doing It Foundation

do for you, Kyle?"

I startled at the question. The whole pregnant-wom-an-having-contractions scare made me forget all about where I was and what I was doing here.

"Have you finally come to take Val's challenge? Here to pledge your abstinence?"

If that's what it took…

I pulled my shoulders back and puffed out my chest. I refused to let this woman see how nervous I was about this. "As a matter of fact, I am." I dangled my bracelet for Robin to see. "I wasn't lying last week. I've already been abstinent for eight months. I thought Val would like it if I made it official."

Robin blinked and pulled a pair of flip-flops from a drawer in her desk. She bent over to try and put them on. She couldn't reach very well, so I squatted down and slipped them over her feet for her.

"Well, aren't you just full of surprises," she said.

"See, I can be a nice guy. You shouldn't be so skeptical."

"Thank you for the help with my sandals, but I was actually talking about you pledging the abstinence challenge. Do you really want to do it?"

She held her hand out to me as if she literally needed my help to get out of her chair. Actually, she probably did. "Are you sure you should get up? I think you should rest."

My concern amused her. "Five o'clock," she said, smoth-ering a laugh. "Quitting time. I was just getting ready to leave when you walked in."

"Oh. Sorry." I helped her out of her chair, surprised that I was disappointed I wouldn't get to explain my plan to her.

She walked with me to the door, and as she turned out

the lights she asked her question again. "Do you really want to sign up for the abstinence challenge?"

I shrugged. "Why not? I've already given up casual sex, and I think signing up for the challenge would make Val happy, so…"

"So you'd go on record—officially—and tell your fans that you're doing the V is for Virgin abstinence challenge just to make Val happy?"

"Yes." Robin held the door for me and then locked it after we were both outside. "I would do that for Val. She deserves it. Here's the thing, though. If I'm going to do this—officially—then I'm going to do it all the way. I want the whole freaking world to know that Kyle Hamilton's not doing it. I want to be a spokesperson for you guys, like Val was."

Robin stopped walking so abruptly that she stumbled out of balance. The momentum of her giant belly nearly made her fall over. "Are you *kidding* me?" she asked when I grabbed her by the shoulder to steady her.

Robin's was basically the same reaction I got from my managers when I'd revealed the plan to them earlier today. I decided to give her the same argument I'd given them. "I have to do a press tour to promote my new album, and people are going to ask anyway, so I thought I could sort of combine the two things."

"You want to promote the Not Everybody's Doing It Foundation on your press tour for your new album?"

Ok, it sounded ridiculous when she said it like that. "Val's the reason I wrote my new song and it's about *waiting* for her. She's the reason I started writing again, the reason I decided to put out a solo album. I almost *have* to explain it.

Plus, I've already agreed to donate a portion of my record sales to The Not Everybody's Doing It Foundation, like Val did with her jewelry, so I'll have to bring that up in interviews anyway. I may as well be an official spokesperson, right?"

Robin leaned her hand against the brick wall of the building and gaped at me with wide eyes. "Holy crap, you're serious," she breathed.

"Would you please sit down before you hurt some-thing?" Was it possible to shock someone into labor? "Maybe I should talk to someone else about this. You're in shock. I don't want to make you have a baby on the sidewalk."

"I'm fine," Robin promised, still dazed. "I just can't believe it. With your fame and your reputation, and espe-cially your history with Val, do you know how much press you would get? Do you know the kind of good you could do? How many lives you could touch by doing this?"

Ugh, this was the part I was least looking forward to. I didn't want her gratitude, or anyone's. I didn't want people to make me out to be some kind of saint. I wasn't good like that. I wasn't like Val. I might be doing something good, but my motives were hardly pure.

"Look, don't get all mushy, okay? Don't mistake me for a do-gooder. I don't really care if I touch people's lives. I'm doing this for Val, not anyone else. It's completely selfish. I'll leave all the caring and making-a-difference stuff to you guys."

I was officially uncomfortable and wanted more than anything to be far from that office and away from Robin's speculating eyes. I pulled one of my manager's cards out of my wallet and handed it over. "My managers are ready to work with you guys to set something up. You just need to have whoever's in charge contact them at this number. They'll be waiting for the call."

Robin took the card as if it were the Crown Jewels of England. Once she got over her shock, she put the card in her purse and looked up at me with another calculating expression. "Walk with me," she said.

"What?"

"You and I need to talk, and there's a Taco Bell a block down the street calling my name." She rubbed her belly and the smile on her face didn't match her next sentence. "This little devil-munchkin is determined to turn me into a hippopotamus before he arrives."

I laughed but didn't follow her. I was appalled at the thought of her walking anywhere. Seriously, pregnancy looked awful. I was so glad I'd been born a guy. "Fine, but I'll drive. I'm not letting you walk anywhere like that."

Robin laughed and changed course for my car. As I helped her into the passenger seat, she grinned up at me. "You'll make a good father someday."

"I hope so. Someday."

BETWEEN THE TWO OF US, WE PRETTY MUCH ORDERED THE entire menu at Taco Bell. I'd managed to make it to the table without being recognized and Robin managed to make it without needing an ambulance, so we were both in good spirits as we started in on our mound of food.

"So what did you want to talk about?" I asked, once I'd eaten enough to politely hold a conversation between bites.

Robin put down her nachos and gave me a hard look. "Are you in love with Val?"

The question made me choke on my burrito. I coughed a minute and took a long sip of soda before I answered. "No. Of course not. That's crazy."

Robin sat back and crossed her arms over her chest. "Is it?"

Why was my heart suddenly pounding in my chest? I wanted to shake some sense into Robin and force her to stop asking me about this. Val and I definitely had a connection, but how could I love her? "I hardly know her," I said. "I haven't seen her in four years and I barely knew her back then."

"Then why go through all this?"

"Because I want to know her. Val and I have a connection that's worth exploring. This is the only way she'll give me a chance."

Robin studied me for a minute. I'm not sure what she was trying to find, or what she thought she knew, but the look in her eyes scared me. She stared me down with a determination I hadn't seen in anyone except for maybe myself and Val.

"I'm going to be honest with you, Kyle. This idea scares me," she said, digging into her nachos again.

I was a little offended. "Why?" I heard the disappointment in my tone and knew Robin heard it, too. "I'm only trying to help you. I could give your foundation so much publicity. I could do you guys a lot of good. Val would want me to do this."

"That's just it. You don't really understand how *much* it would mean to Val. You don't understand how much *you* mean to her."

That was the last thing I'd expected her to say. "What do you mean?"

Robin sighed and pushed her food away. She pierced me with a grave look. "If you start this and then screw it up, you will break her heart in a way she'll never recover from."

Whatever she meant by that, she was one hundred percent serious. I put down my burrito, no longer in the mood to finish it. "Explain."

"Val told me all about what happened between the two of you after the concert that night. She cried on my shoulder for days after you left. She was afraid she'd made the wrong choice. She started second-guessing herself, worried that she expected too much from people and that she'd thrown something special away when she let you go. She was in *love* with you, Kyle."

I reared back in my chair, shocked by Robin's confession and how much she meant it. Every word she said felt like a physical blow. I wanted to believe her, but I didn't want to hear it at the same time. I hated to think that I'd hurt Val.

I didn't like the thought that I'd made her question herself. The fact that she was so confident and determined, that she knew who she was and what she wanted, was the thing I liked the most about her. We were the same that way.

Robin continued on with her lecture, refusing to pull a single punch. "Val always hoped that one day you'd understand her choice and respect it, but she never dreamed you'd actually see things her way. She wouldn't let herself dare to hope you'd ever be willing to wait for her."

"But I am now. Why is that a bad thing?"

Robin tried to smile for me, but it was a sad smile. It was full of pity. "Val has faith in you," she said. "She's always had faith in you. She saw something good in you even when she didn't want to. Even when I tried my best to convince her otherwise."

"Gee, thanks," I teased, but the jab was halfhearted. I understood why Robin would want to warn Val away from me.

Robin shrugged, unapologetic. "If you do this, if you commit to this cause, you'll give her the hope that she's been denying herself for years. You'll suddenly be the perfect man, the hero, the dashing prince come to give her the happily ever after she's dreamed of her whole life. She'll fall again, Kyle. Hard and fast. You have to think about that. Don't play with her heart."

"Are you saying that I have to be ready to marry her if I want to ask her out?"

"No, but—"

"I'm not playing games with this," I insisted, voice low. I was seriously frustrated. I took a breath and forced myself to stay calm so that I wouldn't call attention to myself. "There's something there between Val and me. You know there is," I said, daring Robin with a look to deny it.

"I know," she admitted hesitantly, but the defensiveness in her tone had lessened.

When I spoke again, it sounded like a plea. "I want to see what would happen if we gave each other a real chance, but she won't give me that chance if I can't commit to the abstinence thing first. I'm not thrilled about it, but she's worth it, and I want her to know that. Doing this will help her see that I'm serious."

Robin shook her head. "I get that," she said. "And I think it's great that you're willing to try. But I don't think you understand what you're committing to. You said you're only doing it for Val, which means you still don't really get it. The abstinence challenge isn't a game. It's not a joke. There are so many people who take it seriously, and with you being who you are, your pledging would be a big deal to a lot of people."

I started to argue, but Robin wouldn't let me interrupt. "This is different than fame," she insisted. "Pledging to the cause and becoming a spokesperson would make you a role model. People would look up to you. They'd put their faith in you. One mistake and you'd let them down. Some you'd disappoint, and others you'd simply prove right. They'd have a field day with your failure. If you screwed up even once, you'd do a lot of damage to yourself *and* to Valerie and the campaign she's put so much work into. You could destroy everything she's built. Are you ready for that kind of responsibility?"

"I—"

I didn't know what to say. I'd driven to the foundation this evening, so sure of myself. I'd spent hours arguing with my managers and that had only strengthened my resolve, but suddenly I was sweating.

Robin reached her hand across the table and squeezed mine. The anger and skepticism were gone, replaced with endearment. I didn't understand the mood swing. I'd just decided she hated me and thought I was a lost cause, so I wasn't sure why I was getting a smile from her now.

"You're a good guy, Kyle," she said. "I know you care about Val, and I know she still cares about you. I love her and I want to see her happy. Believe it or not, I think you could do that. You're right. There's something between you guys. There always was. I would love to see the two of you work it out. I just want you to understand that Val comes with strings attached. You need to know what you're getting yourself into, and you need to be sure it's what you want before you do it. Maybe you should talk to Val first, too. You might want to make sure she wants to date you before you pledge your abstinence to her in front of the whole world."

Maybe I shouldn't have eaten that last burrito. I suddenly felt sick to my stomach. "Do you think she won't give me a chance?"

"Nothing personal." Robin shrugged. "She's been hurt quite a bit over the last four years. It's made her wary. She's a stubborn, busy, determined woman, and dating doesn't really fit into her agenda right now. If you're going to convince her, you've got your work cut out for you."

Well, that was disheartening. And extremely good to know.

I sat back and let everything she'd said today sink in. This was going to be a lot more complicated than I'd originally thought.

After a minute, Robin broke the silence. "She *is* worth it, Kyle," she whispered, giving my hand another squeeze.

The second she said that, I knew. "Yeah," I agreed. "She is." I pulled myself out of my own head and smiled at Robin. "Thanks for the talk."

"Sorry if I was too harsh. Pregnant women have no patience, you know."

I shook my head. "I needed to hear it. You're a good friend to look out for her like that. You must really care about her."

"I do."

Robin and I were quiet for the short ride back to the foundation office. As I helped her out of my car and into hers, I said, "I care about her, too. Enough that I'm in even if she doesn't want to date me. Have your boss call my managers."

"Are you sure?"

She pinned me with another serious look, but I saw the hope in her eyes as well. That hope lifted my spirits. She wanted me to win Val as much as I did. "I'm sure," I said with new resolve. "Try not to stress too much. When I agree to do something, I do it right. I'll be an awesome role model."

Robin buckled her seatbelt and grinned up at me. "You'll definitely make it interesting."

"And sexy."

That made her laugh. "And that," she agreed. "Good luck, Kyle."

I pointed to her massive belly and said, "You too."

9

G IS FOR GIRLFRIEND

VAL'S NEWEST PROJECT, A NONPROFIT ADOPTION AGENCY
called F is for Families, is in Sunnyvale, California, just a
short trek from Stanford where Val has been living for the
last four years. Like the Not Everybody's Doing It Foundation, the office called an older strip mall home. This one, at
least, was sandwiched between a dentist and a chiropractor
instead of a laundromat and a pawnshop. The front window
was clean too, with a nice decal, so that was a step up.

This office was bigger, a lot brighter, and more cheerful.
It had a small waiting area in front of a reception desk and
a few cubicles tucked away in the back. It actually felt like a
legitimate business, whereas the Not Everybody's Doing It
Foundation felt like a couple of do-gooders had decided to
start a club in their parents' basement.

The sight of this office brought me a sense of pride. Val
had done this. This whole organization was her creation.
Was there anything she couldn't do? (Besides *it*, of course.)

"Welcome to F is for Families. May I help you?"

The woman behind the reception desk stood up to greet me. She was somewhere in her mid-fifties, had a long brown braid that reached all the way to her butt, and wore a rainbow tie-dyed sundress that screamed hippy activist. I was so out of my element here.

"Hi. I'm looking for Valerie Jensen. Is she here?"

Hippy Lady smiled at me. "Of course. She's with a client at the moment. Have a seat. I'm sure she'll be out of her meeting soon. I'm Rain. If you need anything, just let me know."

"Will do. Thank you, ma'am."

I took a seat in the hard plastic chair and reached for a magazine. *Women's Health, Parenting, and Reader's Digest.* Ugh. I decided against the stellar reading material and pulled up a game on my phone.

"Did you have an appointment, Mr.…?"

Rain was eyeing me with the hungry gaze of an expert busybody. She hadn't recognized me, but she was obviously very curious who the strange young man visiting her boss was.

Far be it from me to withhold juicy gossip. I flashed her my best smile. "I'm Kyle. I don't have an appointment. I'm just here to take her to lunch."

Rain's eyes sparked with excitement. "*Valerie* has a lunch date?"

Wow. Robin hadn't been kidding when she said Val didn't go out much. The astonishment in this woman's voice suggested the concept was impossible.

I felt bad enough for the lady that I threw her a bone. "Actually, she doesn't know she has a lunch date yet. I'm an old friend. I just happened to be in town and I thought I'd surprise her."

Rain's smile fell a little in disappointment. "From out of town?"

"Los Angeles."

"Could be worse," she decided, narrowing her eyes at me. "Are you single?"

I laughed. She was all right. "Very single, and very interested."

"Well, now that's more like it!"

Rain pulled a chair from a neighboring desk and patted the seat. "You just come on over here, Kyle, and tell me all about yourself. Can I get you a cup of coffee?"

She was already on her feet, heading for the coffee pot, so I said "Thank you" and came to sit in the chair next to hers.

"Cream and sugar?" she called out.

"Coffee is coffee. I'll accept it in any form."

Rain grinned as she handed me a cup and sat down. She took a moment to look me over before shaking her head, as if to clear it. "Well, you are just a downright handsome young man, aren't you? What brings you to town? I hope you're here for the whole weekend. Valerie needs to be taken out on a proper date. She's such a catch, that one, but she won't step away from work long enough to let the men know it."

"Well, *I* know it."

"You do?" Rain bit her lip in an attempt to contain her excitement.

I leaned toward her and whispered, "Can I let you in on a little secret?" Rain hunched forward, her eyes glittering with anticipation. "I didn't 'just happen' to be in town. I came here specifically to see Val. I have no plans other than to woo her, and I'll stay for as long as it takes."

Rain was too overwhelmed to speak. She clutched at her chest, as if trying to make sure her heart didn't burst from it. Before the moment could get awkward, a door opened and Val stepped out into the main office with a teary-eyed couple and a pregnant girl that couldn't have been more than fifteen or sixteen.

Val shook the man's extended hand as the woman dabbed at her eyes with Kleenex. "We can't say 'thank you' enough."

"There's no need to thank me. That's what this program is for. Don't forget to schedule your next appointment with Rain before you go."

The teen suddenly threw herself at Val, enveloping her in a tight hug. "Thank you so much, Miss Jensen!" she blubbered.

Val hugged the girl back and brushed her thumb over the girl's wet cheeks. "Dry those tears now, Colleen. Everything's going to be okay."

The girl nodded, gaping up at Val with a look of hero worship. I could relate. Val was amazing. Watching her with those people stirred something in my chest. I could understand why Robin had been so hesitant before. This was about more than just an abstinence challenge. Val really did make a difference in people's lives. I could help her with that…or I could screw it up for her. I absolutely *couldn't* screw it up for her. Not now, not ever. No matter what I had to sacrifice.

"She's definitely worth it."

I didn't realize I'd spoken out loud until Rain patted my knee and said, "Yes, she is."

Our conversation caught the attention of Val and her clients. "Kyle?" Val gasped at the same time the teenager shrieked.

"*Kyle Hamilton?* Mom! Dad! That's *Kyle Hamilton!*"

The girl bounded over to me with fresh tears in her eyes, ignoring her parents' protests. "I'm sorry! I just love you soooooo much!" she cried.

"Thank you, Colleen, was it?"

I stood and opened my arms—an invitation for the girl to hug me. She screamed again and plastered herself to me as if she planned on staying there forever. "I can't believe I'm meeting you! You're my favorite singer in the whole world! I was so sad when Tralse broke up!"

I laughed and hugged the girl back. I winked at her parents over her shoulder to let them know it was okay. They gave me matching, chagrined smiles. "Have you heard the new song yet?" I asked Colleen, my eyes drifting to Val as I spoke.

"Yes!" Colleen squealed. "I saw you on the Connie Parker Show last week! It's amazing! And *so* romantic!"

"*Amazing,* you say? And *romantic?*" I couldn't help the grin I shot Val. "Imagine that."

When I chuckled, Colleen pulled her face out of my chest and glanced down at the *A* dangling from my wrist, nearly swooning from shock. "I still can't believe *you're* doing the abstinence challenge."

Maybe her disbelief should have been insulting, but it made me laugh. "A necessary evil if I want to date the fair virgin."

The girl's eyes widened.

"All right. I think that's enough of that." Val stepped

between Colleen and me. After giving me an exasperated look, she apologized to Colleen's parents for the interruption and marched them to the front desk. "The Mastersons have been approved and need to schedule an appointment."

Rain's answering smile was sincere. "Wonderful."

Once the family was out of the building, Val whirled on me. "What are you doing here?" she hissed.

"Taking you to lunch." I held my hands up in a gesture of surrender. "Why am I in trouble? What did I do?"

My questions made Val realize she'd just snapped at me and startled her out of her bad mood. She rubbed her temples and sighed. "I'm sorry. I'm just surprised to see you."

"You didn't call me. I waited for two weeks. I don't have your number anymore, so what else was I supposed to do?"

She looked at me with that same sad expression she'd worn at the studio. "You shouldn't have come."

"Why?" I demanded. I knew she'd try to blow me off, and I wasn't going to let her get away with it.

Val glanced around the room at our growing audience. Everyone in the office had stepped out of their cubicles to see what was going on. Rain watched us, transfixed. Val's face pinched again and she grabbed my hand. "Let's go talk in my office."

I yanked my fingers from her grip. "So you can blow me off before giving me a chance? No way. Not this time."

"Kyle, we can't do this."

I reeled her in and slipped my arms around her waist so she couldn't escape me. "Tell me you haven't been thinking about me since the second you saw me."

She didn't answer, but the truth was in her eyes.

Her brows fell into a frown and she closed her eyes as

if to shut me out or make me disappear. It hurt that she wouldn't even look at me. Why did my physical presence seem to cause her so much pain? What had I done that was so wrong?

"We're a lost cause, Kyle," she whispered. "You know we are. Do you really want to put us both through that again? It's been four years and I still feel heartsick over it every now and then."

She was making this more complicated than it had to be. My heart ached at the pain in her voice. I had to make it stop. I had to take away whatever sorrow she felt toward me. "There's a time and a place for everything, Val. We weren't ready then. But now?"

Holding her tightly to me with one arm, I tucked her hair behind her ear and forced her chin up. My fingertips lingered on her cheek. I couldn't seem to pull them away.

She shuddered at my touch and placed her hands on my chest as if to push me away, but she made no real effort to escape me. "Now?" she repeated, her voice so faint I barely heard her.

"I'll wait for you. I'll wait all the way to the altar if we make it that far."

Startled, her body went stiff and her breath hitched. Her beautiful brown eyes, glossy from a layer of unshed tears, stared up at me with both fear and hope. Vulnerable as she was in that moment, she was the most beautiful thing I'd ever seen.

"I've been waiting for you since the moment I put on the bracelet," I said. "And you're waiting for me, too." I smirked at the question in her eyes. "Four years and you've never fallen for anyone else? You're not over me. You still want this as much as I do."

Val's head finally cleared and she came back to herself. "Still completely arrogant, I see," she said, her voice returning to its normal strength.

I smiled at the old insult. "But no longer slutty."

Her lips curled up, though I could tell she was trying very hard not to smile. The action drew my gaze to her lips and my whole mouth turned to paste. I lowered my face halfway and waited for her to meet me in the middle. I wanted to kiss her again, but I needed her to make the move. I had to know she wanted me as much as I wanted her.

"Give us a chance."

"It'll never work," she said. Her eyes were on my mouth now too, and her breath was coming fast.

"At least if it doesn't, it won't be because we didn't try."

She swallowed hard and wet her lips but didn't move to kiss me. The distance between us was torture. "Kiss me," I whispered.

"But, Kyle, I think we—"

"Don't think. Just kiss me."

Finally, she let her eyes flutter shut and slid her hands up over my shoulders as she brought her lips to mine. She wrapped her arms around my neck and I lifted her up onto her toes to deepen the kiss. I waited until my body screamed at me for air before I set her back on her feet. Panting hard, I leaned my forehead against hers and took a moment to catch my breath. "It doesn't get more right than that, Val." My voice sounded husky and full of emotion.

Eyes still closed, she let her arms fall to her sides and laid her head on my shoulder, resting against me as if she needed a hug. I obeyed and wrapped her in a gentle embrace.

"You live in L.A., Kyle," she whispered sadly. "My life is here. I'm starting grad school in a month, and you'll go off on tour with your new album."

"But I'm here now. Give me one day. Just today. If that works, then give me tomorrow."

She pulled her face out of my neck and looked up at me with glossy eyes.

"We'll take it one day at a time," I promised. "Let's just see where that gets us before we worry about anything else."

She searched my face for answers, clearly worried about what the future might hold for us. Whatever she was looking for, I was determined to show it to her. She was so strong all the time, in every other aspect of her life. In this one area I could take that burden from her. I could be the strong one this time. I could be her rock if she needed one.

I didn't know what our future held. I had no idea how we would overcome the obstacles already set in our path. But I knew I wasn't going to throw in the towel without putting up one hell of a fight first. Giving up wasn't something I knew how to do.

That's the great thing about life. Anything is possible if you want it bad enough. And right then, holding Val in my arms, with the taste of her kiss still on my lips, there wasn't anything I wanted more than I wanted to make things work with her.

"Okay," she finally said.

Cheers went up all around us from the handful of people in her office. I'd forgotten we had an audience. Val looked as if she'd forgotten that fact, too. She blushed bright red but laughed and accepted the congratulations from her coworkers.

"So…" I slipped my arm around her waist. "Can I take you to lunch?"

Val sighed. "Actually, I can't. Bryce, Jacinta, and I are meeting with some potential patrons this afternoon."

A petite black woman interrupted Val, clapping her hands excitedly. "He can go in my place." She shook her head when Val started to argue. "You can schmooze without me. I'm just the numbers, and the Greshams already know all the numbers. You and Bryce are the heart of this organization. It's the two of you they're really investing in. You don't need me."

My brain slammed into a mental brick wall. Bryce? Who the hell was Bryce? And why did it sound like he and Val were some kind of golden couple?

Val looked torn for a minute as her eyes darted back and forth between her coworker and me. "You sure it'll be okay?" she finally asked. "The Greshams are very conservative, and Kyle is…"

I smirked and filled in the blank for her. "Capable of behaving himself." At her skeptical look, I added, "When I have to."

"Actually, having him along might work in our favor," a smooth, deep voice said.

If the six foot tall, blond haired, hazel eyed, preppy, pretty-boy douche stepping forward was this Bryce person, then "golden" was a very apt description.

Val smiled at the newcomer and said, "Kyle, this is Bryce Carmichael. He's the legal half of our F is for Families family. I never could have gotten the organization up and running without him."

Bryce laughed. "Not true. She'd have found a way.

Nothing stops Val from getting what she wants." The jerk stuck his hand out to me, flashing a big pearly-white smile that had the nerve to look sincere. "It's nice to meet you. Val's told us a lot about you. Welcome to the Family."

"Thanks."

I tried not to be a jackass and crunch the guy's hand as I shook it, but I kept my reply short because I was nowhere near the actor Cara was and I doubt I could have hidden my instant dislike of this guy. I was jealous as hell, because while I knew they weren't dating I had to wonder if they used to. It was obvious that they were close.

I reminded myself that two seconds ago Val was kissing me, not him. And she'd just agreed to be my girlfriend. I smiled at the thought and decided I didn't need to hate the guy. I held Val just a little tighter to my side. She smiled at me when I squeezed her and turned her gaze to Bryce. "You're really okay with Kyle coming tonight?"

"Sure. He's your greatest V is for Virgin success story, Val. What could be more convincing?"

Val's face lit up. "Excellent argument, Counselor," she said. "As always." She turned her bright eyes on me and said, "You want to be my show-and-tell for the afternoon?"

Hell yes, I did.

10

B IS FOR BASEBALL

Val and her best friend Bryce Carmichael carpooled to work every day in Bryce's very expensive BMW convertible. It was flashy and pompous, and something my parents would have approved of. And Val loved it. Girls and convertibles. I will never understand it.

I was squished in the tiny backseat because Bryce had offered to drive wherever it was we were going, and I was too much of a gentleman to let Val ride in the back. "Home first, Jeeves," Val said as she buckled herself in. "I need to change."

Both of them were dressed in business attire. Val in a pencil skirt, blouse, and heels, and Bryce in a dress shirt and slacks—though he wasn't wearing a tie, which I had to admit, earned him a couple of cool points.

"You're fine how you are," Bryce said. Val cut him a serious look that made him groan and argue. "Your house is out of the way."

"Bryce, don't even try it. You know this is a battle you will lose."

"But the Greshams are serious Giants fans."

"I won't hold it against them," Val replied flippantly.

Bryce groaned again and switched lanes to get on the freeway going the other direction. Their familiarity with each other was almost as annoying as having no idea what they were talking about. "What's going on?" I asked, hoping my irritation was well buried.

"Val's getting her way," Bryce said, "same as always. And adding twenty minutes to our drive because of a hat."

"It's a *lucky* hat," Val said, as if that explained everything. She turned in her seat and grinned at me. "The Greshams are a very wealthy older couple from Palo Alto. They could never have children of their own and fostered kids for over twenty years. Now that they're too old to foster children, they're looking to back an adoption agency as a way to stay involved, but they're very particular about what kind of agency they want to support. We're one of the handful of nonprofit agencies they're considering."

"If we can convince them we're the right fit," Bryce said, glancing my way in his rearview mirror, "they'll fund the majority of our expenses for years. Then we could put a lot more effort into placing children rather than making sure we stay afloat."

I was surprised by the zeal in his voice. I recognized passion when I saw it. He was every bit as sincere as Val with this whole adoption thing—a true do-gooder just like her.

"So what does any of that have to do with a lucky hat?" I asked when Val caught me frowning.

Her grin doubled in size. "Robert Gresham is a huge baseball fan so he's taking us to a game. The Giants are playing the Angels today. I can't go to an Angels game without my lucky hat."

She was a baseball nut? I was so surprised I didn't even know how to respond. Never in a million years would I have guessed that. "Are you a sports fan in general or just baseball?" I asked.

"I'm an athlete." She shrugged. "I appreciate competition no matter what sport it is. Volleyball is my favorite, but baseball is a close second, and the Angels are my team." She shot Bryce another no-nonsense look, then said, "The hat is necessary. My dad gave it to me when he took me to my first game. I was six. I've worn it to every Angels game I've been to ever since. Over the years I've gotten a handful of my favorite players to sign it."

I smiled, despite being cramped in the back of a typical rich-guy car. Finally, something we had in common. I loved sports. Couldn't play them to save my life, but I loved watching them. Personally I was a huge Lakers fan, but baseball was cool too, and I'd happily take Val to all the Angels games her heart desired.

"What about basketball?" I asked hopefully. "Do you like the Lakers at all?"

"I'm not religious about them, but I wouldn't turn down tickets to a game." She wriggled her eyebrows and added, "Especially not where your seats are. You should have tried that approach four years ago. If you'd dangled courtside seats in front of me, I might have said yes to a date."

Whatever look was on my face made both Bryce and Val burst into laughter. "How do you not know this about Val?" Bryce asked.

His question pissed me off, but only because he had a point. As much as I liked Val, she was practically a stranger to me. I tried not to glare at the guy and said, "She never gave me a real chance to get to know her." Swallowing back my hostility, I forced myself to smile and added, "But I'm looking forward to learning everything about her now that she finally will."

We pulled up in front of a small one-story house. It was a few decades old but well-maintained. Painted yellow with white trim and shutters and rose bushes beneath the front window, it looked like something a grandmother would live in, and yet, somehow it made sense that Val lived here.

"Two minutes!" she promised as she jumped from the car and ran inside.

I used the opportunity to ask Bryce some questions that I'd been dying to know since I first saw him. "So, how long have you know known Val?"

Bryce turned in his seat to face me instead of looking at me in the mirror. His answering smile was friendly—as if he didn't consider me a threat at all. "Since she moved here. I was in my second year in law school and was a TA for one of her classes her freshman year. I knew of Virgin Val—I'm adopted too, and I'd always thought her story was cool—so I recognized her instantly. I asked her to coffee, we swapped adoption stories, and we've been really good friends ever since."

Really good friends? Yeah, right. No guy is just "really good friends" with a woman. "Did you two ever date?"

Obvious? Yes. But I didn't care. I wanted to know.

Bryce laughed. "I would have in a heartbeat if I'd ever thought for one second that Val was interested, but she's never acted anything but platonic with me. Over the years I've learned to accept her friendship for what it was. I care about her enough that I just want to see her happy."

While I sat there trying to decide exactly how much he was in love with Val, he studied me with an expression I couldn't decipher. He glanced back toward the house and the smile fell from his face. "I've never seen her respond to anyone the way she did to you in the office earlier," he said, concern etching his brow. "Seeing the two of you together made a lot of things about her make sense."

"What do you mean?"

Instead of answering my question, he said, "Be careful with her. Don't hurt her."

"I don't plan to."

I must have sounded defensive again because he lifted his hands as if to say he was backing off. "I know," he said. "I can tell you're sincere, but it's hard to not worry. I've seen her hurt before and it's not something I want to see again."

My curiosity piqued at this hint to Val's dating history, but before I could ask, Val came back. She'd changed into jeans and a snug Angels T-shirt that made me forget all about the conversation I'd been having with Bryce. Her hair was in a ponytail and pulled through the back of an old, faded baseball cap. Sure enough, it was covered with signatures.

This was a brand-new side of Val that I'd never seen. Usually I'd describe her as beautiful, hot, gorgeous, or sexy, but right now she was just plain cute. A smile crept over my face and Val grinned to match it.

"I approve of the lucky hat," I said. "Sports Fan Val is a look I could get used to."

.   .   .   .   .

THE GRESHAMS SHOWED UP AT THE BASEBALL GAME DRESSED for a golf tournament. The only indication that they were in the right place was the San Francisco Giants cap Mr. Gresham wore on the very top of his head trucker-hat style. He looked like a jackass, but he'd sprung for amazing seats right behind the away team's on-deck circle, which thrilled Val to pieces, so I didn't begrudge him his lack of style.

They stood when we arrived, and Mr. Gresham gaped at Val's attire. "The *Angels*?" he gasped, not quite insulted, but almost.

Val gave him a very solemn look and said, "Mr. Gresham, I'll be frank with you. I could really use your money for the agency, but I don't want it badly enough to root for the Giants when they're up against my Angels. Not now, not ever."

I almost burst into laughter. It was a bold move that I don't know if I'd have made, but Val would forever be Val. Whether she was standing up for her right to not have sex, or root for the away team against the boss, she would never compromise her personal standards.

Mrs. Gresham chuckled under her breath while her husband blinked at Val in astonishment. Then, without warning, he threw his head back and let out a big belly laugh. "A woman of true principal," he teased. "I can respect that."

Val gave him a smile that would one day win her an election, and they fell into comfortable conversation. Until the Giants took the lead with a three-run homer in the bottom of the second, that is, and Val started shouting insults at the Giants. By the seventh, the Angels were behind six to one and Val had gone beyond slinging insults to arguing with the umpires and trying to coach the Angels.

The Greshams seemed as surprised and amused as I was, but the resigned look on Bryce's face suggested he'd sat through many games just like this. "She's like this every time," he said, reading my thoughts.

Laughing, I pulled Val's hand into mine and laced our fingers together. "Should we go get some corn dogs or something?" I asked. "Let you walk off a little steam before you get us thrown out of the park?"

Val slumped back in her chair with a disgusted sigh as one of the Angels struck out and ended the inning. "He went down *looking*," she groaned. As the player walked back toward the dugout, she shouted, "You can't hit the ball if you don't swing, Trout! That's twice in a row!"

Unfortunately we were only two rows away from the field, which was well within hearing range, and that comment earned her a glare from the center fielder in question. When she caught his attention she blew him a kiss and yelled, "Don't worry, you're still my favorite!"

The guy tried to hold his glare, but he broke down and laughed. "Thanks, gorgeous. I'll hit the next one just for you," he said as he disappeared into the dugout.

I chuckled to myself. Nobody could resist the woman. "Should I be worried about the competition?" I teased, bringing her hand to my lips.

"Only if he homers it on his next at bat."

She met my eyes and sighed, a lot of her aggression gone. "Sorry. I'm just frustrated because they're better than this. It's one thing to lose if you're trying your best, but they've given up."

That made Bryce laugh. "She's like that in the office, too. Never lets anyone slack off, and never gives up."

"I'm not the only one," she replied. "You're the one who sees every adoption we handle through to the end."

That comment finally got them all discussing the reason they were meeting today. I'd been worried that I would be bored while they talked shop the rest of the afternoon, but this meeting seemed more like they were interviewing Val to become one of the family. I found the get-to-know-you session fascinating and extremely enlightening. I learned more about Val in those last two innings than I had the entire time I'd known her.

The Greshams did ask a lot of questions about the adoption agency she ran, and there was some business talk, but for the most part they were more interested in the people running it than the organization itself. They wanted their money to be in good hands.

It was during the bottom of the ninth that the real question of the hour was finally brought to the table. Val's BMW convertible driving, friendly to everyone, Stanford Law do-gooder, fellow adoptee, best guy friend said, "Well, I believe Val has now told you everything there possibly is to know about herself, and with her team currently losing an embarrassing eight to one, you have now seen her at her worst."

I chuckled at that along with the Gershams. Val was definitely not a gracious loser. (Not surprising, considering she wasn't personally capable of losing.)

"The only question left," Bryce said, "is can F is for Families count on your patronage?"

As much as I hate to admit it, I understood why that woman in Val's office had spoken of Val and Bryce as if they were some sort of power couple. Bryce was basically the male version of Val, and together they were downright formidable. They had me sold, but the Gershams hesitated.

"You've seen the numbers," Bryce persisted. "You've met the staff. You know what F is for Families is all about. What else is it that has you unconvinced?"

Mr. and Mrs. Gersham shared a look and then Mr. Gersham said, "We heard that Miss Jensen was planning to leave the organization. Is this true?"

They obviously weren't thrilled with the news, but Val wasn't the least bit ruffled. "It's true," she said, nodding. "I will be handing the reins of control over to Bryce at the end of the summer. I'm starting grad school in the fall and I intend to pursue a political career after I graduate."

"So you're leaving permanently?"

"The agency will always be mine in my heart, but yes. I will be leaving permanently. I can promise you, though, that my leaving will change nothing about the organization. The transition will be seamless. You'll be in very good hands."

As Val stared the billionaire couple down, silently daring them to disagree with her and turn her down, I marveled at her courage. She was the most confident woman I'd ever seen. She was fearless.

Val won the staring contest but still didn't get the "yes" she was looking for.

"It's my turn to be frank with you, Miss Jensen," Mr. Gresham said. "My wife and I were drawn to your organization because of *you*. We know your history and are impressed with everything you've done. We like what you stand for. Mr. Carmichael seems like a man with a good heart and smart head on his shoulders, but it's *you* we trust."

"So trust her," I said. I'd been pretty quiet through this

whole meeting after the initial introductions, not really fitting in with all these Ivy League let's-save-the-world-one-adoption-at-a-time people, but it was hard to keep quiet when they questioned her.

The conversation died and the Greshams, Val, and Bryce all turned to give me their full attention. "This organization has been her life's work for years now," I said. "She's put her heart and soul into it. I just met Bryce today, but I wouldn't have to have met him at all to know that he's perfect for the job. There's no way Val would be able to hand over something she cares so much about if he wasn't the exact right person."

Both Bryce and Val looked surprised that I'd come to Bryce's defense. Val's eyes misted over the tiniest bit and she gave my hand a grateful squeeze. I leaned over and kissed her cheek. "It's true."

Mr. Gresham cleared his throat to gain my attention. "I can see your point," he told me. "But that's an awful lot of blind faith you're asking for. Can you honestly tell me you would support an organization simply because Miss Jensen did, even if she was no longer in charge?"

I laughed. "I already have. Val's only involved in the V is for Virgin campaign by reputation anymore, and I don't even really believe in the cause, but I still agreed to be their new official spokesperson last week."

Val's head whipped around and she gasped, "You *what*?"

"You heard me," I said, laughing at her expression. "It's all finalized and everything. I'm holding a press conference next week to make the announcement and take the official abstinence pledge in front of a camera. I signed the contract yesterday, agreeing to donate ten percent of all my profits from the new album to the Not Everybody's Doing It Foundation."

Her shock right then was worth the promise I'd given Robin. She slapped her hand over her mouth and her eyes welled up with tears. She blushed as she accepted a tissue from Mrs. Gresham.

"I'm sorry," she said, dabbing at her tears. "I'm just— Kyle, I can't believe it! Are you *serious*?"

I shrugged.

Val laughed as another round of happy tears slipped from her eyes, and she threw her arms around my neck. "Thank you!"

As I hugged her back, Mr. Gresham spoke again. "You see? It's this kind of thing that we're impressed with, Miss Jensen. You inspire people to act."

Val let go of me and turned back to Mr. Gresham. "If that's the kind of person you're looking for, then you have to choose F is for Families. It's because of Bryce that I even started the agency. *He* inspired *me* to act."

I'm not sure whose curiosity was more piqued: the Gresham's or mine. I wanted to be sick to my stomach. It was bad enough that Mr. Carmichael was basically perfect for Val in every way, and had everything in common with her down to the Stanford Alumni status, but to hear that he was also the person who *inspired* her? It was vomit inducing.

"Mr. Gresham, the truth is, Bryce is far better suited to run F is for Families than I am. I may have started the agency, but it was Bryce's original idea. He was the one with the vision. I just helped him make it a reality. I have aspirations for a different career after I'm finished with grad school, but Bryce will stay with the organization for the rest of his life. He grew up in the foster care system and wasn't adopted until he was fourteen."

The Greshams gasped at the revelation and stared at Bryce. Their expressions instantly melted into looks of sympathy and admiration.

"I got lucky being placed with a couple when I was twelve who took a liking to me and chose to adopt me," Bryce said. "I'd been bounced around from foster home to foster home since I was five years old. I didn't stand a chance at succeeding in life until the Carmichaels offered me a real home, and now look at me. I'm a Stanford Law graduate. I know how important adoption is, and for these kids to have stable homes with good parents. This job is personal for me."

Val broke the reverent silence that had fallen upon us with Bryce's story. "Every staff member at F is for Families has a personal connection to adoption in some way and has chosen to work there because they are passionate about the cause. I guarantee you won't find a more dedicated agency to put your money behind, and Kyle is right—Bryce is the perfect man to head the organization. You would be fools to choose another agency simply because I'm not in charge."

My jaw fell slack at Val's very blunt speech. The Greshams were just as surprised, but when they looked at one another and both cracked smiles, I knew Val had won. The Greshams wouldn't be choosing another agency. They'd just found a home for their money.

Virgin Val had struck again. Even Mike Trout homered his next at bat, bringing in two more runs for the Angels, as if he simply couldn't let Val down. He winked at Val on his way back to the dugout after crossing home plate, mouthing the words "for you." She gave him two big thumbs-up.

Seriously, the woman was a force to be reckoned with.

And she was finally mine.

11

D IS FOR DATING

VAL AGREED TO LET ME TAKE HER OUT ON A PROPER DATE TO celebrate her victory after the game. I agreed to give her an hour to shower and change, and then checked myself into a hotel so I could do the same. Believe it or not, it was our first real date, and that had me anxious to make it perfect.

Standing on her doorstep in my sport coat holding a bouquet of roses, was a major high school throwback. I felt like a freshman going to his first homecoming all over again.

When Val answered the door in a strapless red cocktail dress that hugged her frame and stopped mid-thigh, I died. I pulled at the collar of my shirt, trying to release some of the heat that was suddenly consuming me.

I'd never seen her so dressed up before. Usually she sported a business casual look—preppy enough that my country-clubbing parents would adore her. There had been a few times she had gotten sexed up in a sassy, let's-hit-the-club way, but I always assumed those times were of Cara's doing.

This look was different. It was classy. Tasteful. It was

elegant and fun at the same time—a perfect blend of casual and formal. She was maddeningly sexy without trying. Probably without even knowing it. I wondered if she had any clue how tempting she looked.

"Kyle?"

How long had I been standing there just staring at her?

"Shit, Valerie," I muttered. I couldn't decide if I'd landed in heaven or hell. She'd transformed herself into the stunning beauty she was now just for me, and I wasn't allowed to touch. This night might kill me. "How the hell am I supposed to abstain from anything with you looking like that?"

I wasn't kidding.

She eyed my jeans and chewed on her bottom lip as she looked down at her own outfit. "You didn't say what we were doing, so I wasn't sure how to dress. I'll go change into something more casual."

"No!" I nearly tackled her when she turned to leave. "You will absolutely *not* go change. Not now, not ever again. You look…" It took me a long time to pick a word. "Breathtaking." It still didn't seem adequate enough.

She blushed at the praise, but when I pulled her to me by the hips and my hands automatically started roaming, her smile fell flat and she sighed. "I should go put on some jeans."

"No, you really shouldn't."

My hands rounded the curve of her butt and she raised a challenging brow. I chuckled and somehow peeled my hands off her body and shoved them in my pockets.

"Sweatpants and a scrubby T-shirt, then. I'll be right back."

When she turned to leave again I grabbed her hand and

pulled her out onto the step. "I am serious. You are not taking that dress off."

Me, on the other hand...

Damn it! I was so screwed. She wasn't even out the door
yet and I was tempted to skip the date altogether and sweep
her straight into bed.

"Kyle?"

I shook myself out of my trance. I had to get it together.
"I'm good," I lied. "I've managed for eight months now; I
can do this. Nobody's taking your dress off. Not you...and
not me, either." *Even if it kills me.*

Val blinked, finally grasping the true depth of my inter-
nal struggle.

I tugged her away from the house before she could run
screaming, and gave her a sheepish smile. "We'll duct tape
my hands behind my back if we have to."

She finally laughed. "Hopefully it won't come to that,"
she said as I walked her to my car and opened her door for
her, "but don't think I won't if you make me."

I took her into San Francisco. I had reservations on one
of those dinner cruises where they take you out on a big
yacht and provide a romantic candlelit dinner while they sail
you around the bay. This one came complete with a grand
piano and a stringed quartet. Not my usual taste in music,
but I looked forward to a nice slow dance with Val after we
ate.

Val followed my gaze around the room and then smiled
down at the table as if she were enjoying a private joke. It
made me smile too, even though I didn't get it. My curiosity
got the better of me. "Something funny?"

She met my gaze with a twinkle in her eyes. "I thought

you weren't a fan of places that set out more than one fork."

I chuckled, surprised she remembered that about me. "Not usually," I agreed, "but I figured, since this was our first real date and all..."

Val thought about it and smiled. "It really is our first, isn't it?"

"The first one you agreed to willingly. It seemed like a special enough occasion to merit multiple forks."

"I'd say so. It's only been five years since the first time you asked."

I let my eyes rove over her again. Her hair was twisted up, leaving her neck and shoulders bare. Her skin shimmered slightly in the soft light.

She was beautiful, but when I looked at her, it was the memories we shared that made me smile. I was glad we had the history we did, otherwise I might not see past the beauty. I wouldn't appreciate her the way I did now.

"It was well worth the wait, Val, I promise."

My words changed something in her countenance. Her smile slipped into a look I couldn't decipher. Her voice was soft when she said, "You haven't asked me what I think about your new song."

My stomach lurched, but I managed to sound calm when I responded. "I've been trying very hard not to. I learned my lesson the last time."

Val blushed, chagrined. "I deserve that."

"You were honest," I said. "I can't ask for more than that."

She reached across the table suddenly and set her hand on top of mine. "I love the new song, Kyle."

I hadn't realized how much I needed to hear that until

I let out the breath I'd been holding and felt a million times lighter. "I'm glad," I said, forcing down a lump in my throat.

I flipped my hand over and tangled our fingers together. Val looked at our joined hands as if she didn't understand what was happening. "Did you really mean it," she asked, "or was it just a good idea for a song?"

It hurt that she needed clarification. "I'm here, aren't I?"

"Yes, but I don't understand *why*." She seemed mystified. "It's been four years. You were engaged to someone else. Why write another song now? What on earth even made you think of me after all this time?"

I sat back with a sigh and took a sip of my wine. Val pulled her hand back to her side of the table and waited for an answer.

"It's a long story," I warned, "and I'm pretty sure talking about your ex-fiancée on a first date is some kind of faux pas."

Val wasn't going to let me off the hook that easily. "I need to understand. I want to believe that you're sincere. It's not that I think you're lying, but you're *Kyle Hamilton*. You're larger than life and whimsical. You're so passionate about everything...for five minutes at a time. I can't help having doubts about what exactly it is you're looking for with me."

She still saw the old me. The younger, stupid, cocky, rock star who only knew how to live in the moment and never considered the future. How could I make her understand that I was different?

"I'm here because I'm tired of 'five minutes at a time.' I'm looking for the chance to have something real."

Val considered this a moment. "And you believe you'll find that with me?"

I nodded. "I don't think you'd be capable of anything less. You aren't the type of woman a guy picks up at a bar and takes home for the weekend, Val. You're the kind we see going out with other men that makes us wonder what the hell we're doing wrong."

Val sat, frozen, staring into my eyes as my words settled in. I refused to look away. Eventually she managed a smile and took a sip from her glass. "I still can't believe you're the new king of the abstinence crowd."

Her teasing tone brought the light mood back and I laughed. "Me either."

After dinner we went out on the ship's deck. Even though I was born and raised in Surf City, USA, I'd never been a surfer. But I loved the ocean. As a kid, I grew up boating. My parents have their own yacht and although I hated going to their stupid yacht club events and mingling with snooty people in uncomfortable clothes, I always loved going out on the boat. I loved the feel of the water rolling beneath me, and I loved the fresh breeze with that saltwater and seaweed smell.

Cruising around the San Francisco Bay was nice because while the water was a little calmer than being out on the open ocean, the view more than made up for it. At night the city lights were amazing, and the bridges spectacular.

Val walked to the edge of the ship and leaned against the railing as she stared out at the approaching Golden Gate. "It's beautiful," she whispered.

Standing behind her, I was sure my view was a little better. I took off my blazer and wrapped it over her bare shoulders. It may have been the first week of June, but in San Francisco that still only meant low sixties after the sun went down. With the breeze, it was quite chilly.

"Thank you," she said, gripping the jacket tightly around her.

"My pleasure. Now I have a reason to do this..." I pulled her back against my chest and wrapped her in my arms. "If you're going to wear my jacket, then it's your job to keep me warm."

"Deal," she said.

She sucked in a deep breath when I placed a soft kiss on her neck. She shivered and rested her head against my shoulder. We stayed silent for a while, enjoying everything about this moment. When the boat glided beneath the bridge, I broke the silence. "I'll never understand how man accomplishes some of the things they do." Staring up at the massive structure from its underbelly, my mind was a little blown away.

There was a smile in Val's reply. "I'll bet there are people who think that very thing about you and the things you've accomplished in your life."

"I sing. I don't engineer miraculous structures that will stand for hundreds of years."

"But the songs you write will last forever. Your music has already touched hundreds of thousands of lives and will be remembered as part of this country's history."

The compliment was surprising and warmed me on the inside, but at the same time it felt a little ridiculous. It was only music. It's not like I singlehandedly brought down the national teen pregnancy average.

"You're one to talk," I teased, wanting, for once, to take the attention off of myself. "Look at the things you've accomplished just in the last five years. You were so amazing they had to make a movie about you."

Val smiled up at me over her shoulder. "I'm pretty sure there was a character in that movie named after you, too."

"Yeah, but I think I was the villain."

She laughed, and I leaned down and pressed my lips to hers. The kiss was chaste—a simple peck—but just the fact that I could do it, that Val was here with me and that I was allowed to kiss her whenever I had the urge, felt like as mind blowing a feat as building the bridge we were sailing under.

Val blushed bright red. She gave me a shy smile and turned her gaze back to the water. "This is a little strange, isn't it?" she asked.

I gave her a tight squeeze and said, "I like to think of it as inevitable. I knew from the first time I saw you that I wanted you to be mine. This feels like…sweet victory."

I knew instantly that I'd put my foot in my mouth and said the exact worst thing, but it was too late to unsay it.

Val stepped out of my arms and turned around to face me. She looked as if she were about to throw her hands on her hips and start tapping her foot. "'Sweet victory'?" she asked. "And now that you've finally won your coveted prize, how long before you get tired of me and move on to the next challenge?"

I sighed. I could be such an idiot sometimes. I knew Val was concerned about my sincerity. I knew she was going to feel insecure at first.

"Never," I promised. "I could never get tired of you."

She didn't look like she believed me.

"Do you really think I'm going to toss you aside the first chance I get?" I asked.

"It's taken me five years to get this far. Am I excited that

I've finally achieved it? Of course. Right now I feel like the luckiest guy on Earth, and I'm scared to death that any minute you're going to realize you're too good for me and send me packing."

Her frown turned into a wry smile.

"It's the truth," I insisted. I stepped closer and took her face in my hands. "Trust me, I do not want to screw this up. Okay?"

She searched my eyes a moment and nodded. "Okay."

Crisis averted, my smile came back. "Good," I said. "And now that we understand each other, I think it's time I reap some of the spoils of my victory."

Before she could argue, I lowered my face to hers again. This time I kissed her good and hard. The heat of it was probably inappropriate for a public display but I didn't care; I wanted her to feel it. I wanted to start a fire inside her that would leave her burning all night.

I pushed her back against the boat railing and leaned in until our bodies were flush against one another. My hand slipped inside the blazer she wore, and I ran my fingers up the side of her body. Nothing separated us except the thin material of her dress, but it wasn't enough. My hands fell to her butt and I squeezed her against me, hoping her closeness would relieve some of my need for her. She gasped.

"Gross," a young female voice said.

There was a round of snickers and then a male voice that said, "Yeah, get a room."

I thanked the Lord for his divine intervention and disentangled myself from Val. I apologized when I saw her startled expression. "Sorry. I guess I got a little carried away."

"Yeah," she breathed.

We were interrupted again by a third voice. "Aren't you guys, like, way too old to be dry humping each other in public?"

I laughed. Whoever our make-out police were, they had sass. "I'm a rock star," I said, turning my attention to them. "It's expected of me."

There were six teenagers all dressed in formal attire, donned in corsages and boutonnieres. They'd been sneering but when I turned around, the frowns left their faces and their eyes all went wide simultaneously.

"Kyle Hamilton?"

"The one and only." I flashed them my best smile. "Please, feel free to jump up and down and squeal a little if you need to. I don't mind."

Val snorted softly. I snagged her around the waist and reeled her to my side. "Same goes for you," I told her. "Any time you want to fangirl out on me, you go right ahead."

"Yeah, that's gonna happen...never."

I heaved an over-the-top sigh, making the girls in front of us giggle. One of them stepped forward holding a phone. "Can we take a picture with you?" She blushed and her eyes flicked to Val. "Would your girlfriend mind?"

Call me a dork, but I felt a thrill at hearing Val's new title. "What do you say, *girlfriend*?" I asked, casting Val a look that made her laugh.

"I'm not his girlfriend."

And suddenly that thrill was gone. I stopped paying attention to the kids and frowned at Val. "Um, yes, actually, you *are* my girlfriend."

"Um, no, actually," she repeated sarcastically, "I'm not. This is just a date."

I narrowed my eyes at her. Was she serious? I totally thought that conversation in her office earlier today made it official. I could have sworn she was right there with me, too. Why was she fighting me on this? Well, if she wanted a fight, she'd get one.

"I've got news for you, you gorgeous, stubborn commit-aphobe. This is not just a date. It's the start of a relationship."

"This is a date to see if you deserve a relationship."

"You know I do. You're just being difficult. Maybe it's not me that likes the chase. Doesn't matter, though. Whether you admit it or not, we're totally going out."

She rolled her eyes and held her hand out for the girl's phone. "I'll take the picture for you," she said. She held up the phone and added, "Everybody squish in close. It's going to be hard to fit you all in with Kyle's ego taking up so much space."

Everyone laughed, and Val proceeded to take a number of pictures with several different phones. As I smiled for one last shot, the girl clinging to me gasped. "Oh my gosh, I *knew* you looked familiar! You're Virgin Val, aren't you?"

Val gave the phone back to the girl and smiled sheep-ishly. "You caught me."

The girl squealed and ran to Val, forgetting all about me. It was a little surreal. I can't say that's ever happened to me before.

"I can't believe this! I've wanted to meet you for forever. Your movie inspired me so much." The girl lifted her arm to show Val the virgin bracelet on her wrist that had been hidden beneath her corsage. "I wear it all the time. Can I take a picture with you, too? Please? It would mean so much to me."

"Of course."

Val slipped my jacket off to pose for a picture. As she handed it to me I winked at her. "Look at you, stealing my fans."

She smirked. "I think you'll survive."

When she turned around, the girl gasped again. "Oh! You're even wearing your necklace!"

"Always." She laughed as she put her arm around the girl. "Especially now that I'm on a date with Kyle. He needs the constant reminder."

"It didn't look like the reminder was working very well," one of the guys muttered.

Val blushed and I burst into laughter. "Can you blame me?" I asked. I waved a hand toward Val. "Do you see how insanely hot this woman is?"

After Val posed for a few pictures of her own, the girl who recognized her hugged her and said, "I can't believe you're dating Kyle Hamilton."

Val sighed but I laughed. "Neither can I," I said. "It only took me five years and a vow of celibacy to get her to say yes."

The girl's eyes bugged and she bit her lip to hold back a squeak of excitement. I stole Val back from the girl and slipped my arm around her waist. "Now, if you guys will excuse us, since this is our first date and all, I think I should take the lovely lady back inside for a spin around the dance floor."

Before I could drag Val away, the girl yelled out, "Will you kiss her for us again?"

I stopped and smirked.

"What?" Val asked.

"Twist my arm."

I started to lean in, but Val clasped a hand over my mouth. "Wait," she said, laughing. "Didn't you guys just ask him to *stop* kissing me?"

The girl blushed but said, "Please? My older sister is a huge Virgin Val fan, too. She's never going to believe that you guys are really together."

Val shook her head. "I told you, we're just on a date. We're not—"

Val gasped in surprise when I swept her into my arms and dipped her back. "Not together?" I asked and kissed her long enough for those girls to get all the pictures their hearts desired.

When I finally set her back on her feet, she sighed. "Must you always cause a scene?"

"Well, you know, it's like I told them." I pointed my thumb toward the teens. "I'm a rock star. It's in the job description."

12

M IS FOR MEDIA

As much as I hated having to wake up alone the next morning, having my own place to sleep while I was in town was a necessary evil of dating a woman I wasn't allowed to have sex with.

I thought I understood temptation. I'd been tempted to ditch my bracelet plenty of times in the last eight months and managed to stay strong. But those times I'd just been saying no to casual sex with a stranger. Val was not a stranger and there was nothing casual about the connection I felt to her.

When I dropped her off on her doorstep at the end of our date, I was slammed with a desire so intense it almost brought me to my knees. I stood there, leaning against the doorframe, scared to take even a single step inside as I kissed her good night.

I warned her to deadbolt the door once I left, just in case I changed my mind in a few hours when I was still suffering from the painful side effects of our abstinence. She got all misty-eyed and told me how much she appreciated my understanding and willingness to try. That's when I drove straight to the closest hotel and took a nice, cold shower. Now it was the morning, and I wondered if I'd be able to take a warm shower ever again.

The nearest hotel to Val's house didn't have room service but they boasted free breakfast. Not one to ever pass up free food, I made my way downstairs around eight thirty on the hunt for what I hoped would be a waffle and some eggs.

I'd just poured myself a cup of coffee when I heard Val's voice. It took me a minute to find her because I didn't think to check the television.

"I'm sorry, but what are you all doing here?" she grumbled.

The TV in the hotel lobby was set to the local news. A highly annoyed-looking Val stood at her front door in her pajamas with disheveled hair.

"We saw your picture on the cover of this morning's *Celebrity Gossip* magazine," the reporter said. "Is it true that you've reconciled with Kyle Hamilton and are now dating him?"

I laughed. So the fans we'd met last night were the enterprising kind. I should have asked for a cut of the money they made selling our pictures to the tabloids.

"Kyle and I reconciled our differences over four years ago, and yes, we went on a date last night. I still don't understand why that constitutes a press conference at my home at eight thirty on a Saturday morning."

I chuckled again. Val wasn't a morning person, then. I wouldn't have guessed that about her. I'd assumed she was one of those women who was always perky and completely put together.

"Where's Kyle?" a man holding a large camera asked. "Can we talk to him? What made you decide to break your vow to wait until marriage?"

Val's eyes widened when she finally realized what they were all so worked up about. She let out a breath and rubbed her head like it hurt. "I haven't broken my vow," she said. "I went on a date. That's *it*. Kyle took me to dinner and brought me home around eleven thirty last night. I went straight to bed. *Alone*."

"Then whose car is that in your driveway?"

"I have a roommate."

I forgot about breakfast when I saw the hurt in Val's eyes. Val needed to be rescued. She was trying her best to keep her composure in front of the cameras, but she was insulted by the questions.

Val's house was only three blocks from the hotel and I got there in less than five minutes. I honked to get everyone's attention as I pulled up and jumped out of the car, saying, "Okay, people, move it along now. Nothing scandalous going on here. If Val dumps me because you guys questioned her virtue, I'm going to be very pissed."

The small group of paparazzi went into a frenzy. They bombarded me with questions, but cleared a path for me to Val's front door as they took their pictures and videos.

Val stepped out onto the porch, rubbing her upper arms. Maybe she was cold, or maybe she was just trying to hide the fact that she wasn't wearing a bra. She was dressed in a pair of sweatpants and a tank top. She was barefoot, makeup-less, and her hair was a mess. I decided the just-rolled-out-of-bed look was very sexy on her. Still, I pulled my jacket off and wrapped it around her. Only I should be able to enjoy her like that.

"Good morning, beautiful," I said as I pulled the jacket closed and kissed her cheek. "Did you know you're live right now?" I pointed to the van parked on the curb that said Channel Nine. "I saw you on TV at the hotel and couldn't let you have all the fun by yourself."

She frowned at me but melted into my arms and said, "Thanks for coming. How do I get rid of them?"

I laughed. "You smile and answer their questions."

That earned me another frown, but Val sucked it up. "Fine," she said and forced a smile for the cameras. "What do you guys want to know?"

Everyone yelled questions at once, but there was one that stood out. "Is it true that you broke up with Adrianna Pascal because of Val?"

"I broke up with Adrianna because she went home with the wrong guy on my birthday. I mean, I know Brian played me in the *V is for Virgin* movie, but the resemblance between us really isn't that strong."

"Are you guys officially together, then?"

Val said "no" at the same time I said "yes," and the crowd laughed.

I flashed the paparazzi a big smile and said, "Excuse us a minute." I turned to face Val and said, "Come on. Didn't you have a good time last night?"

"Yes."

"Don't you want to go out again?"

She hesitated to answer, as if waiting for a trap. Have I mentioned she's an intelligent woman?

"Yes…," she said slowly.

I grinned. *Step right this way into my snare, Ms. Jensen.* "And wouldn't you be really mad if I started dating someone else right now?"

She didn't answer, but she narrowed her eyes and clenched her jaw. Bingo! Game. Set. Match. Winner—Kyle Hamilton. Girlfriend—Virgin Val.

"You're sexy when you're jealous," I teased. "Now that we've established that I'm not allowed to see other people— which, you're not, either, by the way—would you kindly admit to these fine people that you're my girlfriend?"

She looked up at the sky and let out an exasperated breath. "Fine." She sent a deadpan look toward the cameras and said, "I guess it's official."

I grinned like an idiot and pulled her to me. "Thank you." I gave her a peck on the lips before presenting her to the cameras. "Everyone, say hi to my new..." I looked at Val again. "What's the word I'm looking for? You're my what?"

She rolled her eyes but still cracked a smile when she said, "I'm your girlfriend. I'll even make sure to update my Facebook status."

Who's the man?

The crowd began firing off their questions again. It was the Channel Nine news guy who got his answer when he held his microphone out to me and said, "How are you guys going to handle the sex issue?"

I held up my wrist with a grimace and waited out the gasps.

"You really agreed to abstain from sex?"

I shrugged. "She wouldn't go out with me otherwise."

"Isn't that going to be difficult for you?"

I barked out a laugh. "Are you kidding? Not being able

135

to touch her last night was so hard I almost drove her to Las Vegas to get hitched just so I could finally have my way with her."

The reporters went crazy over that comment. They crowded closer, snapping their cameras again and shouting more questions—most wanting to know if we were engaged. I started to laugh until Val swatted my arm. "Kyle!" she shrieked.

"What? I said I was tempted. Not that I planned on following through."

She glared at me and I couldn't help laughing at her. I've always loved when she was mad at me. "Okay," I said. "I'm sorry." I turned my attention to the reporters. "Val and I are *not* secretly engaged. We've only been on one date, so you can all calm down. No one's running to any chapel. We don't even know if things are going to work between us. Yes, this not having sex with my girlfriend thing is going to be insanely difficult, but I am going to try my best. Now, if you all don't mind, I'm going to take Valerie inside and make her some hot coffee. She's practically turned into a popsicle standing out here in her bare feet."

Val looked relieved when I opened the door and pushed her inside, ignoring the questions still being thrown our way.

I THOUGHT THE INTERVIEW WENT GREAT, BUT IT BECAME obvious that I was the only one enjoying myself the minute the door was shut between the reporters and us. Val let out a long groan as she took off my leather jacket and sank down onto her sofa.

"It wasn't that bad," I said, joining her.

I held out my arms for her to snuggle into and got a glare instead. "Vegas, Kyle? Now everyone thinks we're secretly engaged, and that you're only marrying me so you can sleep with me."

I seriously didn't see what the big deal was. "Who cares?"

"*I* do."

"Sheesh. Somebody's grouchy this morning." Her mood was contagious and I found myself working to keep control of my temper. "Look, people know me, okay? And they know you. They might think I'm capable of it, but nobody is ever going to believe that you'd run off to Vegas with me. It was just a joke."

"No, it was a *circus act*. Everything with you always is." She stood up and wandered over to her front window. Pulling the curtain back, she scowled. "You haven't even been back in my life for twenty-four hours yet and I've got the media camped out in my front yard."

She dropped the curtain and turned back around to face me. "I'm starting an intense graduate program in September at one of the most competitive schools in the nation. I'll never get through it if the paparazzi are hounding me 24/7."

She rubbed her temples again, seriously stressed. I wanted to help somehow, but there was nothing I could do about the reporters and photographers. They would always be there. They were a part of life for me.

I got up and crossed the room to her, relieved when she let me take her hands in mine. "This is just because we're new right now," I promised. "The media frenzy will die down before you start school."

She slammed me with a severe look. "No, it won't. You're an instigator, Kyle, a showboat. You ham it up for the cameras and they follow you around like dogs hoping you'll throw them another treat. Your life will always be *that*." She thrust her hand toward the door, indicating the reporters on the lawn. "I don't want that. I hate the craziness."

Her tone was angry, accusing, and it hurt my feelings as much as it pissed me off. "Oh, and like dating you is going to be a picnic?"

Val flinched, so I tried to pull back my temper. "I want to have sex with you," I admitted. "More than anything." At her surprise, I held my hands out and shrugged helplessly. "I want to take you into your bedroom right now and do things to your body that will have you screaming my name in ecstasy. I've never wanted anything more in my entire life. I hate that I can't touch you. I *hate* it."

Val pulled her hands free and took a step back—a step away from me. "But…" Her eyes fell to the bracelet on my wrist. "You're already abstaining. You gave up sex on your own."

"I gave up *casual* sex," I clarified. "I gave up sex with strangers. I've abstained because I haven't had anyone I really cared about. I don't want making love to be meaningless anymore. But if I'm in a committed relationship, that changes things."

She looked stunned.

"I'm sorry, Val, but I happen to think sexual intimacy is a vital part of a relationship. I can admit now that sex is special and that you should wait until you care about someone to be with them, but I will never understand why you have to have a marriage stamp on it first. I'll definitely never agree with it. I still think you're making a stupid choice. Waiting for marriage is pointless."

Val's eyes filled with tears. I didn't want to hurt her, but she needed to know how I felt. I had to be honest. I was going to struggle with this, and she needed to know that.

"Then what are you doing here?" she asked. "If you hate it so much and you think I'm being an idiot, then why come back? Why ask me to be in a relationship?"

That was the question of the hour, wasn't it? "Because you're worth it."

I stepped toward her again, and when she tried to back up I kept moving closer until I had her backed against a wall. She turned her head away, but I pulled her chin up and forced her to look into my eyes. If there was ever one thing I wanted her to understand, ever one thing I needed her to believe, it was this.

"I'm willing to make the sacrifice because I think you're worth it. I'm not going to like everything about you, and you're not going to like everything about me, but that doesn't mean we can't make this work."

Val shut her eyes against more tears. As much as I hated that I was the cause of her sadness, I thought she looked beautiful with the water tangling in her lashes. A drop escaped and fell down her cheek, and I wiped it away with my thumb.

"We have something special," I said in a low voice. "I can feel it. I think you can, too. So I am going to take the bad with the good and ask that you try to do the same. I can't help the fame. Not only is it my job, I love it. I'm a complete attention whore. I know that. I'm not going to deny it. I'm asking you to accept it. I know you hate it, but it's as much a part of me as the virgin thing is a part of you."

Val swallowed back her emotions and nodded. "Okay." The promise came out small and strangled. "You're right. I can't expect you to make all the sacrifices. I'll find a way to deal with the fame."

A weight lifted off my chest that I hadn't realized was there, and I let out a breath I'd been holding in my lungs. "Thank you," I said as I pressed a light kiss to her lips.

She finally opened her big, beautiful brown eyes and stared into mine. Her uncertainty and fear shone through in her gaze, but along with the vulnerability I saw hope. "Please be worth it," she whispered.

The doubt should have stung, but instead it settled my nerves. She wasn't sure about us, but she was willing to take the chance. That took courage—something Val's always had in abundance, and one of the things I liked best about her.

I felt the corners of my mouth curve into a smile. "I'll do my best," I promised and kissed her again. This time I let it linger, and she wrapped her arms around my neck. I pulled her away from the wall and wrapped her tightly in my arms, needing the connection as much as I'm sure she did right then. We pulled apart when we heard a loud sniffle.

"That was so beautiful," a weepy voice said. "You guys are totally going to make it."

I turned to see a bathrobe-clad blonde smiling at us from the mouth of the hallway. She dabbed her eyes with a tissue and held out the box. Val laughed as she took a tissue. I was pretty sure I was missing an inside joke.

The two women hugged, and then Val pushed her friend toward me. "Kyle, this is my roommate, Stephanie.

Stephanie just got engaged a couple of weeks ago and it's made her a bit emotional. She cries at everything now. Movies, songs, books, girl talk…there was even this one time when she was doing laundry."

Stephanie playfully shoved Val. "I'm just so happy," she said. "Austin and I have been together for three years. I didn't think he'd ever ask. The engagement was a complete surprise."

I didn't ask questions. Cara and Adrianna had both been all gooey, emotional messes after they got engaged, too. Eventually, that phase passed and the bridezilla stage kicked in. I didn't think this woman needed to hear that she'd soon give up her tears of joy and become a neurotic, anal control freak, so I just held out my hand and said, "Congratulations."

Stephanie's face flushed as she shook my hand. "It's nice to finally meet you," she said. "I was there through most of the events of senior year, but I'm sure you don't remember me. Back then you only ever had eyes for Val."

My eyes automatically went back to Val and I smiled at her pink cheeks.

"I guess not much has changed."

When I realized I was staring, I laughed and pulled Val back into my arms. "Some things have changed. For instance, I'm allowed to kiss her now."

I went ahead and proved my point.

"So about the rest of the weekend…," I said.

Val shrugged. "I've got no plans until work Monday."

Just what I was hoping to hear. "Good. I've got more than enough plans for the both of us, but I'm afraid they'll require you to be showered and dressed." Unable to resist,

I grinned and said, "Would you like some help with that?"

"Yup." Stephanie laughed again. "Definitely still the same Kyle."

13

I IS FOR INTERVIEW

I WAS STARTLED WHEN MY PHONE BUZZED IN MY BACK pocket. I'd been on edge for days.

Hey rock star. How did the interview go?

Relief flooded me when I saw it was Val who'd texted me. We'd had the most amazing weekend together, and then I flew home on Monday and hadn't gotten anything more from her than a couple of random texts in three days. She'd been swamped at work and I had this interview coming up, so I'd flown home. Val hadn't said anything about when we'd see each other again.

Still waiting I texted back. **Not sure what the hold up is.**

I'd wish you luck but you don't need it. You're going to rock it.

I was new to long-distance relationships. I didn't like that we'd left things open-ended. Val was so caught up in her crazy, full-speed-ahead world. I wondered if she even realized it'd been three days and we hadn't talked. Maybe that was normal for her in a relationship, but I was kind of an all or nothing guy. I didn't want to ask outright if she wanted to come down to L.A. this weekend, but what could I say to drop the hint?

Wish you were here. You should be doing this interview with me.

I wish I were there too. I miss you.

Well, that answered nothing. But at least she missed me. At least I'd crossed her mind once or twice since I left. Another text followed her last one.

Is that lame? Saying I miss you? I know it's only been three days.

I felt a smile creep onto my face. Probably the first one I'd managed all day. She was worried about saying she missed me, while I was struggling not to jump on another plane.

Not lame I typed back. **I miss you too. All my other girlfriends down here aren't as fun as you.**

HA. HA. Not funny.

I laughed. **You're sexy when you're jealous.**

I've got to go. I'm meeting my other boyfriend for lunch.

You're right. It's not funny.

See?

You're not really going out to lunch with some guy are you?

Aw, you're so cute when you're jealous.

Okay, you got me.

Good. I really do have to go though. Late for a meeting. I'll talk to you soon, okay?

Can't wait.

I slipped my phone back into my pocket and tried not

to frown. I knew she was kidding with the boyfriend comment, but I hated thinking about it all the same. Especially after having met Bryce Carmichael, the F is for Families wonder boy.

I glanced around the studio, wondering what the hold up was.

My managers had put the word out that I was pledging the V is for Virgin abstinence challenge and invited a number of different media people to witness it. *Celebrity Gossip* asked to do a cover and a four-page photo spread and interview. Who knew my abstinence would be such front-page news?

They'd really gone all out for this thing, too—lights and cameras everywhere. They had three separate location setups, crafty, and my own private waiting area. At least there was that. I wasn't being hounded by the press while I waited. Seriously, what was the deal?

When I started fidgeting, I pulled out my phone again. This dumb thing needed to start already so I wouldn't just sit here imagining Bryce "P is for Perfect" Carmichael hatching a plan to make the world a better place over margaritas with my girlfriend.

Or Angels' center fielder Mike Trout, for that matter.

"Nervous?"

I glanced up to see Robin grinning at me.

Curse my stupid restlessness. I hoped I didn't look like I was scared to everyone else here. All those reporters sitting on the other side of the studio would just love to tell the world I was nervous right now.

I forced myself to sit still. "I'm not worried about the interview."

"So, you're just excited to pronounce your abstinence?" she teased.

"Yup. That's it. How'd you guess?"

Robin's smile turned to a smirk. "Why does Val have you strung out?"

I grimaced. "That obvious?"

"I know relationship drama when I see it. What's going on? I thought things went well in Nor Cal."

Was I really about to have this conversation? I searched the room again wishing someone was ready for me, but everyone was still just standing around.

Robin crossed her arms and gave me a look that said she meant business.

With a sigh, I put my phone away and gestured to the vacant chair next to mine. "Have a seat, put your feet up."

Robin's face lit up and she sat down. Watching her fall into her seat was painful. She looked around the room and lowered her voice. "Am I, like, breaking some kind of rule by talking to the talent?"

I smirked. "Not when you know them personally. You're a welcome distraction."

"So, what's going on with you and Val?"

"I hope you checked out crafty," I replied. "I warned them there'd be a pregnant lady here today. It should be stocked with plenty of peanut butter and pickles."

Robin laughed and subconsciously rubbed her belly. My avoidance tactic worked, though, and she was distracted. "Sadly, my cravings have been different this time. I'm all about banana pudding and gas station taquitos. Gross, I know, but…"

"Ooh, those pepper jack ones? I love those."

She laughed again and threw her arm over my shoulder. "Kyle, I believe you might just be a kindred spirit."

Robin was all right. I leaned over and spoke softly, as if I were sharing a huge secret. "You want to see something cool? Watch this."

I looked up and waved over the first person I saw. The kid was about eighteen or nineteen and had his hands full of a tangled heap of wires. He looked thrilled to have my attention. "What can I do for you, Mr. Hamilton?"

I winked at Robin and then said, "We have a pregnant lady emergency on our hands. I need someone to run to 7-Eleven and get a couple of those pepper jack taquitos they make and a banana-flavored pudding cup."

I smirked when the kid flagged down one of his crew members and handed over the wires. "Can you take this to the DP? I've got to run an errand for Mr. Hamilton." He turned back to me and said, "Two taquitos and a banana pudding cup?"

"The pepper jack kind."

"I'm on it."

I stopped him before he walked away. "Actually, make it four." I patted my stomach and smiled. "Sympathy cravings."

Once the kid was gone, Robin burst into laughter. "Is he really going to do it?"

"Oh yeah. He'll hurry, too."

Robin shook her head, saying, "You didn't have to do that," but she couldn't hide her amusement.

"Ah, don't worry about it. He's getting paid. Plus I probably just made his whole day. Now he'll get to go home and tell all his family that he got to meet Kyle Hamilton, and that we bonded over taquitos and pudding."

When Robin cast me another disbelieving look, I grinned. "There are perks to being the talent."

"I guess so." Robin stretched out and let her eyes fall shut. "Unfortunately, bribing me with convenience food isn't going to get you off the hook. Come on, fess up."

"You are worse than Cara." I laughed and decided I'd lost the battle. "There's nothing wrong. It's stupid."

Robin shrugged. "But it's bugging you."

"Well, yeah, it's bugging me. We live six hours apart and we didn't talk about how the distance thing is going to work before I left. The ball was in her court, and she didn't say anything. I've been gone three days and she still hasn't brought it up. I'm not usually this needy and stalkerish, it's just she's always so busy. What if she can't manage to pencil me in for a month?"

I was surprised I'd just admitted all that. I felt like an idiot, but Robin didn't laugh. She was quiet for a minute, then let out a long breath. "I'm not going to lie, that's always going to be an issue with Val. She and I aren't as close as we used to be in high school. We're still good friends. We keep up on Facebook, I see her a couple times a year, and I took over all the V is for Virgin stuff for her when she went to college, so I still work with her quite a bit. I know how she operates. She's always busy, always got too much on her plate. She lives by the schedule on her tablet. You'll probably always have to compete for her time."

I frowned. Wasn't this girl-talk crap supposed to make you feel better? Wasn't that why women were always so insistent on talking?

"But," Robin said when she saw the look on my face, "she's always there when you really need her. And, she has a way of working out the impossible. I think she might surprise you."

I couldn't ignore the sincerity in Robin's voice, and it did actually make me feel better. Robin knew Val, and if she thought we'd make it work, then I would have faith, too.

Just then, a door slammed and a pair of heels clacked across the floor in a hurry. I didn't know why that made Robin smile so big until I heard Val call out, "I'm here! I'm so sorry! There was an accident coming over the Grapevine. Traffic on the freeway was stopped for almost two hours. What can you do?"

I whirled on Robin, feeling a bit like I'd been betrayed. "You knew this whole time she was coming?"

Robin laughed, really enjoying my shock. She patted my leg and winked as she hoisted herself out of her chair. "I arranged it."

She left me sitting there in bewilderment and hurried over to Val. They hugged and chatted for a minute before Robin pointed my direction, and Val looked over. My mouth must have still been hanging open because Val pursed her lips together in an attempt not to laugh.

I got up to greet her and she met me halfway. "Hey."

There was a hint of insecurity in her answer. "Surprise?"

I was still a little stunned as I pulled her into my arms and gave her a quick kiss. "You came down to do the interview with me?" My disbelief was starting to melt into gratitude, and I finally managed a smile.

"Actually…" She hesitated, worrying her bottom lip in her teeth. "Bryce talked me into taking the summer off. My parents said I could stay with them until school starts. They were pretty thrilled, actually."

I couldn't believe what she was saying. "You quit your job?"

She shrugged as if to play it off, but her cheeks turned pink. "I've been training a replacement anyway because I knew I was going to have to hand the organization over once I started grad school. I just handed it over a couple months early. Honestly, I could use the break."

She waited for a response, but I didn't know what to say. I just kept picturing a giant day planner with its entire schedule erased and replaced with the word KYLE in big block letters.

When I couldn't speak, she started to ramble. "There will still be the random conference call, and I've got some maid of honor stuff for Stephanie's wedding that I'll have to—"

I cut her off with a kiss. The woman had just quit her job for me. I needed her in my arms. I pulled her close and kissed her until she melted. She looked up at me, face flushed, with a shy smile. "So, it's okay that I came?"

"Is it okay that my girlfriend wanted to spend the summer in the same city as me?" I pretended to think about it. "I think I'll survive."

Her smile became more confident. "And is it okay if I share your spotlight with you today? I had so many people contact me after that escapade in front of my house; I thought doing the interview together would help answer a lot of questions. When Robin mentioned it to your people, they seemed pretty excited."

"First she steals my fans, then she wants to take over my interview," I said with a playful sigh. "And you say *I'm* the attention hog."

Val rolled her eyes and I couldn't help kissing her again. "Thanks for coming."

THE FIRST THING THEY DID WAS SIT VAL AND ME DOWN FOR an interview where we announced that we were officially dating. I explained that I'd given up sex for her and that I'd be teaming up with the V is for Virgin campaign and the Not Everybody's Doing It Foundation. I showed off my bracelet, told them about the percentage of the album sales I'd be donating, and I even sang "Worth Waiting For" unplugged.

Then there was a brief Q & A session. Most of the questions were directed at Val. What she thought of the new song. How we originally met. How she felt when we were reunited. How I'd managed to finally win her over.

"Oh, that's easy," she said. "He won me over when I saw the photos four years ago after he was dubbed that year's Sexiest Man Alive."

Val pretended to fan herself, and the entire room burst into laughter. I laughed along with them, but on the inside I was shocked. In all the years I'd known her, she'd never once flirted with me. I flirted—all I ever did was hit on her— but she'd never reciprocated. She'd never even once told me she thought I was good-looking. I knew she was attracted to me because she always responded to me on a physical level whether she wanted to or not, but she'd never admitted it out loud before.

"Really, though," she said when the laughter died down, "I'm not sure when he won me over."

She looked at me in contemplation and shook her head slightly as she said, "He drove me so crazy, but in a way I always liked him from the first time we met. Underneath the ego, he's an amazing man. He's passionate and driven. We're the same that way; we've just always had our eyes on different prizes. He still drives me nuts sometimes, but now that the sex issue isn't standing in our way"—she lifted a shoulder and blushed—"he's kind of hard to resist."

Val smiled at me and I grinned back, trying my hardest to hide the fact that I was struggling with unexpected emotions. This was a side of her she'd never shown me before. I knew she cared about me, and I knew she was this way with others, but I'd personally never experienced the flirty, loving Val who was nice and thought highly of me and complimented me. Until now, she'd always been on her guard with me.

"You're awfully quiet, Kyle."

The statement was more of a question and came from someone sitting in the crowd. I wondered how long I'd been sitting there, spaced out.

"I'm just a little shocked," I joked. "I'm not sure who this incredible woman sitting next to me is, or what happened to the snarky, sarcastic, defensive girl I remember from four years ago."

Val squeezed my hand and, in a voice dripping with heartfelt sincerity, said, "She grew up."

Something thumped in my chest and made me feel like

I couldn't breathe. I had to wrap up the interview after that because Val was twisting me all up inside.

They filmed me signing the official V is for Virgin abstinence pledge and I presented the certificate to Val herself. "Here," I said, acting as if I had just signed my life away and was being tossed into a prison cell. "I am officially abstinent. You win."

She glowed in a way I'd never seen as she accepted the document with my signature on it. She smiled down at the paper, then threw her arms around my neck and kissed me. "And I'm officially yours," she said, "so I guess you win, too."

AFTER THE INTERVIEW, THEY SENT ALL THE PRESS AWAY AND took a series of couples photos of Val and me with Val wearing her *V* necklace and me showing off my *A* bracelet. I'd done a lot of photo shoots over the years, but I'd never had as much fun with one as I did with Val that day.

I was used to crazy photographers, but she wasn't. Every time the guy told her to gaze into my eyes and then jumped around us yelling directions like "We're so happy! We're so in love!" or "Now we're sexy! Abstinence is sexy!", Val would lose her composure. I think the poor photographer was ready to throttle her after like the sixth time she lost herself in a fit of giggles. Several hours in he gave up, declared her a hopeless case, and said if the pictures were terrible, it wasn't his fault. I assured him they'd be perfect.

It felt like a lifetime before we were finally done and I was able to have Val all to myself. It was too early for dinner, so we decided to leave our cars parked in the studio lot and go for a walk. Not that downtown Burbank is especially exciting, but it was always a good idea for me to stay away from the tourist spots, and it was a beautiful day.

"So," I asked as we strolled down the street hand in hand, "you're going to stay with your parents while you're here? Are they still in Huntington Beach?"

Val nodded absently. "It's home."

I sighed, and Val cast me a sideways glance. "Why? Where do you live these days, Mulholland Drive?"

I pretended to be offended by the assumption, but it was hardly believable when I had to answer, "On the PCH up in Malibu."

Val snorted softly and shook her head. "Of course you do."

"What? It's a nice place."

She laughed again. "I'm sure it is."

"It's also a really long drive from Huntington Beach."

Val sighed a little as she conceded to my point. She countered with, "It's better than Sunnyvale."

"True." I lifted Val's hand to my lips. "I'm glad you're here. Thanks for coming down."

We came across a farmer's market and took our time wandering through the different vendor booths. Val was interesting to watch. I pulled my cap low over my eyes and stayed pretty quiet, happy to blend into the crowd, but Val interacted with almost everyone she crossed paths with.

She'd stop to coo at a baby or pet a dog, always engaging the strangers she talked to with questions or compliments that sounded sincere. She talked to all the different vendors, complimenting them on their prize-winning tomatoes or asking how their crops had been this year. She was a ray of sunshine that left a trail of smiles in her wake wherever she went. I'd never known someone like her.

"You should stay with me," I blurted randomly as she bought a glass of lemonade from a young girl who was selling them out of a little red wagon alongside her parents' fruit stand.

She was still crouched down in front of the little girl, but she glanced up at me and arched one of her eyebrows.

"Sometimes at least," I insisted.

I waited while Val paid the little girl, complimented her on her excellent lemonade, and told her to keep the change. She stood back up and met my gaze with a serious look. "I don't think that's a good idea, Kyle."

I tugged her along to the next booth and away from little ears before I whispered, "It's not like you'd have to get naked with me. You could even have your own room. It would just cut out so much driving time."

She was quiet a minute. When she finally shook her head, my heart sank in disappointment.

"I'm sorry, Kyle."

"You don't trust me?"

"Not in the least." Val laughed at my frown. "I have no doubt you would do things like strut around the house shirtless, looking all hot and tempting, trying to drive me crazy on purpose. You're not the only one I don't trust here, mister. I may be the stronger of the two of us, but my restraint only goes so far. Me staying at your house would be a train wreck waiting to happen, and you know it."

I was taken aback by the sudden turn of this conversation, and the weakness she'd just admitted to. It's sad how excited her confession made me. I stopped walking and pulled her to me, slipping my arms around her waist. "I'm sorry. All I heard there was that you find the idea of me shirtless to be completely hot and tempting."

She rolled her eyes but still laughed. "Like that's front page news?"

"It is to me. I didn't realize you had any hormones."

She laughed again. "I'm a virgin, but I'm still human, and a female at that. There's not a straight woman in the world that wouldn't find a shirtless you hot and tempting."

"True." My trademark egotistical smirk made an appearance. "I do put the 'abs' in 'abstinence,' don't I?"

Val stared up at me, completely speechless for a moment, then slapped a hand over her face and shook her head. She tried really hard not to laugh, but she couldn't manage it.

"You never cease to astound me," she said as she gave me another look that suggested I was ridiculous and started walking again.

I laced our hands together and felt her still shaking with laughter.

"I have an idea," I said. "Let's go to the beach."

She gave me another look. "The beach? Really? So you can peacock around in nothing but your swim trunks? Do you really need to feed your ego that badly?"

"Are you kidding?" I grinned. "Now that I know taking my shirt off will get you all hot and bothered? I'm tempted to strip down right here and now."

"And that is exactly why I will not be staying the night at your place. Ever."

I tried to make her feel guilty with my most convincing pout, but she only laughed and turned us around in the direction we'd originally come from. "Come on, let's head back. I promised my parents I'd have dinner with them tonight."

14

V IS FOR VIDEO

VAL SPENT THE NEXT COUPLE OF DAYS IN HUNTINGTON Beach with her parents, and met her half-brother for the first time on Friday, but she came up to L.A. on Saturday to watch me film the video for "Worth Waiting For."

I was really excited for this video. The song was sick, we had Carlos Gutierrez directing—who'd done the most number-one videos of any director in the music industry—and we had the sexiest, award-winning (daytime) actress starring opposite me. Since Cara had done the "Cryin' Shame" video, I'd talked her into doing this one as well. She was an excellent actress and gorgeous to boot. This video was going to be killer, and the enthusiasm on set was high.

When I got there, Cara was already shooting her solo shots. They had her standing in front of a wind machine, looking beyond hot in a man's dress shirt. I'd be joining her as soon as they had me dressed and in makeup.

Shane was standing just off to the side, watching her as he sipped a cup of coffee. I walked over and slapped him playfully on the back. I leered at Cara for a moment and said, "Man, I love my job."

Shane cut me a sideways glance. "Prick. Could you at least try to pretend you're not excited to spend the day in bed with my wife?"

For the video, they'd gone with the concept of me alone in bed with my fantasies. My girl would be there, haunting me in my dreams, and then I'd wake up alone. Artistically, it fit the song perfectly and would be amazing. *Real*istically it meant that I was about to spend the day in bed—shirtless—with Cara hanging all over me and kissing me, while wearing nothing but my dress shirt.

"It's going to be a horrible day's work," I deadpanned.

Shane shook his head, but his lips quirked up into a smile. "She is sexy, though, isn't she? Do you think I can get one of those wind machines to take home with me?"

I laughed and looked at my phone. Val said she'd come up sometime before lunch, but I was ready to see her now. Who knew going three days without seeing her would be so hard? It was worse knowing that she was close and we just hadn't been able to get together.

"I wonder how long this will take today. Val wants us to go to dinner with you guys after, but I need some alone time with her tonight too, and the woman refuses to stay with me at my place. Can you believe that? I even offered her the spare bedroom. She flat-out told me she didn't trust me."

Shane snorted. "That's what you get for dating a smart woman. She sees through all your bull."

"Hey. I could keep my hands to myself."

Shane took another sip of his coffee, then said, "I'm counting on that today, dude." He slapped my stomach with the back of his hand, hard enough to knock the wind from me. "Don't do anything that I'll have to punch you in the face for."

"What the hell! Does *nobody* trust me?"

"I trust you," Cara said, coming up to us. She jumped into Shane's arms, wrapping her bare legs around his waist. "Hey, lover. Don't be jealous. Kyle only gets to have me in his dreams. You get to have me for real." She kissed him, then turned to me with a wicked grin. "I'm finished with my solo shots. You ready to get your fantasy freak on?"

I looked down at the jeans and T-shirt I had on and gave her a big, cheesy grin. "Sure. Just let me slip into something more comfortable."

"Please tell me you don't actually use that line for real."

"He wouldn't be the great Cheerleader Seducer if he didn't have better material than that," Shane offered helpfully.

I laughed all the way to wardrobe, where I was handed a pair of silk pajama pants and shoved into a changing room. Next, I was attacked by hair and makeup. You wouldn't believe how much product it takes to give you a "sexy bed-head" look. At least they went light on the makeup. I'll admit I go a little heavy on the eyeliner for a show, but I'd look like a giant douche with it caked on when I was supposed to be sleeping.

The morning went by quickly. Everybody was in a great mood, Cara was a great actress, and Carlos said Cara and I had great chemistry—enough that Shane was threatening to have my face replace Rico's on his dartboard.

Everything was running smoothly and we were moving through the shots quickly. We'd moved through the lighter shots and had finally gotten to some of the heavier scenes.

For this one, Cara had to crawl up the bed until she was straddling my lap. She'd kiss my chest and eventually make her way to my lips. Everything was slow and sensual and so, so, so hot.

After a particularly steamy take, Carlson yelled "Cut!" and people cheered. "That's definitely the one!" Carlos announced. "We've got what we need there. We just need to get the second angle now. Can you two stay put for a minute while we frame it, then you can take ten?"

I glanced at Cara and smirked. "Twist my arm."

"How about you, Cara?" Carlos asked. "You going to be all right like that for a few minutes? Legs not going to fall asleep?"

"Legs are good," she called. She winked at me and added, "I can think of worse positions to be stuck in."

Across the room, Shane groaned. "That's it. Cara's never allowed to do another video for you again, you ass!"

Cara and I both laughed. We knew it was mean, but Shane was just too easy. "Don't worry, baby," Cara called to him. "We'll take a break in a minute and I'll let you show Carlos what real chemistry is. Kyle's cute and all, but he's nothing compared to you, shnookums."

"That's right, baby!" Shane called back. "You better recognize, Kyle. You may be the front man, but I'm the one with all the real skills."

He went there. I couldn't let that stand. "Hey, Shane, you ever hear the one about the lead guitarist who was in tune?"

"No."

"Yeah, neither did I."

Cara smacked my chest. "That was lame," she said, but

she was still laughing.

From across the room, Shane flipped me the bird. "How do you know when a lead singer's knocking at your door?" he asked. "He can't find the key and doesn't know when to come in."

"Thanks, douche."

I'm not sure if it was my brilliant comeback or the joke that made everyone on set laugh, but at least Shane was laughing. Cara and I liked to give him a hard time, but I didn't want to push him too far.

"Sounds like a party in here!"

I grinned like an idiot at the sound of Val's voice. "Finally."

I scanned the room and saw Val carefully making her way through the studio, escorted by a PA. She was dressed in another nice suit—a pants suit this time instead of a skirt—and she was having a hard time navigating the sea of electrical chords in her heels. The spike of her shoe caught on a chord and she stumbled. I laughed to myself. If I hadn't seen Baseball Val, I'd wonder if she even owned a pair of jeans anymore.

Cara made a surprised choking noise. "You invited Val to this today?"

"Why wouldn't I? She said she wanted to come."

Cara looked at me as if I were the biggest idiot on the planet. "And you couldn't have invited her to the shoot *yesterday* when it was just you and the band on a soundstage?"

"I did invite her to that, but she had something with her birth family yesterday. She was so bummed about missing the shoot that I told her we were filming today, too. I didn't even think about it. I just said to come."

Cara shook her head. "Well, I wish you luck, moron. You're so getting dumped."

"Yeah right. Val will understand. It's the job. She knows that."

Cara didn't seem convinced. "I guess we're about to find out." She forced a big smile on her face and said, "Val! You came! I'm a little surprised to see you here." She sent me another look that suggested I was completely obtuse. "But I'm glad you could make it."

Val finally spotted us and came to a stumbling stop. The PA had to reach out to steady her this time so that she wouldn't fall.

"Hey, honey. You could have worn tennis shoes," I teased. "Hollywood generally keeps the work environment pretty casual."

Val blinked back and forth between Cara and me and breathed, "I guess so."

I sighed when her face paled. "I guess I should have given you some warning, huh?"

Val swallowed, and her voice was still faint when she said, "Probably would have been a good thing."

"You didn't even warn her?" Cara hissed under her breath.

"I didn't think about it."

"Idiot."

I glared at Cara and turned my attention back to Val. It was hard to see her face because flashes had started going off in my face as a couple of people buzzed around Cara and me, testing the new lighting set up. "Sorry," I said. "They'll be done here in just a second, then I'll have a few minutes to show you around. Sound good?"

Val nodded and let the PA drag her off to find a chair without saying another word.

"Definitely getting dumped," Cara muttered.

Before I could fire a comeback, the DP gave Cara and me the okay to get up. I practically pushed Cara off of me and had Val in my arms before she'd even managed to sit down. "Hey," I said, pulling her to me for a kiss. "I'm glad you made it."

The kiss she gave me back was polite and her smile was a little forced. Concern tinged my brow and I squeezed her tighter to me. "I'm really sorry I forgot to warn you about today. I didn't even think about it. I was just so excited to have you come. You okay?"

"Yeah, of course," she said.

I wasn't sure I believed her, but she was trying to be brave. I hadn't meant for this to happen, but after a moment I figured it was a good thing. Unfortunately, this was part of the job. It didn't happen for me as often as it did for Cara, but it *did* happen from time to time. The sooner Val was exposed to it, the less it would bother her. Shane never liked it much either, but he dealt.

"You sure you're good?"

She nodded. "I'm fine. It was just a surprise."

"Well, let me show you something then, so there won't be any more surprises."

I threaded her hand through mine and started dragging her across the room to a large corkboard where the story-board artist had tacked up the sketches for each shot of the video. Each sketch had the corresponding song lyrics pinned above them. They were crud drawings, but they were enough to help you visualize the entire project so you'd know how it would come together.

"Cara's playing the role of my fantasy girl today," I explained. "The story is that I'm dreaming because I have to wait, so we can't really be together and it's driving me crazy. I can't touch her in real life, so she's haunting my dreams. See how I wake up alone at the end?"

I pointed to the last few sketches and waited for some kind of reaction from Val. She'd been so quiet while looking at the drawings, and I was dying to know what she thought. I loved it, but this was her song. I wanted her to love it, too. She'd hated "Cryin' Shame" so much and had dreaded seeing the video. I'd wanted to make sure that didn't happen again. I'd worked hard to find something I thought she would appreciate when I'd sat down with my team and discussed concepts.

"I'm actually really excited about it," I said when she continued to examine the boards. "It's a very low-key shoot. Not flashy at all. I was really happy that they agreed to go with a more haunting—almost mysterious—feeling, and not just over-sex everything to the point of tackiness like a lot of music videos. The song is about so much more than just wanting to get her in bed. It's deeper, you know. He's trying to do what she wants, but he's struggling. This video's going to focus on the struggle. It's going to showcase the emotion in the song."

Val finally pulled her eyes away from the storyboards to meet my gaze, but she still didn't say anything. It was as if she were at a loss for words. Her brow was creased and she chewed on her bottom lip as if she was worried about something.

"Carlos is a great director," I assured her, guessing at her worry. "I've worked with him before. We talked a lot about this song and what it means to me. He really gets it, and that's going to come through in the final product. It's going to look fantastic. Nothing trashy, I promise. It'll stay PG-13."

Val swallowed and then forced another smile.

"You don't like it?" I tried not to let that disappoint me.

She shook her head quickly and forced more pep into her face. "I do like it," she said. "I'm sure it's going to be a great video."

"Then what is it? Something's wrong."

"Nothing's wrong. I promise. I was just expecting… something different. I thought there'd be a band and lights and smoke machines. I expected to watch you sing the song so many times in a row that I'd be dreaming about it for a month."

I chuckled and pulled her into my arms, relieved she was only disappointed that she wouldn't hear me sing. "That was yesterday, but if you're that desperate to hear the song, I'll call the guys and make them come play it for you when we're done."

She finally gave me a genuine smile and leaned against me, letting me hold her for a minute. She dropped her cheek onto my shoulder and her hands slid around my waist. The moment she realized I wasn't wearing a shirt and that she was touching my bare skin, she froze. A heartbeat passed and then, slowly, she let her fingers glide over my back. The delicate touch set me on fire, igniting me from the inside out.

It was crazy how the simplest touch from Val affected me in ways a whole legion of Lakers girls could never accomplish. I suppressed a shudder and forced my hands to behave. I couldn't help the way my grip tightened, though, and eventually I simply had to kiss her.

She kissed me back with more enthusiasm than I'd expected her to, and it took every ounce of self-control I had not to scoop her into my arms and throw her down on the bed across the room. Thankfully, Carlos interrupted us before that happened. "This must be the muse," he said, holding back a laugh.

I proudly pushed Val toward him. "The one and only. I was just getting a refill on inspiration before we start shooting again."

Carlos chuckled and pointed to a corner of the room. "That must be what Cara's doing, too."

Val and I followed his gaze to where Cara was attacking Shane. "Nope." I laughed. "That's just Cara and Shane. They're always like that."

Carlos's nose wrinkled in a way that made me laugh even harder. "Well," he said, "I'll let you break them up. We're ready to get started again. We're ahead of schedule, too. General consensus seems to be push through the lunch break so we can wrap early. I think we can be out of here by three."

"Sounds good to me." I looked to Val. "Do you mind?"

She shook her head. "Only if you don't mind if I invite Robin and Alan to join us for dinner. She called and said *Celebrity Gossip* sent her the mock-up for the article on us. She wanted to show us."

"That's fine," I agreed.

"I'll let the others know." Carlson hurried off.

Val tried to start walking back to her chair, but I wouldn't let her escape. "As long as we are negotiating," I said, reeling her back into my arms, "I'll go to dinner with everyone if you agree to let me take you out afterward, just the two of us."

Val pretended to think about it. "I suppose I can do that. If I really must."

My anxiety melted away at the taunt. If she was teasing me, then she would be fine. I squeezed her to me again and bent to kiss the soft spot beneath her ear. "Oh, yes," I whispered. "You really, really must."

When my lips touched her skin, heat coursed through me. I dragged my mouth down her neck and back up along her jawline. I was seconds away from getting inappropriate, but I couldn't stop myself. Everything inside of me ached with desire. My chest heaved as I fought to keep air in my lungs. I pulled the neck of her shirt back and kissed along her collarbone.

"Kyle, stop," she gasped. "We're in public."

She put her hands against my chest. I think she meant to push me away, but her fingers curled against my skin instead, spurring me on even more. "Sorry," I said, barely suppressing a groan. "Sexy shoots like this one always build a lot of tension."

Val's hands stilled against my chest. "You're turned on right now?"

I chuckled, low and throaty. "I'm not the only one. Did you see Cara? At least she's had an outlet all day." I pulled her even tighter against me. "I've been dying for you for hours. I'm seriously going to need you to help me get rid of some of this tension later. We'll definitely have to implement the duct tape rule, though, because there is no way I will be able to keep my hands off you."

I couldn't keep them off her now. They were already

roaming over everything they could reach that wouldn't get me slapped. "Come to think of it, handcuffs might be safer. Don't worry, I have a pair you can use."

Apparently, I'd pushed her a little too far with the handcuffs comment because she deflated in my arms. "Let's just hurry and get this over with," she said, shoving me toward the set.

It was a good thing she did, because I wouldn't have had the willpower to do it myself.

15

N IS FOR NEEDY

I WAS ON CLOUD NINE THAT NIGHT. THE SHOOT WENT BET-
ter than any shoot I'd ever done, and then I got to go out
with my best friends and Val afterward. As I sat down with
Val in the restaurant in Pasadena where we were meeting
Robin and her husband, I pulled her close against me and
grinned across the table at Cara and Shane.

Ever since I'd put on my bracelet and started writing
again, my relationship with Cara and Shane had steadily
gone back to how it was before Reid's death. I hadn't realized
how badly I'd missed my best friend until I had him back. It
was as if the last few years of my life I'd been living in black
and white, only I never knew it until Val suddenly brought
everything back into Technicolor.

"You know, this is what I always wanted back in the day
when you guys first got together," I said, gesturing around
the table. "The four of us hanging out."

"Me too," Cara agreed. "I tried to make it happen so
many times." She sent a tentative smile to Val. "I'm really

glad you're here. It never felt right without you."

Val's answering smile was timid, and it made me sad. Cara and I had always had the same vision, but Val had never wanted it. Cara and I trying to push this foursome on her is what ultimately destroyed Cara and Val's relationship. Their new friendship was even shakier than Val's and mine.

They were trying to come back from being completely broken. It was working to an extent, but things weren't the same between them anymore. They weren't as close or as comfortable with each other as they used to be. I wasn't sure they ever really would be again.

I felt terrible about the tension between them and wished Robin and her husband weren't meeting us for dinner so that they could have more time to patch things up properly, but I couldn't say as much to Val. I knew she was struggling to make sense of this new life I'd asked her to live. I figured including Robin was her way of bridging the gap.

If I hadn't been completely sure of that before, the way she jumped up and grabbed Robin into a hug when she arrived proved it. It was like watching her grab desperately to a life buoy in the midst of a raging ocean. She was so relieved when Robin and her husband showed up. The question that bothered me was, why had she been so uncomfortable that she needed the lifeline?

"When you texted me the location, I thought it was a joke. A rock star and a TV star dining at *Coco's* at four o'clock in the evening?" Robin said as she plopped down into a chair. "Not that I'm complaining. I do like their pie."

I laughed. Val had once had the same reaction. "There aren't many places a rock star and a TV star can go without being recognized," I explained. "The sixty-five and up crowd aren't really our demographic. Well, they're not mine, anyway. Miss Daytime over there is probably at risk of getting mobbed by the old ladies."

"Jealous of my old ladies, Kyle? I didn't realize you had a thing for false teeth and rose-scented perfume."

Val cleared her throat, pulling Cara and me from our banter. "Guys, you've all met Robin, but this is her husband, Alan. Alan, this is Kyle, Cara, and Shane."

Val was still acting weird, so I decided to put on my best manners. I stood and held out a hand to Alan. As he shook our hands and said hello to us all, his greeting was polite, but he was definitely wary of our group. I couldn't blame him. He looked very much like the suburbia American dream. His hairline was slightly receding, he had a few extra pounds around the middle, and I'd bet money that he wore a white shirt and tie to the office every day. Not that there's anything wrong with that, but it was just so completely opposite from the world that Cara, Shane, and I lived in. The difference between us was painfully obvious, and I tried to ignore the fact that Val seemed to have a lot more in common with him and Robin than with any of the rest of us.

Things were slightly awkward but at least the waitress came to take our orders fairly quickly, breaking the tension a little. When she got to Robin, I was shocked to hear the pregnant woman say, "Nothing for me, thanks."

"Nothing for you?" I blurted. I hadn't seen the woman without food in her hand since we met.

She laughed and said, "My stomach's feeling a little off. I'm not that hungry, so I'll just have a few bites of Alan's spaghetti."

"No, you won't," Alan said. He glanced up at the waitress

and said, "Bring us two plates of spaghetti."

Robin frowned. "Hon, I don't need my own plate."

"Yes, you do, because I would like to eat my dinner and if you don't order your own, you will eat all of mine."

"No, I won't."

"You always do." He looked at the waitress again and held up two fingers. "Two plates of spaghetti."

"And the chocolate crème pie."

"No pie," Alan said sternly, earning another frown from his wife. The sour look didn't change his mind. "You know what the doctor said. You're borderline gestational diabetic. No more sweets."

"'Borderline' is not diabetic," Robin grumbled.

Alan shook his head at the waitress. "No pie, thank you. Just the spaghetti."

"Two plates," the woman replied with a smile.

I don't know what she was smiling about. Observing Robin and Alan was like watching a dizzying ping-pong match. If they stayed like this all night, I'd get a headache. I couldn't help wondering if Shane and Cara would end up like that.

"So," Robin said cheerfully after the server retreated to the kitchen. She smiled as if the argument with her husband had never taken place. "How are you enjoying your vacation, Val?" She snickered as if she'd just made a funny joke. I didn't understand.

Val groaned. "You know me."

Robin laughed, but my face fell into a pout. Whatever they were joking about, I was missing the punch line. Another person who knew Val a lot better than me. That wasn't a good feeling.

"You guys want to explain to the rest of us?"

"Oh, it's nothing." Val leaned into my shoulder and squeezed my hand, making me relax a little. "I just get restless sometimes."

"Sometimes?" Robin laughed. "The woman can't do vacation. She's completely incapable. She's been down here for four whole days, which means she's going out of her mind already not having anything to do."

I'm pretty sure I was frowning again. "What do you mean nothing to do?" I asked Val. "Your schedule's been so packed I had to wait three days for you to come back and see me."

"Visiting family and catching up with old friends is great but it still feels very…idle. Plus, I've finished seeing everyone, so my schedule is completely empty now. I can only sit around for so long. Without a job or school, I'll need something to do this summer."

"I thought *I* was your something to do this summer."

When Cara and Shane both snickered and Val gave me a flat look, I had to think back on what I said. I smirked at the innuendo, unintentional as it had been. "That's not even what I meant."

"For once," Cara quipped.

I glared at her and brought Val's hand to my lips. "I thought you came down here to spend time with me."

Val smiled at me as if she found me completely adorable. It wasn't condescending, but it still pissed me off a little. It made me feel as though she were indulging a whiny kid.

"I did," she promised. "We'll have lots of time to spend together, but you're going to be busy during the days. Your tour rehearsals are starting soon and you'll have a ton of press appearances for your album."

"But you can come with me to all of those things. It'll be fun. Like today."

Val's smile faded. "You thought today was fun?" she asked quietly.

"You didn't?" I was so confused.

My question made the blood drain from Val's face but, for the life of me, I didn't know what the problem was. Today hadn't just been fun; it'd been amazing. One of the best days I'd had in a long time.

"Kyle, today was—" She bit her lip as if she didn't want to say what she was thinking and then changed her sentence. "I can't just follow you around all summer sitting on the sidelines for hours while you do your thing. I'd be bored to tears."

She wasn't being mean, but I still felt like I'd been slapped, and I forgot all about the fact that she'd completely skirted the question I'd asked her. "You think what I do— my music—is boring?"

"Of course not," she said quickly. She pinched up her face as if I were making her head hurt. "I just meant that I couldn't help you with anything while I was there. I couldn't participate. You'd be busy and I'd just be sitting there. Going to a dress rehearsal or the occasional interview is one thing, but watching your practices and workouts all summer? I couldn't do that any more than I could sit on a beach reading and sipping margaritas all summer."

She squeezed my hand again when I frowned. "It's okay that you work, Kyle. I don't need to be with you every second of the day. I'll be fine. I just need to find something to do. I need a project or something."

I truly didn't understand this woman. "You think I asked you to come to my rehearsals because I'm worried about having to entertain you?"

"What other reason would there be for you to drag me to work with you?" she asked, baffled.

We clearly didn't speak the same language. She was just as confused as I was. "Um...how about that I just like your company and want you there?"

She blinked up at me as if I were insane.

"Kyle, she's not a *groupie*."

Val and I both turned to see Cara biting back laughter. "You'll have to forgive him," she said to Val. "His last girlfriend actually *was* a groupie and was fused to his side 24/7 the entire time they were a couple. He's not used to a girlfriend who has a life of her own that doesn't revolve around him."

Everyone had a good laugh at my expense. I tried to be a good sport about it, but I wasn't very happy. Now Cara had me thinking about Adrianna, and that was never a good thing. I could see all the reasons she wasn't right for me now, but the one thing I'd always loved the most about her was how much my music meant to her. She'd been my biggest supporter for years. She was always by my side—loving me, encouraging me, and appreciating what I did.

Val was different. She wasn't even a fan. From the first time I'd met her, she'd never been impressed with my job. In fact, Cara told me on many occasions not to take it personally because Val simply didn't care much about music in general. If it was on, she'd listen, bounce her head along to a catchy beat or hum with the songs she knew, but she didn't connect with it the way Cara, Shane, and I did.

I knew Val respected my job and what I'd accomplished. She was happy for me and glad that I loved it. She understood how much it meant to me, but she didn't really care about it personally. I knew that about her, and I'd accepted it, but it still depressed me. I wished there were a way I could make her love it, too.

I'd hoped my new song would do that for her—give her a real connection to music. She said she'd loved it, and she'd agreed to date me, so maybe it had helped a little, but she'd clearly hated the video shoot today.

I was shaken from my thoughts when our food arrived—a welcomed distraction. I dug right in, and after my first bite Val laughed softly next to me. The quiet sound lifted my spirits a little. She hadn't laughed much today. Something was bothering her.

"What's so amusing?" I whispered.

Her eyes sparkled as she smirked up at me. "Your sweet tooth," she said, swiping some of the whipped cream on top of my French toast.

My mouth went dry when she sucked the cream off her finger. She was teasing me, but not in the way she meant to. She was clueless about the effect she had on me. I decided her naïvety was dangerous for us both and needed to be expunged.

"You never steal a man's whipped cream, Val." I gave her a warning look that she promptly laughed at. "Do it again," I challenged. "See what happens."

She considered my threat and reached for my plate. I snatched her hand away and smeared whipped cream across her mouth. Before she could wipe it off, I leaned forward and kissed her, gently sucking the sugary cream from her lips.

The move shocked her. Clearly she'd never played with her food before. She was so surprised she'd probably never even realized it could be done. And that it could be sexy.

This was definitely sexy—so incredibly sexy that I couldn't control myself. Her startled gasp lit me on fire. I took advantage of her open mouth and deepened the kiss.

She pushed me back and shook her head, her cheeks flushed. "Can you please not do that in public?" she whispered.

I pulled her closer and nearly growled my reply. "Fine. Then let's go someplace not public." I needed her. I needed her right then. As much of her as she'd let me have.

She surprised me with a severe glare, but she quickly checked her anger as if she hadn't meant to let her emotions slip. Her face smoothed out into an unreadable expression and she didn't explain when I questioned her.

"No mauling me in public," she warned with a laugh I was fairly sure was fake.

Robin snorted a laugh. "Yes, definitely no more of that. You're nauseating, Kyle, and if I lose my appetite you'll be in big trouble."

No doubt that would have been a very bad thing, but there was no danger of her failing to eat. She saw the smirk on my face and rolled her eyes.

"Fine. What were we talking about before I so rudely attempted to get some hot, sweet lovin' from my wickedly irresistible girlfriend?"

Val rolled her eyes, not amused, but at least the rest of the group laughed and the last of the awkwardness disappeared.

"We were discussing Val's need for a summer project,"

Cara said.

Alan hadn't said much so far tonight, but he cleared his throat and spoke up. "You should come work with Robin at the foundation. They've been a little swamped since Christina took that job out East."

Robin loved that idea. "Yeah, you totally should! You could help me get so much done before this little nightmare arrives. We're going to have to get a *temp* while I'm on maternity leave." She shuddered at the thought.

Val sighed and sat back, not touching her plate of food. She was still upset about something and trying to hide it. Was it because I kissed her? I didn't think so, but I couldn't figure out what else it could have been.

"I'm sure I can do that sometimes," she said, answering Robin's question. "It's just such a drive from Huntington to come up every day."

"Like I said, my door's always open."

My joke did nothing to cheer her mood. If anything, it made things worse. "We've talked about that and it's not happening," she said, exasperated. "Besides, Malibu is just as far from Pasadena as Huntington Beach."

While we were busy frowning at one another, Shane threw his arm over Cara and said, "Pasadena to Laurel Canyon isn't a bad drive. We've got a spare room or two if you want to stay with us."

Cara's eyes went wide and she squeaked. "Really? You wouldn't mind?"

Shane shrugged. "Why not?"

I had to give the man props. He wouldn't admit it, but he was trying to help repair Cara and Val's relationship. I wanted that too, so I nudged Val and said, "That's a great idea."

"V, you have to!" Cara squealed.

I smiled at the nickname. Cara was the only person who ever called Val "V" and I hadn't heard her do it since they were reunited. Val liked hearing it too and finally smiled the tiniest smile. "All right. I suppose it would be nice to spend some more time together."

"The best."

"Oh!" Robin shouted suddenly. "I've got it! You can start that L.A. office for F is For Families you've been talking about for months."

Val perked up at the suggestion and immediately fell into serious thought. The wheels in her head were spinning. I knew the look on her face—determination and excitement. I was the master of that look. She'd just found her project.

"Could you get one up and running in two months before school starts?" Robin asked.

"Not easily," Val admitted. "But if I could get the permits and the grants pushed through somehow, I could set it up enough that Jacinta could come down and take over when school starts. She wants to be back in Southern California anyway."

I was glad Val's mood seemed to be improving, but didn't like the sound of that. "I don't know about this, Val. It doesn't sound like a project; it sounds more like an all-encompassing, time-consuming, life-sucking, girlfriend-stealing nightmare."

Val finally gave me a smile—albeit, a small one—and patted my hand. "I won't forget to make time for you, but Robin's right. I've wanted to do this for months and it's the perfect opportunity. I can't pass it up."

"But what about your vacation? What about taking a break before school?"

"Kyle, before you showed up, I hadn't been on a date in longer than I care to admit. This will still feel like a vacation. I promise."

"But—"

"Kyle, stop being so needy," Cara interjected.

I frowned across the table at her. "I'm not needy."

She actually laughed at me. Even Shane laughed, the traitorous bastard.

"You're the neediest person I know," Cara said, flashing me a sympathetic smile. "But don't worry—we love you anyway. It's not your fault you're a spoiled rotten celebrity who gets everything he wants whenever he wants it so much that he can't live without having his heart's every desire at all times."

My jaw dropped open. "I am not a diva!"

"No," Cara said. "Just needy, with a tendency to pout when you don't get your way."

I frowned at Val, and she patted my hand sympathetically. "I'm not needy," I insisted, and everyone laughed again.

"Hey," Shane said, smirking in my direction. "You know the difference between a lead singer and God?"

I rolled my eyes. I'd heard this one a million times, but everyone else waited for the punch line.

"God knows he's not a lead singer."

I flipped my best friend off as I waited out the laughter. And believe me, there was a lot of it. Jerks.

16

P IS FOR PRUDE

VAL HAD PERKED UP A LITTLE THROUGH THE REST OF DIN-
ner, and she'd loved the mock-ups of the *Celebrity Gossip* article, but I knew something was still bothering her. Actually,
I think it was obvious to everyone because they cleared out
suspiciously fast, leaving the two of us standing in front of
the restaurant.

"Alone at last," I teased, hoping to keep the mood light.
"What would you like to do now? Want to go back to my
place? You haven't seen it yet."

Val's face paled at the suggestion. "Actually, I think I'm
just going to go home, if that's all right. I've got a headache."

I'd seen her reach up to rub her head several times
tonight, but it was still an excuse to bail and we both knew
it.

"Val, what's the matter?"

I tried to pull her into my arms and she immediately
stepped away. "I just don't feel like going out tonight. I'm

going to go home. I'll call you tomorrow."

There was a moment after Val walked away from me where I simply stood there staring after her retreating figure in shock. She'd just reached her car when I snapped out of it and caught up to her.

"Val."

"Not right now, Kyle," she said in a tired voice, pulling her keys from her purse.

I took her hand before she could open the car door and forced her to look at me. There were no tears in her eyes, but she was definitely struggling to keep them back. My throat was tight, knowing that I'd somehow upset her so badly, and at the same time, I was completely frustrated with her. "I don't speak 'girl.' You have to tell me why you're so upset with me if you want me to fix it."

Confessing that I had no clue why she was angry seemed to make the problem worse. She shut her eyes against her tears, but one escaped and rolled down her cheek. I pulled her into my arms, but she quickly pushed me away. "Please don't," she said. "I don't want you touching me right now."

I stepped back, my eyes snapping wide and my arms dropping to my sides as if they weighed several tons each. She may as well have said she hated me and never wanted to see me again. I repulsed her. I saw it written in her eyes in the few fleeting glances she bothered to give me.

For a moment, I said nothing. Didn't move. I couldn't make sense of the emotions in me. Then, my injured pride forced me to walk away. I heard her call my name but I ignored it. What was I supposed to say to her? I hadn't been more shocked since Adrianna asked me to sing "Cryin' Shame" on my birthday.

How could I always be so caught off guard by the women I cared about? I'd seduced a hundred women. I'd always prided myself on understanding what they wanted and how to give it to them. What a joke.

There were a couple of wooden benches perched on either side of the main door to the restaurant that served as a waiting area on crowded evenings. It was still early enough that they were both empty. I headed for the nearest one and threw myself down onto it. I folded my arms tightly across my chest and stared at my feet. I was sulking. I knew it. But how the hell was I supposed to feel after that kind of rejection?

Cara and Shane had been together for five years and made it look effortless. Then there was Robin inside, about to pop out her second child and bickering with her husband over a piece of pie because he cared about her enough that he wanted to make sure she and their baby stayed healthy. Two completely different relationships, yet both couples were light-years beyond me. I felt like a total jackass, incapable of having a relationship deeper than a night of body shots and crazy sex.

A pair of close-toed, black high heels stepped into my view.

"Kyle, I'm sorry. I'm trying to deal with this as best I can, but it's a lot harder than I thought it would be."

I didn't want to look up at her, but I couldn't help searching her face for clues. I knew I was glaring at her, but I was powerless to stop myself. I was angry. Hurt. Confused.

"Deal with what?" I snapped. "All I did was kiss you tonight, and ever since then you've recoiled every time I touch you. I've agreed not to have sex, but I can't help the way you make me feel. I can't just shut myself off. Believe me, if I could have, I would have already done it. Is it really so terrible that I want you?"

A flash of intuition sparked in Val's eyes. I envied her whatever it was she thought she'd figured out. I'd have killed for even a hint of understanding.

Her expression softened and she sat down next to me on the bench. I made no move to get closer. She laid her hand on my leg and I gritted my teeth. It was okay for her to touch me, just not the other way around?

"How am I supposed to feel," she asked, "knowing that you can't keep your hands off me because you're all turned on from having spent the day making out with another woman?"

I sighed as the picture finally became clear. "You're upset about the shoot today?"

I should have known. I was an idiot for not getting it right away, but at least the anger and the hurt were gone now. She wasn't rejecting me, she was feeling rejected.

I finally reached for her hand. Relieved that she let me take it, I laced our fingers together and let our hands rest on my leg. "It was just a job, Val. It didn't mean anything—to me or Cara."

"I know," she said quickly. "I told myself the same thing all afternoon. I'm trying not to be jealous, but you *liked* it, Kyle. You enjoyed kissing her. Didn't you?"

I could have lied to her—she was staring at me with big, vulnerable eyes begging me to deny it—but I've never been big on lying. Telling someone what they wanted to hear only hurt them in the long run. That's why I'd always been straight with the women I'd dated in the past—even if it painted me as the world's biggest jerk. They all knew I was only looking for a night of fun and that we'd never get past that. It gave them the chance to opt out if they couldn't handle it. It saved them heartache.

It was the same with Val. I could tell her what I thought would make her feel better, but, eventually, when I couldn't end up being the perfect guy I led her to believe I was, she'd get hurt much worse. Better to be honest and let her opt out now if she couldn't accept it.

"What do you want me to say?" I asked, hoping my gentle voice would soften the harshness of my words. "Of course I liked it. She's a beautiful woman and kissing her is very pleasant. Liking it is basic human nature. I can't help that. But I wasn't there mentally, Val. All day long, you were the only thought in my head."

She turned her head away from me but didn't pull her hand out of mine. I gave it a squeeze. "I'm sorry if that's not good enough, but I can't apologize for my job. I don't even want to. I'm proud of what I do, and I'm proud of how that video is going to turn out."

Val slowly turned her face back to mine. "I know," she whispered. "And I'm proud of you too, Kyle. I know how much your career means to you. I know how much you love it, and I know there are certain aspects of it that are always going to bother me. Logically, I get it. It still hurt watching you do things with my ex-best friend that I'm not even sure I'd be comfortable doing with you myself. You got further with Cara today in front of a room full of people and cameras than I've ever been with anyone."

I was stunned. I'd never thought of it that way. I met her eyes, and the control on her emotions broke. "She's so beautiful," she said. "They all are. You've been with so many of them and I—" Her voice broke and tears sprang into her eyes. "I know what I am, okay? I know I don't measure up, and I know I can't give you everything you want."

I was so shocked I actually gasped. "Val…" My voice trailed off when I couldn't think of anything to say. How could she think that? How could she possibly be so insecure?

"Watching you today, I just felt like such a silly, naïve, little girl. I couldn't stop thinking about all the women you've been with. So many that being half-dressed in bed kissing your best friend's wife in front of your girlfriend meant absolutely nothing to you. It was so not a big deal that you didn't even consider the possibility I might be upset. It was just normal for you. I can't even fathom how prude I must seem to you and your friends."

I sat there shaking my head. I kept moving my mouth, though nothing would come out of it.

She wouldn't look at me now. She'd pulled her hand out of mine and shifted on the bench so that she was slightly turned away from me, as if she felt completely ashamed.

This intense wave of passion washed over me. My need to make her understand how much she meant to me was so strong it pushed against me, making my body tremble as it fought to escape.

"Val, no." I grabbed her legs, turning her body my direction again, and took her face in my hands. "Cara may have been the actress in the video today, but that song is about you. The lyrics—the feelings I expressed in them—they're real, and they're all for you. I wrote the song for you. I'm abstaining for you."

I placed a soft kiss to her lips, and she closed her eyes as another tear escaped down her cheek. "I can't do anything about my past," I said softly. "I've done a lot of things with a lot of different women, but I've never waited for any of them."

I stopped talking and waited until she opened her eyes. When those soft-brown beauties found mine, I smiled and said, "Do you understand? You are the only one. This is a first for me, so we're both rookies right now. This is something I'm doing for you, and only you. There's no other woman on the planet I'd even consider making this sacrifice this for. I'm doing the abstinence thing because it's the only gift I can give you that will make you understand you mean more to me than any other woman I've ever been with."

I wiped the moisture from her cheeks and tucked her bangs behind her ear. Her eyes were still shiny with tears, but they held a glimmer of hope in them now.

My entire body melted beneath her gaze. She withered me into something so soft she could mold me into any type of man she wanted and I'd conform. I was Play-Doh in her delicate hands.

There were so many things I wanted to say, so many feelings I wanted her to understand. I've never been good with speeches. I express myself lyrically, so I did the only thing I knew how to do—I quietly sang the words to her song.

> *Forever I'll wait, it's drivin' me mad*
> *Driven by memories I've not yet had*
> *Hanging on a promise of you and me*
> *Hope springs eternal for things that could be*
>
> *You ask me to wait, don't know if I can*

Too scared to lose, I'm only a man
But I can't let you go, can't shut the door
Heart's telling me you're worth waiting for

"It's *you*, Val. It's not Cara. It's not any woman from my past. I don't see a silly little girl. I see an incredible woman. Your prudishness and naïvety are what make you so special to me."

Her gaze came into focus and she narrowed her eyes the tiniest bit. It made me smile. "Sorry, I can't deny that you're a naïve prude. We both know you are one," I teased. "But I love that about you. I find your innocence so…what were the words you used…hot and tempting."

She blushed and I laughed again. "I'm serious," I said. "That's why I can't ever keep my hands off you—because you're too damn sexy for your own good. You are so much more *hot and tempting* than anything else in the world—even more than me without a shirt on."

Her lips finally curled up and I kissed her. "There's my smile." I laced our hands together again and sighed when she gave me a reassuring squeeze. "What more can I do to make you feel better about us? How can I help you?"

Val gazed out in front of her and shrugged. "I don't know. Get me a dartboard with the Lakers' cheer team on it for Christmas?"

A startled laugh burst out of me. "I'm never going to live that one down, am I?"

"Never."

We laughed a minute, but my giggles gave way to a sigh. "Are we good, then?" I asked. I really hoped the answer was yes.

She leaned forward and pressed her lips to mine. "We're

good. I'm sorry I'm such an insecure mess."

"Well." I snuck my arms around her waist and kissed her again. "I can hardly blame you. You are dating *Kyle Hamilton*, after all. That's a lot to compete with."

Val brought her arms around my shoulders and let me give her a kiss that was more than just a peck. "Am I dating Kyle Hamilton or his ego?" she asked.

I grinned against her lips. "We're a package deal, actually. Lucky you, you get us both."

"Lucky me."

We lost ourselves in each other for a minute, both of us needing the connection after our fight. But eventually I had to stop before I laid her back on the bench and got us both arrested for public indecency.

"So," I asked, pretty sure I was the insecure one at the moment, "do you still want to go home?"

Val sighed and leaned her head on my shoulder. "Not really. You up for seeing a movie or something?"

It wasn't a quiet night at my place, but I'd take it. "So long as it doesn't star Brian Oliver, I'm good with that."

17

B IS FOR BROTHERS

BEFORE I KNEW IT, A MONTH HAD PASSED AND THE FOURTH of July was upon us. Cara and Shane were throwing some huge party, but I was determined to spend the night alone with Val. I needed the attention.

After Val settled in at Cara and Shane's house, she'd found her groove and gradually got busier and busier. She dove headfirst into starting her F is for Families office and spent a good deal of hours with Robin doing Not Everybody's Doing It stuff. She'd also flown back to Northern California twice so far for meetings she couldn't do over Skype and maid of honor stuff for her best friend's wedding.

Still, she always made sure to schedule time for me, even if I was literally being penciled into her planner. It was hardly romantic, but at least she gave me the password to her Google calendar so that I could pencil myself in whenever I had something I wanted her to attend with me, or if I simply needed Val time. For her, that was the equivalent of exchanging keys to each other's houses.

This weekend, I definitely needed some Val time. I'd blocked out all of Friday night, Saturday, and Sunday on Val's schedule with a written note that any changes would result in severe punishment. (Robin had the password to her schedule too and liked to move my Kyle time around on occasion.)

Somehow I'd managed to keep the entire weekend mine until Friday morning when Val's birth mom asked her to spend the Fourth of July with her and her son. I knew Val was still really anxious about her new relationship with her half-brother, so I gave up my alone time and told her we should go.

Val's birth mom lived all the way out in Lancaster. It was a crap drive, but there was a huge festival set up in the city park where they were going to shoot off fireworks at dark, so we met Val's birth mom and brother, Brody, for dinner before heading over to the park a couple of hours before the fireworks.

Brody was fifteen and moody as all hell. The kid had been a total punk since the second we showed up. He'd barely said a word to any of us all through dinner, and if he said a word to Val at all it was snide. His attitude got worse when we went to the festival and he started seeing a lot of kids from his school. It was getting very hard to ignore.

We were at a booth where you had to shoot basketballs into hoops to win a teddy bear when Val Sr. tried to break the ice for the hundredth time. (I don't know if the titles of junior and senior apply to girls—Val certainly laughed whenever I used them on her and her mother—but it seemed the easiest way to distinguish the two of them.) After

Brody made three shots in a row—consequently winning a ridiculously large stuffed bulldog—she said, "Val, did you know Brody was on the varsity basketball team this year? He was the first sophomore to make the team in over five years."

"That's awesome!"

Val was genuinely impressed, but Brody didn't appreciate her enthusiasm. The punk sneered at her, making me want to punch him in his frowning face. Val's smile faltered, but she pressed on, determined to be nice. "I'm a bit of an athlete, too. I'm not very good at basketball, but I played college volleyball for Stanford."

"Good for you," Brody muttered, then walked off without looking back.

If I were his mom, I'd have knocked him upside the head for that, but she only sighed as she watched him stalk off. There was a sheen layer of tears in her eyes. "My husband knew about Val, but I'd never told Brody about her until I saw the movie," she confessed. "He's been having a hard time with it. He's been very cold to Val."

"I noticed," I muttered.

I was surprised at how hard it was to control my temper. I'm not really the overprotective type, but I knew how much Val wanted to have a relationship with her brother and how hard she was trying. It bothered me that he wouldn't give her a chance.

A hand slipped around my waist, easing some of the tension from me. "He's been getting bullied by the kids from school since the Connie Parker Show," Val said. "Even by his teammates."

Valerie Sr.'s eyes filled with tears. "They were saying very hurtful, derogatory things about both Val and me. They're spamming his Facebook with nasty comments, teasing him when they see him. It's been pretty bad."

Teenagers were cruel. I felt bad for the kid, but he shouldn't have been taking it out on Val. It wasn't her fault.

"I can't blame him for hating me," Val said sadly. The way she sighed I knew she was already resigned to the idea of never having a good relationship with her brother.

I had no idea what I could do or say to make things better, but both Val and her mom looked so sad that I had to do something. I looked at the kid manning the basketball booth and said, "How much for a ball?"

"Sorry, they're not for sale."

I pulled a hundred dollar bill out of my pocket and held it up. The kid's eyes popped wide open and he glanced back to make sure his boss wasn't looking before he pocketed the cash and handed me the ball.

"We'll meet up with you guys in a little bit," I said, kissing Val's cheek.

Her grateful smile was all the motivation I needed.

The city park was huge. All of the carnival rides, games, and vendor booths were set up on the acres and acres of grassy fields. But on the other side of the massive recreational area—beyond the restrooms and playground—the tennis, volleyball, and basketball courts were unaffected by the festivities and still open for public use. It was this last attraction that I was sure held Brody's interest when he'd ditched us and left the festival.

After saying good-bye to Val and her mom, I headed toward the basketball courts, dragging a gaggle of starstruck high school students in my wake—most of them girls. That was pretty standard anytime I went out in public, but it was unusual that no one had approached me so far. They simply followed me around, trying to be discreet while snapping pictures of me on their phones.

I think they were holding back because I'd been with Brody and his mom. It was clear that most of the kids following me went to his school. The news that I was here hadn't taken long to spread once the first of Brody's classmates had seen us, and throughout the night I'd gathered a bit of an entourage.

Normally I would have stopped to talk to them, but Brody had been such a jerk to Val that I hadn't been in the mood. Now I was on a mission, and being elusive to the kids that knew Brody was going to work in my favor. I ignored them all and headed straight for Brody.

I found him sitting on a bench next to the basketball courts. There was a pickup game in progress on one of the courts, but he hadn't joined.

"Heads up!"

Brody caught the basketball I threw at him just before it took his head off. Judging by his nasty look, I may have put a bit too much force behind my pass for it to be considered friendly. "What the hell, man?"

"That's what I'd like to know," I said.

I came over and sat down next to him without waiting for an invitation. He gave me a wary glance but didn't tell me to get lost.

I studied him as he sat there trying to ignore me. He didn't look much like Val—his complexion was darker and he had brown hair instead of blond—but he had the same deep brown eyes as Val and he shared her height. At only fifteen, he was already about six-foot-four or five. It was no wonder he played basketball.

Eventually he broke the silence with a scoff. "They sent *you* out here to talk to me?"

"Nope. It's worse than that. I sent myself because my girlfriend was upset."

When Brody shot me a questioning look, I grimaced and pointed at myself. "Totally whipped."

Brody shook his head, but he cracked a small smile.

We both turned our eyes to the pickup game. After a short pause, I said, "She's pretty cool, you know. You should give her a chance."

Brody leaned forward and began bouncing the basketball on the ground between his knees. "Why?" he asked. "She's ruining my life."

I scoffed in disgust. What a whiner baby. "No way. If your life is getting ruined, it's because you're letting it. You think Val's never been teased? Hell, I bullied her myself and I did it in front of the entire world. At one point my fans dubbed her the most-hated girl in America. Her house got vandalized. She got death threats. She was lied about in tabloids. People called her a liar, a hypocrite, and a whore." Brody flinched at the harsh words. "But do you think she let it ruin her life? No. She stood up for herself and made people respect her instead of sulking around like a little punk-ass bitch."

The basketball stilled in Brody's hands and he shot me a wounded look. Val would have been pissed at me for calling him out like that, but seriously, the kid needed to man up.

"What do you know about it?" he grumbled, turning his gaze back to the basketball game. "I bet you've never been made fun of in your whole life."

I laughed and shamelessly admitted, "Not once. Some people are just too awesome for that." When he gave me another dirty look, I said, "So, I have no idea what you're going through. But you know what I am an expert in? Being popular. I can fix your social status problem right now, if you want."

Brody glared at the ball in his lap as if he were offended by the offer, but it was too good to pass up. After a moment, he sat up straight and gave me another wary look as he spun the ball in his fingertips. "You'd really help me?"

"Sure. One condition. You give my girl Val a chance."

I got pissed when he scoffed. "This wasn't her fault, either," I said. "She didn't seek out your mom; your mom went looking for *her*. Your mom's the one who decided to make her connection to Val public. It's her fault your friends are teasing you; not your sister's."

If looks could kill, the blazing glare Brody gave me would have fried me on the spot. "She's not my sister."

I didn't back down. "She wants to be. She doesn't have any other siblings. She was excited when she learned she had a brother, and you're an ungrateful idiot if you can't appreciate that there's an amazing person who wants the chance to be a part of your life. Don't be such a selfish prick, man."

I propped my elbows up on the back of the bench, content to chill there staring Brody down all night even if he never said another word. He was quiet for a minute, but he eventually smirked. "You're kind of a jerk."

I smiled. "Takes one to know one."

Brody finally laughed. "Okay, fine. I'll cut her some slack. But she better not turn out to be a total buzzkill."

"Dude." I got to my feet and stretched as I turned to

face Brody. "I'm a freaking superstar. I could get as many women in the world as I want, including your mom. You think I'd tie myself down to just one woman and give up sex for her if she wasn't the coolest chick on the planet?"

Without warning, Brody threw the ball at my face. I barely caught it in time to keep my nose intact. "Stay away from my mom, you jackass," he warned.

He was trying to give me a tough guy stare down, but he couldn't hold it. I laughed when he cracked a smile. I glanced over my shoulder at the pickup game going on behind me and said, "You know those guys?"

He followed my gaze and nodded. "Some of them. A couple of them are on my team."

"What about them?" I nodded toward the group of girls who'd followed me across the park as if they suddenly had the deepest desire to ditch the festival and watch a random pickup basketball game.

This time, when Brody scanned the crowd I was looking at, his cheeks turned slightly pink. "I recognize most of them from school, but I don't know them. They're older. Popular girls."

"Perfect."

I flashed Brody a wicked grin that made the blood drain from his face. "What are you going to do?" he asked.

"I'm going to solve your bully problem by making you too cool to pick on."

"Wait a minute," he said, hopping to his feet. "I have to go to school with these people. I don't think—"

I quit listening to him and headed for the basketball court currently not in use. The gaggle of girls tittered with excitement as I shot—and luckily made—a basket from the free throw line.

I got in a layup as well before Brody finally caught up to me. I threw him the ball—with a lot less hostility this time. "First to twenty-one wins. Call your own fouls."

"You want to play ball?" Brody asked, confused.

I cast a glance at the girls who were already moving from their place on the sidelines of the pickup game to sit along the edge of our court. Brody realized what was happening and blushed again. The poor kid had no game—at least not with the ladies. Basketball wise, though, he was going to wipe the floor with me. "Or we could go back to the fair," I suggested, "and you could apologize to your mom and start kissing up to your sister instead."

Brody snuck another look at the girls before tossing the ball back to me, a confident smirk finally spreading across his face. "I'll let you tip-off. You're going down, *superstar*."

Atta boy, I thought. *Show those ladies you've got confidence.*

I set the ball on the ground and bent over to touch my toes. "It's on," I said, "just as soon as I stretch."

"For real?" Brody asked, but I noticed he'd pulled one of his arms back behind his head.

"Yeah, for real. Do you know what my personal trainer would do to me if I pulled a hamstring in a random pickup game?"

"You have your own personal trainer?"

I laughed. "Dude. Being famous isn't all parties and women. I mean, it *mostly* is, but a body like this—" I pulled my shirt off and threw it aside, winking at the group of girls when they all squealed. "—doesn't come naturally. I spend two torturous hours every single day with my trainer and that's *after* he makes me run a two-mile warm-up."

Brody blinked at me, bewildered, and finished his stretching in silence. Then, as predicted, he proceeded to cream me in a game of one-on-one. He was good, but the fact that I sucked only made him that much more impressive. By the end of our game, the girls on the sidelines had become his personal cheering section, and the guys playing on the court next to us had stopped to see what all the hype was about.

I gave it my best, though, and by the end of the game I was sweaty and exhausted. Once the winning two points were scored, I crashed down onto the grass not far from the crowd in an attempt to cool off and catch my breath.

Brody, after shyly accepting a round of congratulations, sat down beside me and whispered, "Did you let me win?"

I chuckled and didn't bother to lower my voice. "I wish. I'm a singer, not a baller. I genuinely suck that badly at all sports. What's worse is your sister said I'll have to play volleyball with her at that beach barbecue we've got coming up in a couple weeks—you are coming to that, right?"

My parents had decided it was time to meet Val. They could never do anything simple without having the chance to show off, so they decided to invite Val's family—birth and adopted—to their country club in Huntington Beach for a barbecue. I could tell from the guilty look on Brody's face that he'd been planning to skip it until now.

"Yeah, I think my mom said we were going."

"Good. Then you can play Val for me and spare me the humiliation of getting schooled by my own girlfriend."

Brody laughed and nodded his head. "I suppose I could do that. I'm pretty decent at sand volleyball."

I waited a moment and louder than necessary said, "So,

Mr. Basketball, are you a Lakers fan?"

Brody raised a brow at me. "Is my sister a virgin?"

I chuckled. He actually wasn't too bad when he wasn't being a whiny brat. "It just so happens that I am also a huge Lakers fan. I happen to be a season ticket holder, and I'm not talking the nosebleeds. My seats are spitball distance from Jack Nicholson's."

"No freaking way!" Brody shouted. He shook his head with a small measure of disgust. "It pays to be rich and famous."

I threw my arm over Brody's shoulder. "It also pays to know the rich and famous. I'm going to miss a lot of the games next season because I'll be on tour. I thought maybe you could keep my seats warm for me while I'm gone."

Brody's jaw fell open, and for a moment he was completely speechless. After the shock wore off, he shouted again. "Are you freaking *serious*?"

"I don't joke about the Lakers, kid," I said solemnly. "You should take your mom sometimes, or maybe your girlfriend…"

Brody ducked his head a little to hide his blushing cheeks. "I don't have a girlfriend," he mumbled.

"What? No girlfriend?" I practically shouted it, and I glanced around, making eye contact with several cute girls. "Well, we'll have to fix that, and soon. Are you coming to my album release party?"

"Uh…yeah?"

He glanced at the crowd and blushed again. There must have been thirty or forty kids standing around listening to our conversation and all of them were now gaping at Brody in shock.

"Awesome. Anyone you want me to add to the guest list? Any particular starlet you'd like to meet?"

Brody looked up at me with eyes that seemed to ask if I was serious. "Uh…"

"I've got A-list access, dude. Take advantage."

"Um." He thought for a moment and said, "Miley?"

I couldn't help bursting into laughter. "Aiming high, huh? I like it. I always say go big or go home."

I got to my feet and held out a hand to help Brody up. "Miley's already RSVP'd," I said as I brushed some grass off my pants. I snatched the ball from Brody's hands. "She'll be there. Unfortunately for you, your sister would *kill* me if I hooked you up with her. How do you feel about Bella Thorne, though? I've heard she's a sweetheart."

Brody's pout melted into a hopeful grin. "Bella Thorne? Hell yeah."

"Done." I shook my head. "And speaking of your scary sister who holds the leash to my invisible collar, we should go find her before I get in trouble for ditching her all night."

18

S IS FOR SURPRISES

I GRUMBLED AS I TUGGED AT MY SHIRT COLLAR, AND SECRETLY cursed the people who'd made it necessary for me to wear a tie. My album release party was a little too swanky for my taste. My managers had chosen to have it at this new hipster sushi restaurant, so while it wasn't a black-tie event, it was all cocktails and raw fish. I'd have killed for a cheeseburger, but I couldn't complain about the night too much because the little black dress Valerie wore made it worth it.

The décor of the place was pretty cool; I'd give them that. Aquariums throughout the building gave it a very under the sea, mysterious, romantic feel. They'd even gotten some fog machines going along the floors, so we were all walking around in a sea of clouds. The atmosphere was great, they were pumping my new album through the speakers, and I'd had final say over the guest list, so the company was great. If not for the stupid tie, uncomfortable shoes, and fancy food, the party would have been perfect.

"Let me guess," Val whispered as she finally found her

way back to my side. The woman was a born mingler and had been a very popular guest tonight. "Right now, you're wondering how rude it would be if you took off your tie and ordered some pizzas."

She won. I smiled. She watched my pout disappear and bent forward to kiss my grin. "That's a much better look on you," she teased.

I wrapped my arms around her before she could pull away. "If you want it to stay, then you can't keep wandering off on me."

"I'm just being a good hostess. You're the one who keeps hiding from your own guests."

"I'm not hiding from my guests. I was just trying to lure you into this dark corner. And look! My evil plan has finally worked. It took a while, but the wait was worth it."

I adjusted Val so that she was sitting on my lap. She gave me a look that I ignored, and I kissed her again. The blessed woman indulged me more than I thought she would and for a minute we made out like a couple of teenagers.

Energy renewed, I finally got up and dragged Val back into the foray. I had a surprise for Val, and he had just texted me that he'd arrived. "Congressman Richards is that guy you like, right?"

Val blinked and gave me an odd look. "Random. How did you know that?"

I grinned. "My good friend Google seems to know you pretty well."

"You Googled me?"

I was hoping to find some nude pictures but—"

"Kyle!"

I laughed. She was just too easy. "Anyway," I said, lacing

her hand in mine. "Did you know that our wonderful congressman's youngest daughter is fifteen years old and happens to be a big Kyle Hamilton fan?"

"I did know that Congressman Richards had a teenage daughter, and I could have guessed she was a fan—most teenage girls are—though I'm wondering how *you* know that."

I led Val through the crowd where I saw the congressman and his starry-eyed daughter walk through the front door. "I know that because when I called to invite her father to this thing tonight he told me I take up more space on his daughter's bedroom walls than One Direction."

Val gasped mockingly. "More than *One Direction*? That's impressive—wait, did you just say when you called to invite him here tonight?"

I laughed and turned her toward the man standing in front of us. "Val, I'd like you to meet—"

"Congressman Richards!" she gasped. Her face flushed as she gingerly shook his hand. "Wow! I'm sorry—I'm just so surprised. It's so good to meet you."

The congressman chuckled. "I didn't expect to be recognized at an event like this."

"No, it's an honor. I've followed your career since you were elected Mayor of Huntington Beach."

The congressman's eyebrows shot way up. "You couldn't have been more than ten."

Val blushed again. "I was nine. My dad did a lot of volunteer work on your election campaign. He took me to one of the debates and let me hand out buttons. I've been hooked on politics ever since. I just received my degree in political science at Stanford, and I wrote a paper on your congressional platform for my final in one of my poly-psy classes."

I finally couldn't hold back my laughter anymore. It was just so strange seeing Val like this. When I gained the attention of both Val and Congressman Richards, I shook my head and sighed. "I have international superstar status and she goes fangirly over you."

Val blushed again. Congressman Richards and I both laughed as we shook hands. "Congressman, this is my brainiac, future-first-female-president girlfriend, Valerie Jensen. I was trying really hard to impress her tonight, and the Hollywood A-list doesn't seem to do that, so I owe you a big thank-you for coming."

"It was my pleasure, and it was really kind of you to invite Monica as well."

He pulled his daughter in front of him, his smile suddenly transforming him from politician to proud father.

"Thanks for coming tonight, Monica," I said. The girl bit back a squeal when I said her name and trembled as she shook my hand. "You're doing me a huge favor. I have a friend here tonight who was worried that there wouldn't be anyone his age to talk to."

I pointed toward Val's brother. He wasn't hard to spot, towering over most of the people in the room. I gave Monica a second to check him out, then nudged her lightly with my elbow. "Good-looking guy, isn't he?" She blushed and didn't say anything, but her eyes drifted back to him again. "He's nice. Kid of shy, though." I looked at Monica again and added, "Like you, I suspect."

She bit her lip and nodded. I let go of Val and took Monica's hand. "Come on, I'll introduce you while we let the grown-ups talk boring politics."

Val was still talking to Congressman Richards when I returned minus one shy teenage girl. "Don't worry, Congressman. I promise I left her in good hands. He's Val's brother. He'll look after her."

We all turned back to look at the kids. There had been a whole group of girls surrounding Brody, but when I'd mentioned Monica was shy and a little nervous to be there, he'd pulled out a chair for her and given her his full attention. He was introducing her to several girls she clearly recognized.

"Exactly how many famous teenage girls did you invite tonight?" Val asked.

The suspicion in her voice made me laugh. "A few," I admitted.

"And how many teenage boys are here—famous or otherwise?"

I laughed again. "One."

Val rolled her eyes, but the smile on her face was grateful. "You worked a miracle on him. Valerie's called me in tears several times this week. She says he's like a whole new kid."

I shrugged. "He just needed a little attention. You're a hard woman to compete with, Val."

"It's more than that," Val said. "You're really good with him. You should think about mentoring. You'd be great for the Big Brother program. Or, you know, we could even start our own program if you wanted."

She was getting that scary gleam in her eyes, so I stomped out that conversation before it really got started. "Oh, no. No way. No more starting programs for you."

"But that's one you and I could do together."

That was an interesting thought, and not the most horrible one I'd ever heard. "Maybe I'll think about it," I said, "in a few years. Right now you have enough on your plate with your L.A. F is for Families office."

Congressman Richards perked up. "Are you doing that?" he asked Val, surprised.

"I'm trying," she said. "Still waiting on grant approval and a few permits. You know how it is."

Congressman Richards laughed. "Yes, I do. Why don't you send me the proposal? I'll see what I can do to help move things along faster."

Val was overwhelmed. "I—I—that would incredible," she muttered, shocked. "Thank you."

"I would be happy to help. I've actually heard a lot about your V is for Virgin efforts from my daughter this week. She's been nonstop chattering about Kyle since he invited us to come tonight. She showed me the recent article about you doing the abstinence challenge together. I'm the father of a teenage girl, Miss Jensen. There's not a woman on the planet I'd be happier to support than you. In fact, you should call my office and set up a meeting with me sometime. We're going to be interviewing soon to fill a few open positions on my reelection campaign staff. We could sure use someone like you."

Val gasped again. I had to slip my arm around her waist because I was afraid her knees were going to give out. "That's very kind of you," she said once she could speak. "It would be a dream to work with you, but I start grad school in a couple of weeks."

If it was possible, the congressman's opinion of Val went up even higher. "That's unfortunate for me. Still, you should keep my card and give me a buzz after you finish."

Val accepted the business card he handed her and then I made a polite escape, explaining to the congressman that he'd sent my girlfriend into shock and she needed to sit down before she passed out. It wasn't much of a lie. She didn't even notice it when I dragged her to a table and sat her down.

"Did that really just happen?"

I chuckled and was then attacked by my very giddy girlfriend. Her arms came around my neck and her lips found mine. I was more than happy to let her kiss me over and over again as long as she needed to.

"I can't believe you did that for me," she said as she squeezed the breath out of me.

When she pulled back, her eyes were glossy with a sheen layer of tears. The expression on her face did me in completely. Hundreds of women have gazed at me with stars in their eyes, but this was the first time Val had ever given me that look. There was something different about it coming from Val, though. Her infatuation wasn't hollow. There was real emotion in her face. Emotion that meant something. Emotion that had me swallowing back a dry lump in my throat.

"Val," I whispered, bringing my mouth back to hers for a soft kiss. "Let's get out of here. Let's go somewhere, just you and me." She laughed as if she thought I'd made a funny joke. "I'm serious."

"Kyle, we can't leave."

"Sure, we can. It's just a party."

"It's *your* party."

She was right, but I couldn't help wondering if she was making excuses. My good mood deflated and I slumped back in my chair. I was so tired of this. It wasn't even about the sex. It was as if she didn't want to be alone with me at all. Like she had some kind of personal rule against it. We'd been dating for six weeks now and the only time it was ever just the two of us, we were out on a date and it was always someplace nice and public. She'd only even been to my house twice, and Shane and Cara had been there with us both times. It was never just Val and me.

I'd known this relationship wasn't going to be easy, but I was starting to get bitter. I'd expected more somehow. I didn't want to screw this up. Val was the most amazing, perfect woman. She was everything I wanted. I was falling for her, but something wasn't working and I couldn't figure out what it was. If we didn't fix it soon, we weren't going to last.

Val noticed my disappointment. Her worried brow and apologetic smile confirmed to me that her not wanting to leave had nothing to do with offending anyone at this party. I couldn't take it anymore. "What's going on, Val?"

She seemed surprised by the question. "What do you mean?"

"I mean, what's going on with us? Are you in this relationship because you want to be, or because you don't know how to get rid of me?"

Startled, Val leaned over and pulled my hand into hers again. She watched me for a minute, searching my eyes with a concerned frown on her face. "Do you really not know the answer to that?" she asked in a whisper.

I was embarrassed that I didn't. We were to the point where I should have had no doubt. I hated that I needed her to confirm it. I looked down at my lap and shrugged. "I did kind of bully you into it."

All summer I'd felt that this relationship was off balance. I felt as if I cared more about her than she did me. I definitely needed her more than she needed me. No one who knew us would argue that. At first I'd just been thrilled that she was with me at all. Now that my heart was invested, that wasn't good enough. I needed more from her. I needed her to be invested with me, and I wasn't sure she was.

"Kyle." Her hand on my face forced me to meet her eyes. "You of all people should know that I don't do things I don't want to." She smiled a rare, cocky smirk. "I could have told you no. It *is* possible to resist the great Kyle Hamilton, no matter how much you think it isn't."

I wasn't in the mood to laugh, but my lips curved up at the ends. Val's eyes brightened at my smile. "I'm here in L.A. because I want to be," she said. "I'm with you because I want to be. I couldn't ask for a better boyfriend than you."

It was the answer I wanted to hear, but it didn't get rid of the bad feeling in my gut. Words didn't mean much without actions backing them up.

"Okay?" she asked when I didn't say anything.

I wasn't sure we were really okay, but I nodded anyway. She didn't buy it. Sometimes I hated that she was so smart.

She sighed. "Right now is not a good time for this kind of conversation, but it's clear we need to talk. We're going to your parents' barbecue tomorrow, but we don't have anything planned tomorrow evening. Can you wait until then?"

She waited for me to answer, but I didn't know what to say. The phrase "we need to talk" was never good. I couldn't help wondering if we were about to come to another tragic end like we had four years ago. I didn't want that, but sometimes it felt inevitable. It had always felt a little hopeless between us.

"Kyle, whatever is bothering you, I want to fix it. I don't like seeing you upset."

At least she wasn't planning to dump me. That didn't mean it wasn't going to happen, but it helped to know that wasn't her intention. I took a deep breath and tried to pull myself together. I kissed the backs of her fingers and forced a convincing smile. "Okay," I said. "Just you and me tomorrow after the barbecue."

Val roved her eyes over me again from head to toe, as if making sure I wasn't going to break. When I passed her inspection, she smiled and said, "Just you and me. I promise."

19

B IS FOR BABY

MY PARENTS HAD THEIR "LITTLE SUMMER BARBECUE" catered. It was so typical of them. They'd expressed an interest in meeting Val's parents so I'd suggested a barbecue on the beach, and they ended up hosting an event at their yacht club. Aside from the fact that there was sand and water—meaning I could wear swim shorts and flip-flops—it was a swankier event than the album release party the night before.

The guest list wasn't short, either. They'd invited everyone they knew. They'd never thrown a party for Adrianna and me, not even when we got engaged, but I guess dating a nonprofit organization-starting do-gooder Stanford graduate with political aspirations was something they could finally be proud of.

Snobs.

But, they were Mom and Dad, and even though they drove me crazy they weren't the worst parents in the world. I loved them, so I let them have their fancy get-together and grit my teeth through all the painful introductions as they showed my girlfriend off to virtually all of the Who's Who in Orange County.

"Oh, Valerie darling, come here! You have to meet the mayor."

Yes, my mother refused to call Val anything but Valerie.

Val gave my mom a bright smile and turned her attention to the short, fat bald guy in khaki pants and a polo shirt next to her. "Mayor Lambert, of course," Val greeted cheerfully. "It's a pleasure to meet you."

My mom beamed with pride over the fact that Val already knew his name.

I wandered a few feet away back to the hors d'oeuvres table and let them have their introductions.

"My son finally snagged himself a keeper. Valerie is a Stanford graduate," my mother bragged. "She double majored in both economics and political science with honors and is starting her graduate work in a couple of weeks. You'd better keep your eye on her or she might just steal your job in a couple of years."

"Oh, I think Mr. Mayor is safe," Val teased. "I've got my eyes set on a different office."

"It wouldn't be oval-shaped, would it?"

Val shrugged. "Well, rectangle is just so boring."

The three of them erupted into polite laughter.

Sadly, Val seemed to be having a great time. Watching her standing there next to my mother schmoozing with the hoity-toity crowd as if she completely belonged, I realized something disturbing. Aside from the snootiness that my mother had from being raised as a girl with money and privilege that Val didn't have, the two women were actually a lot alike. They were even wearing similar sundresses and strappy sandals.

Shane moseyed up next to me and followed my gaze. "She actually seems to be enjoying herself," he mused.

I sighed. "I'm dating my mother."

Shane snorted. "There's a sort of poetic justice in that that I find amusing."

Val snuck a quick glance around, looking for me. When her eyes met mine, she smiled and rolled her eyes as if she were only humoring my mom. I have to admit, it lightened my mood a lot.

"Okay, so she's not exactly like your mom. You should go rescue her."

"Yeah right. My mother would kill me."

"I'll do it."

Shane and I turned to the new voice and found Brody standing behind us, licking barbecue sauce off his fingers. "I'd be happy to interrupt them and steal that woman's precious show pony from her." He frowned at me and added, "No offense."

"Absolutely none taken," I said with a laugh.

I wasn't offended by Brody's hostility toward my parents. I actually admired the kid for having the guts to stand up to them. My parents had been polite to Val Sr. and Brody, but their disdain for the once-pregnant teen and now-single mom and her son was thinly veiled. I'd wanted to strangle them both a few times today for their subtle snubs.

"If you know a way, please, by all means, go for it. I'd love to see the look on her face."

Brody handed me his empty plate. "Watch and learn, dude."

He licked his fingers one last time and strode over to my

mother, stepping between her and the mayor and tugging on Val's arm. "Excuse me, Mrs. Hamilton," he said with all the false politeness she'd given him today. "Do you mind if I steal my sister for a little while? She promised me a game of volleyball and I have to leave soon." He turned his big, fake smile on the mayor. "Did you know she plays for her college? She's a strong-side hitter."

"And a college-level athlete, too!" the mayor said, his eyebrows rising in surprise. "That is very impressive, Miss Jensen."

"We'll see how impressive it is," Brody said. "What do you say, sis, you and Kyle against me and Mom? Losers have to jump in the ocean fully clothed."

I snickered at the completely aghast look on my mom's face, then burst out laughing when the mayor loved the idea. Val smiled at her brother with genuine excitement and affection. "I say it's going to be a long, uncomfortable ride home for you and your mom," she taunted.

She smiled at my mom and the mayor as if everything were completely normal. "If you guys will excuse me, it appears I need to go settle a little family dispute."

She left before my mom had the chance to argue.

"Good luck!" the mayor called out.

Brody was my new hero until Val kissed my cheek and said, "I hope you're prepared to get dirty. You and I have been challenged. Smack-talk was involved and my honor is now at stake, so we can't back out."

I frowned, so she kissed my lips, hoping to win me over. It worked. "Please?"

"Are you batting your eyelashes at me?" I asked, trying as hard as I could not to grin.

She batted those beauties again and looked up at me from beneath them as she stuck her bottom lip into a pout. "Is it working?"

If her intent was to get herself ravished by me in front of God, her parents, and the Huntington Beach Yacht Club, then yes, it was definitely working. "You had me at 'let's get dirty.'"

She rolled her eyes and pulled me down the patio steps to the sand where a couple of volleyball nets were set up.

"WE GOT HUSTLED," VAL WHINED FORTY-FIVE MINUTES later as we stood on the sand, looking out at the waves.

"You got hustled," I corrected. "I could have guessed Val Sr. was an athlete, seeing as how it runs in the family and all, and Brody knew full well I suck at sports."

She sighed, defeated. "How was I supposed to know there was something you aren't good at?"

Brody laughed and slapped Val and me on the shoulders. "Take a walk, losers."

Val grimaced. "I suppose now is a bad time to mention I'm scared of the ocean?"

"What?" Brody asked, astonished. "You grew up less than two miles from the beach and you're afraid to get in the ocean?"

"There could be sharks," Val said. "And lots of slimy things. What if a fish touches my leg?"

I'd never seen her act like more of a girl.

"Don't worry, Val, I'll fight off the fish for you." I pulled her toward the water and she dug her feet into the sand. "You made the bet, babe, and you lost. Time to take your defeat like a man."

"Rematch!" she shouted to Brody. "Just you and me. Without the handicap, I'd have killed you and you know it!"

"Handicap?" I scoffed. "I wasn't *that* bad."

Val gave me a flat look. Apparently, stress took away her sense of humor. "Kyle, *Robin* could have played better than you, and she's two days overdue."

"Robin?"

There was no way she was going to get away with that, no matter how adorable she was when she was suffering from an anxiety attack. I scooped her into my arms and walked into the waves. I laughed when she started shrieking and had to hold on tight as she flailed in my arms. "Would you look at that?" I taunted. "I guess all my muscles are good for more than just looking at, after all."

"Kyle, I'm serious! Don't you dare drop—"

I threw her into an approaching wave and she screamed. The water was only up to her waist and she came up sputtering seconds later. "Kyle!" she shouted. "You jerk!"

She tried to run for the shore, but I snagged her around the waist and held on tight. "You're not funny," she said as she struggled to break free of my grip.

"You made a bet, woman. That's serious business."

When she realized she couldn't get out of my grip, she wrapped her arms around my neck and clung for dear life. "Fine. I am officially all wet now, so can you please take me back to shore? I really, really hate being in the ocean."

"No way. Swim with me."

I started dragging her out just a little bit further. "Kyle, no. I'm serious. I want to get out."

"I've got you, Val. I'm not going to let go. Just stay here with me for a minute. Please? It's the only place we're safe from my mother."

Val pinched her eyes shut and said, "Fine. Just for a minute, and don't you dare let go of me."

"Never again," I teased.

I picked her up and wrapped her legs around my waist as I waded us into the waves up to my shoulders. I had to push the skirt of her dress way up on her thighs to accomplish it. She gasped and started to protest, but then a large swell came at us that I had to jump in order to keep our heads above water. She glued herself to me like an octopus, clinging for dear life.

"You're okay, Val," I whispered, pushing her wet hair off her forehead with one hand while holding her tightly against me with the other. "I've got you."

She took a deep breath and let her head fall to my shoulder. "Kyle, if something slimy touches me, I swear to you I am going to lose it."

"All right. I'll take you back soon. Just let me hold you a few minutes longer."

Val pulled her head off my shoulder and gave me a searching look. "Are you really this desperate for my attention that you have to hold me hostage in the ocean?"

She'd asked the question seriously, self-consciously even, so I decided to be honest with her. "Yes."

Her eyes fell shut and she sighed as she leaned her forehead to mine. "I'm sorry," she whispered. "I'm a terrible girlfriend."

"If that were true I wouldn't be so desperate for you,

would I?"

She answered me with a kiss that started out soft and quickly turned scorching. As my hands fell down her back, searching for bare skin and finding none, I cursed the bet she made that required she be in the water fully clothed.

"You should lose the dress," I murmured. She curled her hands deep in my hair, and it was getting hard to think. "I've been waiting for your bikini to make an appearance all day."

I expected her to protest, but instead her body tensed and she deepened the kiss. When she let me up for air, her hands fell from my hair to the material clinging to my chest. She yanked on it and said, "Only if you'll lose the T-shirt, Mr. *Abs*tinence."

I managed to let go of her only long enough to help her rip my shirt over my head.

"You're going to lose that," she breathed when I tossed it away.

"I don't care." My words came out in a growl and I crashed my lips back on hers, slamming our bodies together.

My hands rounded the curve of her butt and finally found bare thighs. I pushed the material of her dress further up until my hands were at her bare waist. I paused, waiting to be slapped away, only no resistance came. I was confused, but definitely not complaining.

"Val! Kyle! Come back!"

The shouts sounded distant, second to the sound of my blood pumping in my ears and our ragged breaths. Both of us ignored them.

"You guys! Robin's having her baby!"

"Good for her!" Val shouted, raising her arms above her head, waiting for me to lift her dress off. Before I could, the word *baby* broke through to my brain.

"Did he say Robin's having a baby?"

"KYLE! VALERIE!"

We stopped kissing and turned to the shore where several people were jumping around wildly, trying to get our attention. My mom was frowning at us. "Your friend has gone into labor. She says you drove her here. You need to take her to the hospital."

When it finally sank in, I cursed. "Robin's having her *baby*!"

Val and I hurried back to shore where my mom was waiting for us with towels. I wasn't sure if the disapproving look on her face was because I'd been making out with my girlfriend in the ocean, or because I'd invited a pregnant woman to her party and she'd dared to go into labor in the middle of it.

"Where is your shirt?" she hissed as we hurried up the beach back to the clubhouse.

I couldn't even remember what had happened to it. My mom sighed. "You may take the towels with you. I'll speak to the club owner. The valet has already brought your car around. Your friends are waiting for you."

We hurried across the patio, shouting quick apologies and good-byes over our shoulders. After a fast-paced and dripping walk through the clubhouse, we found Cara and Shane out front standing next to my Escalade.

"That's going to be fun," Cara said flatly as she pointed toward the couple yelling at one another in the backseat.

Shane smirked and held open the driver's door for me. "Better hope you don't hit traffic."

"Traffic?" Alan shouted, slightly panicked. "This is

Southern California! There's always traffic! I warned you, Robin! I told you we needed to stay home today!"

"And *I* told *you* I couldn't spend one more minute in that house with your mother there breathing down my neck! That woman is insufferable! I told you not to invite her!"

"She's my *mother*! I didn't invite her! She just showed up! What was I supposed to do?"

"Lock the doors and point her toward a hotel!"

Wow. I turned back to Shane and his smirk turned grave. "Good luck, man. I'm glad I'm not you."

I took a breath and climbed in the car.

Val kissed my mom's cheek and muttered a quick apology before joining me in the car.

We looked at each other, and then I stepped on the gas.

"You should take her to the hospital here in Huntington," Alan said from the backseat as I pulled out of the county club's driveway.

"No," Robin said.

"Robin, it's a long drive to Pasadena."

"We'll be fine. I was in labor with Asher for ten hours. The contractions are still six minutes apart."

"What if there's traffic?" Alan demanded. "Do you want to give birth to our son on the side of the road?"

Apparently, another contraction hit because Robin grunted and hunched forward.

I couldn't believe this was happening. There was a woman having a baby in my backseat and she expected me to drive? I pulled out my phone, thinking it would probably be better to call an ambulance, and as if she could read my thoughts, Robin glared at me in the rearview mirror. "Drive!" she shouted.

I drove.

"Take us to the hospital here," Alan demanded again.

And then Robin turned into some scary alien monster. "I am not having this baby in a strange hospital an hour away from home with some random on-call quack!" she yelled at Alan. Her red face turned forward again and she cut through me with her glare. "You take me to Huntington Memorial in Pasadena or you are a dead man, Kyle. Do you hear me? You do not mess with a woman in labor!"

I glanced back at Alan with a sympathetic grimace. He understood the look. I was driving to Pasadena because I valued my life and wanted to keep it.

20

L IS FOR LOVE

SO MUCH FOR A TEN-HOUR LABOR. ROBIN'S WATER BROKE around Monrovia, soaking my leather seats in fluids I refused to think about. I was going to need a new car, but at least we made it to the hospital without the baby being born.

Robin asked us to stay—something about not letting Val leave her alone with the idiot who did this to her—so the hospital staff found a shirt for me and I experienced the longest two hours of my life.

Alan sat at Robin's side, holding her hand. Val sat on her other side holding her other hand, and I stood in the far back corner of the room praying I wouldn't throw up or pass out. I had to sit down when the baby's heartbeat dropped and they brought in this vacuum thing and literally sucked the squirt out. The nurses made me put my head between my knees and brought me orange juice.

Val took pity on me then and came to hold my hand instead of Robin's, but the baby was already out, so Robin said it was okay.

I had just decided I'd never ever, *ever* have children, when Robin's baby cried for the first time. I could hardly tell what the bloody, goop-covered bundle was, but then they handed it to Robin and she cradled it as if it were the sun, the moon, and the stars wrapped in a tiny blanket.

Robin burst into tears, and then Val burst into tears, and then even Alan let a drop or two run down his cheeks. He and Robin had been fighting nonstop all day. She'd called him horrible names and threatened to castrate him multiple times. She was pale, sweat soaked, and bleary-eyed, but he stood by her side, smiling down at his wife as if he'd never loved anything or anyone more. There was so much emotion in the room that I was afraid of drowning in it.

"Kyle, come see," Robin whispered. Her eyes never left the baby in her arms.

I wasn't sure I could stand up, but Val took my hand and pulled me over to Robin's bedside. I was startled by what I saw. "What's wrong with his *head*?" I gasped. "Is he okay? And why is he purple?"

Everyone in the room laughed at me. "It's from the vacuum," Robin explained. She grinned down at her son. "It's normal, and it'll fix itself soon enough, won't it, pretty boy?"

"He's beautiful," Val whispered. "Congratulations, you guys."

"Thanks."

Val squeezed my hand as she smiled down at the kid, and I got this strange flutter in my gut.

Robin passed the baby over to her husband and he turned into a puddle of mush. He bounced that baby in his arms and cooed at him as much as Robin had. Then he randomly leaned over and smashed his mouth to hers, careful of the infant in his arms.

"I love you, honey," he said. "You make beautiful babies."

"I love you, too. You give me beautiful babies."

It was as if Val and I weren't even in the room. Robin and Alan were completely lost in each other and their new son. I'd never seen a happier couple. The love they had for each other in that moment was something I hadn't even known existed. I'd thought I understood love, but it turned out I didn't have a clue.

"Well, we should really get going now and let you guys enjoy this," I said. "Congratulations."

Robin and Alan barely glanced up at us to say their good-byes and thank us for the ride. Val promised she'd be back tomorrow to hold the baby once she was free of saltwater and sand.

We were both quiet all the way back to my car, and for a minute we just sat there in the parking lot letting everything we'd just experienced sink in.

"That was incredible, wasn't it?" Val murmured.

I didn't know what else to say but "Yeah. Crazy."

Val snapped out of her daze and smiled at me. "You feeling better now?"

I still felt a little queasy, but I nodded. "You women are tough."

"And you men are really a bunch of big softies." She took my hand and squeezed it. "But that's why we like you."

Val smiled at me so brightly that her eyes shone, and for a moment I imagined what it would be like for us to be in Robin's and Alan's shoes. Obviously I was nowhere near ready for kids—if anything, this experience had pushed kids back a good twenty years on my agenda—but I realized that the kind of relationship Robin and Alan had was something I wanted. Not just that I wanted it, I was ready for it. I wanted what Robin and Alan had, and I wanted it with Val. I just didn't know how to make it happen.

I finally started the car, and Val and I drove in comfortable silence, our hands still entwined, until I missed the turnoff to take her back to Cara and Shane's place. "That was the exit," she said.

"That was the exit for Cara and Shane's place," I said, "but yesterday you agreed to be mine tonight so we're going to my place, at least for a couple hours."

Val opened her mouth to say something but closed it again and went back to looking out the window. I wasn't sure what that meant. I couldn't tell if she was happy or not. I got the impression she didn't want to go to my place, but that she didn't feel like she could argue.

That horrible weight returned to my stomach and I felt like I couldn't breathe. I almost turned around and took her home, but I decided we needed to confront this even if it meant losing her. I couldn't live in this relationship halfway anymore.

We were both quiet the rest of the way home and Val was very tense as she followed me inside. I hated how nervous I felt. She was my girlfriend. We'd been together for over six weeks. I should be able to bring her home to my house without feeling like I'd kidnapped her.

"So." I cleared my throat, hoping to get rid of the lump in it. "Are you hungry? We could order in."

"Actually, if it's okay with you, I think I'd like to wash the ocean off of me first."

Mental images swarmed my head in a dangerous way.

Fantasies that should definitely *not* become reality. "Um…" I had to clear my throat again. Stupid thing was so dry my voice didn't want to work. "I think I can help with that."

I dragged her across the house to the pool in my backyard. I lived up on the bluff, so I didn't really have much of a backyard beyond my patio and the pool. I had one of those infinity pools, so it looked like you could swim right over the edge into the ocean. The view was amazing.

The sun was starting to dip low in the sky, which made the sight all the more spectacular. In ten minutes it would hit the horizon and paint a vivid portrait of oranges and purples across the sky. There's nothing like a Southern California sunset over the Pacific Ocean.

"What are we doing?" Val asked after taking in the view for a moment.

I took off my shirt—a standard green hospital scrub top that the staff had scrounged up for me—and dipped my foot into the water. "We're washing the beach off of us. You're not scared of all water, are you?"

"No, just the ocean and lakes and stuff I can't see through, but—"

"Don't worry, the water's heated. It's a lot warmer than what we swam in earlier."

Val continued to eye the pool dubiously, so I slipped into the water. I dunked myself and scrubbed my hair really good before resurfacing. "Come swim with me, Val. Just long enough to watch the sun set, and then you can go take a shower."

Val sighed, but she cracked a small smile. "You just want to see me in my bikini."

I grinned, grateful for the break in tension. "The thought

had crossed my mind."

I waited, determined to win the staring match we were suddenly lost in. Luckily, she cracked first and pulled her ocean-crusty sundress over her head.

My mouth went dry again. Ms. College Athlete was everything I knew she'd be. Beautiful, fair skin that looked soft and hard all at the same time. She was toned without looking overly so, and her figure was nothing to scoff at. I knew she was self-conscious about her chest, but she filled out that top just fine. And she had this smallish dark pink birthmark high up on her left hipbone just above her bikini. My entire body ached at the thought of kissing that birthmark.

Val caught me wetting my lips and blushed a rosy pink. It only made me want her more. "You're beautiful, Val," I rasped. "So beautiful."

When she slipped into the water, I think it was to hide herself from my hungry gaze. I ducked myself beneath the surface again, trying to clear my head. I had to keep my control, hopeless and impossible a task as that seemed.

When I came back up, Val was within arm's reach. I wanted to pull her to me, but I resisted. She was still on edge. I held out my hand, hoping she'd come to me on her own and was surprised when she did.

"Come look at this."

I took her hand and waded over to the vanishing edge of the pool. I felt her reluctance and pulled her a little closer to me. "You're perfectly safe. You can't really go over the edge."

"I know, but it just looks so dangerous."

"The only dangerous thing in this pool is that swimsuit you're wearing."

The comment earned me an exasperated sigh and a smile.

We reached the edge of the pool and I pointed out the ledge beneath the water that worked as a bench for us to sit on. Val looked relieved to feel the solid concrete beneath her. From the edge of the pool, we could see the edge of the bluff just six short feet away, where the ground really did drop out of sight, and an endless ocean beyond that.

"It's breathtaking," Val whispered.

She moved closer to me, nestling herself against me with a silent command for me to wrap my arms around her. I pulled her back to my chest, letting her sit on the ledge between my legs. She leaned back and her entire body relaxed against me. After a moment she sighed in utter content. "Thank you, Kyle. I needed this after today."

I chuckled. "Me too. I told you my mom's a bit much."

I heard the smile in Val's reply. "She meant well."

"Only because she likes you. She can be ruthless when she disapproves of people."

"Well, we'll just consider ourselves lucky that I made the approved list."

"It is nice," I admitted. "I think you're the first girl I've introduced her to that actually made the cut. Now you can't ever dump me. You're the only redeeming quality I have in her eyes."

"Oh, that's not true. She loves you. She bragged about you all day."

"She bragged about me being able to snag a woman like you. So, really, she was still just bragging about you."

"Well." Val chuckled. "I suppose that really is one of your best qualities. But you do have others. Plenty of them.

And some of them are even redeeming."

I laughed. "Like?"

She gazed out at the horizon as she thought. "Like your passion, and creativity," she said. "What you do with your music, the songs you create, and the way you express yourself is one of my favorite things about you. I don't have an ounce of creativity in me, and I'm terrible at telling people how I feel. I wish all the time I could use words the way you do."

I was shocked by the compliment; it warmed me from the inside out. I never thought she paid attention, much less appreciated me in that way. I felt like my insides were trying to burst out of my chest, so I squeezed her tight as if she would keep me together. Holding her soothed the throbbing in my heart some, but I wasn't able to resist kissing her any longer, so I brought my mouth to her shoulder.

She sucked in a breath and tilted her head to the side, granting me permission to continue what I was doing and giving me access to her neck. "You're also the most thoughtful person I know, when you want to be," she said. "The things you do for me, just to make me happy—like the way you helped me with my brother and helped me to meet one of my heroes—you go above and beyond what most people would do."

My lips brushed over a sensitive spot on her neck, and her body rocked with a violent shiver. "I don't deserve you," she whispered, her voice strangled.

She turned her head up to meet my lips with hers in a sweet kiss. Fire built between us in a slow, sensual burn. Each kiss became longer and deeper until we were completely fused together and unable to let go of each other.

She shifted her body sideways so that she could reach

me better until she was sort of cradled in my arms. Her hands explored my body, her delicate touch leaving a trail of goose bumps wherever her fingers connected with my skin. The feeling was overwhelming.

I tried to keep my hands still because whenever we'd made out in the past she always pulled back when my fingers began to roam, but my control shattered. I wanted to feel her and I wanted her to feel my touch.

My hand fell from her face to her shoulder and trailed down the length of her arm. I found her bare stomach next and brushed my fingertips over her naval. Even with the water dulling the sensations she reacted to my touch. She gasped, and her back arched from the unexpected pleasure. Her eyes fluttered shut and her hands stilled their own exploration as she relaxed.

She was so beautiful like this. So incredibly delicious, just soaking in my attention as if she'd never experienced it before. Then I realized she never *had* experienced it before and my breath got stuck in my lungs.

I knew there were places she'd never been touched, pleasures she'd never felt, and I became desperate to make her feel them. We couldn't have sex, but that didn't mean I couldn't give her a new experience. I could open her eyes to the things that were in store for her. I could let her feel exactly how much I cared about her. I wanted to do that for her. I wanted to share that connection with her. I needed the intimacy.

My hand fell south of her stomach over the outside of her bikini bottom. The second I touched her she choked on a gasp and sat up, pushing my hands away from her. "Kyle, no!"

I was startled from the daze she'd put me in and my arms instinctively went around her, caging her to me before she had the chance to escape. "What's wrong?" I asked, my voice strangled and husky. "I promise I can handle this. The clothes will stay on. I know the rules. No sex."

She scrambled out of my arms and turned to me with such a sad look on her face. "It's more than that, Kyle. I don't want to keep my virginity based on a technicality. It's not just my virginity I'm protecting; it's my *virtue*."

"Meaning...?" I wasn't trying to be disrespectful in any way. I honestly didn't understand.

Val studied my face for a minute, taking note of my confusion, and her face softened into an expression of pity. "Meaning no fooling around at all," she said. "Second and third base are just as off-limits as going all the way."

I should have known. We'd managed to date all summer and had never gotten there before. I should have seen it coming, but it still surprised me. It still hurt. And I don't just mean in an unsatisfied, throbbing kind of way. It was like she didn't want to go there with me. Like she didn't feel anything. How could she stay so cold when I was so damned hot?

I knew I shouldn't take her rejection personally, but I couldn't help it. Hands curled into tight fists, I made a quick retreat from the pool. I needed some space from her.

I grabbed a towel off the back of a deck chair and tried to calm some of my anger as I dried my hair. A hand came down lightly on my shoulder and Val whispered in a tiny voice, "I'm sorry."

I couldn't take it anymore. Something inside of me snapped. I whirled on her. "This is *killing* me!" I took a breath when the blood drained from her face, and waited until I could speak in a somewhat controlled manner. "I've never felt like this before, Val. Not even with Adrianna. Don't you get it? I am in *love* with you. I love you so much that I don't know what to do with myself anymore."

Every part of Val froze except for her eyes, which widened and filled with tears. I had no idea what she was thinking right now, or why my feelings caused her so much pain, but I couldn't stop talking. I'd started this train wreck and I needed to see it through to the end.

"It's not even about the sex," I said. "I'm going crazy because every time I try to get close to you, you push me away. Our relationship is completely surface. Superficial. I keep trying to dive in and you're not following me. I'm afraid you aren't in this as deep as I am, and it has me completely lost."

The last word died on my tongue. I was deflated. I didn't know what else to say to make her understand.

Val stood there for an agonizing moment, letting the tears run down her cheeks. "Kyle," she whispered in a strangled voice, "I'm in this so deep I'm *drowning*."

My brows pulled together in confusion, but hope sparked deep in my gut.

"I love you, too."

My heart stopped, shocked into silence, and I was afraid to start it back up again. She wiped at the wetness on her cheeks and took a hesitant step toward me. I surprised us both when I stepped back, keeping myself out of her reach.

I needed a moment to process. Hearing her say those three words to me pushed my feelings to a point of no return. I wanted it to be true. I needed it to be true, because if she ever took it back I wouldn't survive the loss. But I wasn't convinced that she meant it, so I couldn't let myself accept the possibility yet.

Val swallowed back a mess of nerves and said, "I am crazy, desperately in love with you, and it terrifies me. I fell in love with you the first time we played this game and it tore me apart when you left. I spent four years trying to convince myself I was over it, but I knew I'd never stopped loving you the second you walked out onto that stage at the Connie Parker Show."

I shut my eyes against the sting of emotion and took a calming breath. "I don't understand," I admitted. "If you feel like this, why won't you let me love you back?"

"Because I'm afraid," she whispered. When I met her eyes again, she shrugged. "There've been so many guys who asked me out since high school, and they were all like you. The old you," she amended quickly when I flinched.

She plunked herself down onto a long pool chair and stared into her hands as she spoke. "I was the famous virgin," she said bitterly. "They saw an irresistible challenge and when they realized they weren't going to win, they left me."

She looked up at me, her face fresh with new tears. "I've been dumped by every man I've ever dated, starting from the beginning in high school with Zach and that stupid video. I've watched so many of my friends find love—Robin, Isaac, Cara, Stephanie—and yet I've never managed to have a single successful relationship."

She swiped at her eyes again and sighed as if her situation were hopeless. "You're the one who told me all those years ago that I'm delusional. That I have impossible standards. You said I'm trying to find a man that doesn't exist."

I could have punched myself in the face for saying such horrible things. I finally managed to move my feet and came to sit next to her on the chair. "Val, I was an idiot back then. I was a selfish, arrogant ass who was just pissed that I couldn't get what I wanted from you."

"But you were right," she insisted. "I've proved your theory a million times over. Eventually I got tired of trying and failing, so I quit dating altogether."

"I wasn't right," I insisted, "and I've spent the entire summer trying to prove to you how wrong I was. I think I've earned a little trust by now."

She shut her eyes again and nodded. "You have," she admitted, "but that's what terrifies me. I've been hurt so many times I've lost count and then, suddenly, out of the blue, the one guy I wanted the most and thought I never had a chance with shows up ready to give up sex for me? And, Kyle, you're more amazing than anyone knows. It seemed impossible that a man like you would stick around—*still* seems impossible. It feels inevitable that you'll get tired of this game and walk away like all the others. Like you did before."

My chest was so tight I almost couldn't speak. I had to exert all my energy just to get a single sentence out. "I'm not going anywhere this time, Val. I swear it."

"I want to believe you. I'm trying. But I can't help keeping the distance between us because even though I keep falling further and further in love with you, I'm always waiting for you to break my heart."

If she said one more word, I was going to shatter into a million pieces. I threw my mouth on hers and kissed her like I'd never kissed her before. With the walls between us crumbled, I poured every ounce of love I had into that kiss until I was certain she would stop waiting for me to hurt her. Because after that kiss, she'd know it was impossible.

Once I stopped to catch my breath, I rested my forehead against hers. My eyes were pinched shut, but I could still hear her ragged breaths. I could feel her chest heaving like mine. "Val, eventually something has to give," I choked out. "I don't want to break your heart, but you're always pushing me away and I can't take it anymore. You've got to let me in. You have to trust me."

I took her face in my hand and pushed her hair back. "I know we can't have sex, but I need to feel closer to you. I need this relationship to feel more grown up. I don't know how to handle PG. If you can't be with me physically, then I need you to be with me here." I tapped my finger to her head, then moved it to rest over her heart. "And here. Whatever your next step is, I need it. I need *you*."

A silent sob hiccuped in her chest. After an agonizing moment that felt like an eternity, she looked up at me through her wet lashes and said, "I'll stay with you tonight."

I froze, certain I'd heard her wrong.

"We can order takeout, rent a movie On Demand, and stay in tonight...just you and me." She took a breath. "And I'll stay the night if you want me to. If you think we can handle it."

My mind went blank. When faced with this option, it simply short-circuited.

I knew I should tell her she didn't have to do that. I knew she was only offering this because I'd just asked her to give me more. I hadn't meant staying the night with me, but I wanted it. I wanted it more than I'd ever wanted anything in my entire life, and I am ultimately a selfish man.

"Are you sure?" It was the closest thing to an out I could manage.

She looked nervous and her voice shook a little as she said, "No fooling around?"

"None," I promised. "I'll keep my hands to myself. And, as always, the duct tape rule still applies."

She smiled at that, and something that reminded me of determination crept into her eyes. "Then I'll stay. I *want* to stay." She placed her hand on my chest and inhaled a long, deep breath. "I do trust you, Kyle."

I took her hands and wrapped them behind my neck. "I'm not going to hurt you," I promised as I slipped my arms around her waist and pulled her against me. "I couldn't. I love you too much."

"I love you, too," she whispered, and for the first time since I'd met her, I believed she really did.

21

F IS FOR FANTASY

WE STOOD THERE ON THE POOL DECK KISSING EACH OTHER until we realized the sun had gone down and we were cold and wet. I introduced her to my shower and scrounged up a pair of drawstring sweats and a T-shirt for her. Then I went to order some Chinese and tried very hard not to think about the fact that Val was in my shower.

I had just paid the delivery guy and brought the cartons of takeout into the kitchen when Val appeared. My clothes engulfed her. She was in a pair of navy sweats and my favorite Lakers jersey, and she'd tied her wet hair up in a messy bun. It was the hottest look I'd seen on her yet.

She saw the smile on my face and blushed as she looked down at herself. "I look ridiculous."

I shook my head. "You look sexy."

"You always say that."

"You always look it. Especially right now."

She rolled her eyes and crossed the room to inspect the dinner choices. I slipped my arms around her and grinned.

"Feel better?"

"Much. I smell like a guy now thanks to your body soap, but I'm all clean."

I couldn't resist taking a big whiff. I buried my face in her neck and inhaled deeply, then burst into laughter. "You're right. You smell like a dude. That's...weird."

"Still, it's better than saltwater and chlorine, so thank you. Your manly soap was much appreciated."

"You are welcome to use my shower anytime. And wear my clothes anytime. Or...not wear them. That would be okay with me, too."

Val sighed, but it was playful. "Where do you keep plates? I'll fix this up for us and find something to watch while you shower." She snitched a noodle and said, "You have five minutes or I'm eating without you."

"Slave driver," I teased. I heaved my own playful sigh. "As cold as my shower is going to have to be, I won't need five minutes."

She laughed, but I wasn't joking.

When I came back five minutes later I found Val sitting sideways on my couch, knees sucked up under her chin, remote in hand. There were two heaping plates of Chinese food and a couple of sodas on the coffee table. "I hope you're hungry," she said, gesturing to the plate with twice as much food on it. "I didn't know what you wanted, so I gave you a little of everything."

I looked at the mound of food and grinned at her. "It's a start. Did you find us something to watch?"

The blush in her cheeks sparked my curiosity. "Don't hate me," she said as I sat down beside her, "but I noticed it was on here and I've always thought it would be fun to watch this with you."

I looked at the screen and groaned internally. "*V is for Virgin*? Are you serious?"

She blushed even deeper and bit her lip nervously as she nodded. "Please? Have you seen it?"

This time I groaned out loud. "They made me the villain and they cast the biggest tool in Hollywood to play me."

Val giggled and started the movie without waiting for my official approval. "You kind of were the villain back then," she said, "and I think the casting was perfect."

Right as she said that, the tool in question appeared on-screen. "Brian Oliver?" I asked, insulted despite myself. "You *like* that guy?"

Val laughed at the pout on my face. "Hey, I know what he did to you, but he's a great actor. He did a fantastic job in this movie."

I couldn't believe what I was hearing. She had to be messing with me. "You're joking. Do you seriously like him?"

Her smile faded a little and she shrugged. "It's hard not to. If it wasn't for him, you and I might not have had a second chance."

My retort died on my lips. How could I argue with that logic? Slowly the corners of my mouth turned up, morphing my pout into a grudging smile. "Good answer." I looked at my girlfriend, then glanced at the screen again and almost felt grateful to the bastard.

I let out a sigh. I was now in need of a new archnemesis. "Maybe he's not so bad," I admitted.

Val laughed and leaned over to kiss me before picking up her plate of food. I grabbed mine and found I was actually looking forward to watching this movie with Val. Still, there was one thing I had to put out there. "The guy can't sing for crap, though. They totally had to dub him over with my track."

Val burst into laughter and we finally settled in to eat and watch the movie. We both ate our weight in Chinese and it didn't take long after that for Val to nod off. It was still pretty early, but we'd both had the longest day ever, and, for once, we were together with absolutely no tension between us.

Her head drooped to my shoulder and her hand fell away from mine. When I realized she was asleep, I turned off the movie and sat there debating whether I should wake her or not. I knew she'd be more comfortable in bed, but I didn't know what kind of sleeping arrangements she had in mind. If she was going to lock herself in the guest room, then I'd rather not wake her. I'd sit here all damned night and happily suffer the stiffness tomorrow.

I laid my head against hers and let my eyes fall shut. I was prepared to hold her all night long, but only lasted about five minutes before I broke down and kissed her. She woke up and instinctively kissed me back, but it took her a few minutes before she really woke up. I had her on her back on the couch before she came fully to her senses and realized she'd fallen asleep. She stopped kissing me and sat up. "Sorry," I apologized. I flashed her a sheepish smile. "I guess I'll never be as creepy as a vampire. I tried to watch you sleep, but I apparently don't have the self-control for it."

I knew she was tired when her only response was a small smile. "Sorry," she said, rubbing the sleep from her eyes. "Spending the day at the beach always drains me."

"I think it was all the baby drama that wiped me out."

Val chuckled. "We have had a long day."

"We have." I didn't want to end our night so early, but I could see how exhausted she was. I pushed myself to my feet and held my hand out to her. "Come on. I've got a couple spare bedrooms. I'll let you take your pick, though I recommend the one with the lock on the door, otherwise you might not find yourself alone when you wake up in the morning."

I started to tug Val toward the back hallway, but she stopped me. When I turned to her with a questioning look, she smiled at me as if I'd said something adorable. "I don't have any intention of waking up alone," she said.

That was all the explanation I needed. "You are the best girlfriend ever," I said, smashing my lips on hers again. Once that was taken care of, I switched course for the master suite and dragged her along at a fast enough pace that she laughed at me.

I found her a new toothbrush, quickly brushed my own teeth, then went to go pull the covers back on the bed. I normally slept in nothing but my boxers, but I left my pajama pants and T-shirt on for Val's sake as I climbed into the bed.

I was suddenly buzzing with energy. I knew all we were going to do was sleep, but my body didn't care. It was alive with anticipation at just the thought of having her in my bed.

I took a series of deep breaths and tried to calm myself down. If she had any clue how difficult it was going to be for me to keep my hands off her, she'd run from the house screaming and never trust me again.

I was busy praying for self-control when Val cleared her throat to get my attention. I looked up and—holy shit!

Val had raided my closet. She was standing in the doorway to my walk-in wearing nothing but a white dress shirt just like the one Cara had worn in my music video. The outfit had looked great on Cara, but on Val, with those endless legs of hers…I couldn't breathe.

Her hands were mostly lost in the long sleeves and the top two buttons were undone. I was sure she was still wearing her bikini bottom, but I was fairly certain she wasn't wearing the top. She smoothed the front of the dress shirt once, then met my eyes with a slightly vulnerable gaze.

I swallowed, completely unable to form any kind of words. What the hell was the woman trying to do to me?

As if she were a succubus, born to seduce men to their ultimate demise, she stalked toward me, never taking her eyes from mine as she came to stand at the foot of my bed.

"Val," I whispered hoarsely as I sat up and rested against the headboard. "What are you—"

All the air left my lungs when she climbed up onto the bed and slowly crawled her way up my legs. I gasped when she came to rest, straddling my lap. She tugged my T-shirt up and pulled it over my head. "This was the fantasy, right?" she asked as her hands fell to my bare chest.

I pinched my eyes shut and grabbed handfuls of the sheet beneath me, gripping so tightly my fingers burned. "Damn it, Val." It came out a desperate plea. My entire body was shaking as I battled my restraint.

Her soft hands clasped my cheeks and I felt her mouth brush over mine. "You've been a very good boy this summer, Kyle," she whispered. "You deserve a little PG-13."

She was playing with fire, and she was giving me way too much credit.

When I didn't respond, she nudged my lips with hers, forcing them to open. Then she kissed me more deeply than she ever had. As her tongue dipped into my mouth and she plunged her hands deep into my hair, my control snapped. I wrapped my arms around her and fused our bodies together.

My kisses became frantic and rough. My hands ran the length of her soft, bare thighs and traveled over her hips up under her shirt. They roamed over her back and then came around and brushed the sides of her bare breasts.

She shuddered and the tiniest whimper escaped her, but she didn't push me away. She didn't tell me to stop. She was as overwhelmed as I was, and, heaven help me, I was going to take her.

"Val," I begged. "You have to stop."

"It's okay, Kyle," she gasped, her breath as frantic as my own. "I'm okay. We're okay."

"Damn it, Val, I am *not* okay!"

Startled, she pulled her face back to look into my eyes, but I quickly brought her mouth back to mine. I pulled her hips hard against me, and she gasped again. I knew I needed to stop, but I couldn't. I couldn't stop. I'd lost all control.

"I need you," I growled. It was a warning as much as it was a declaration. "And in about two seconds, I am going to take what I need unless you stop me."

She finally snapped out of it and came to her senses. "Okay," she said and scrambled off my lap.

She sat quietly—insecurely—with her knees pulled to her chest and her arms wrapped tightly around them while I tried to get a grip on myself. It took me a *long* time. I didn't realize she was upset until she whispered "I'm sorry," and I heard the hitch in her voice.

I laid down and pulled her with me. "Don't be sorry," I said as I nestled her against me and wrapped my arms around her. "I'm not sorry. You have no idea how much what you just did me means to me."

"Still. I'm sorry I couldn't give you more."

I kissed her forehead and tangled our fingers together on top of my chest. "This is enough," I promised. "Tonight was enough. Get some sleep, Val." She finally relaxed against me and as I squeezed her in another hug, I whispered, "I love you, Virgin Val Jensen."

She sniffled and whispered back, "I love you too, Kyle."

22

M IS FOR MARRIAGE

WHEN I FIRST WOKE UP I THOUGHT I'D DREAMED IT—THE pool, Val telling me she loved me, spending the evening relaxing over Chinese and a *Lifetime* original, having her play out my fantasy until I nearly exploded from desire, and then falling asleep with her in my arms. It was all too good to be true. I was afraid to open my eyes because I didn't want to find myself in bed alone. But then the bed shifted beside me and I knew it was real.

The smile was on my face before I opened my eyes. Val had rolled away from me at some point in the night and was curled up in a ball on her side. I scooted over and snuggled against her back, slipping my arm over her waist to pull her tight against me. She mumbled something incoherent as she rolled over and nestled herself against me. She stretched her long legs, tangling them with mine, and fell back into a peaceful sleep.

Last night I didn't have the patience to watch her sleep, but now I felt as if I could lie there forever. It was crazy that

I could wake up feeling so relaxed and satisfied even though I'd gone to sleep painfully frustrated.

"Quit smiling so big," Val said suddenly. "No one should be so perky in the morning. It's unnatural." She hadn't moved, and her eyes were still closed.

"I'm not smiling," I lied.

"You're smiling so big I can feel it. It's keeping me awake."

I laughed and dropped a kiss on her head. "Have I told you I find it hilarious that you aren't a morning person?"

"I find it disappointing that you are one," Val grumbled. "You're a rock star. You're supposed to party all night and sleep all day."

"I'm not usually a morning person, but *this* morning seemed worth waking up for."

Val finally picked her head up off my chest and looked at me. She tried to hold a flat expression but couldn't manage it when I gave her a big, cheesy grin. She smiled and pushed herself up to kiss my cheek. "Good morning."

"The best morning of my life."

I'd said it jokingly, but when Val laughed I realized it was the truth. It had been so long since I felt so content. Now I was happy—truly happy—for the first time in a very, very long time. Val made me happy.

"I want this," I said, squeezing her to me as if holding her tighter would settle the sudden tingling in my chest. "I want to wake up with you like this every morning."

"That is definitely not a good idea." Val laughed. "A little temptation every now and then is one thing, but we wouldn't last a week if we did this every day. Kyle, we almost didn't last one night."

"So marry me."

The words were out of my mouth before I realized they were even in my head. Both of us froze, shocked. Val sat up and looked at me with wide eyes, trying to figure out if I'd actually said what I just said. "What?" she asked.

My brain was a scrambled mess, but as I sat there trying to figure out what the hell had just happened, I realized the feeling inside me wasn't panic. It was excitement. I wanted this.

"Marry me," I said. I sounded as astonished as she looked, but it felt right. It *was* right. When I spoke again, my voice went from surprised to insistent. "Be my wife, Val. Be the woman who wakes up in this bed with me every morning for the rest of our lives. Fight with me how Robin and Alan do. Make love to me. Have my children." Her eyes popped so wide that I laughed and said, "You know, eventually, someday."

"Kyle—I—are you serious?"

I hadn't meant to ask her, but now that I had, if she said no, it would kill me. "I hate to admit it, but I've been through enough women to know there's not another one like you out there. You're the one, Val. Whether you accept me or not, there's not going to be anyone else for me."

It took her an eternity to say something. I waited, breath held in my lungs for her answer.

"But we're about to say good-bye to each other," she said, her brow crinkling in concern and her voice falling to a whisper. "Aren't you a little worried about that?"

I'd feared that all summer long, but now I was sure. I grinned. "Val, how many times do I have to say it? You're worth waiting for."

She didn't appreciate the joke. "I'm serious, Kyle."

"So am I. We'll get through the separation. It's only a couple months while I'm touring and you can catch up with me every weekend if you want. We'll schedule long breaks between the US tour and the different legs of the world tour, and I can make sure I have all the same holidays off that you do. You'll be so busy with school the time will fly by." I let out a scoff and added, "Besides, being separated through the entire engagement might be the only way you make it to the altar still a virgin."

Val surprised me with a laugh. "That's definitely the truth," she muttered.

I didn't know what to make of that. Was that a yes? I hoped it was a yes. I hoped I was getting through to her, because the more I talked about it, the more I convinced myself this was meant to be. I was practically giddy when I took her hands in mine and said, "Val, if we can survive a relationship without sex, we're strong enough to survive whatever life throws at us. I love you so much. I want you to be mine forever. Say you'll marry me."

She still hesitated, so I arched a brow to let her know I meant business when I said, "Don't make me do something drastic like ask you on live TV so that you have to say yes. Because you know I will."

She let out a hysterical bark of laughter, and burst into tears as she threw her arms around me. "No!" she cried, and my heart skipped a beat until she said, "Absolutely *no* live TV proposals. I will kill you. This proposal was perfect and the only one you need to make."

I pulled back so that I could look into her eyes. "Is that a yes?"

She grinned through her tears and laughed again. "It's a yes."

She started to say something else, but talking was not something I was in the mood for any longer. I was overcome with passion and overwhelmed with so much love for the woman sitting in front of me that I had to kiss her right that second.

I planned on never stopping kissing Val, but she kept ruining the mood by giggling beneath my lips. Before I knew it, we were both laughing too hard to keep up the kissing. "You like me," I teased her, remembering a joke from ages ago. "You like me one hundred percent."

She laughed again and shook her head. "I like you eighty-nine percent at best. But I love you one hundred percent."

I tried to act hurt but couldn't wipe the smile from my face. "Good enough."

For a minute we sat there grinning at each other like idiots. Val covered a yawn with her hand and stretched. "Please tell me you have coffee around here somewhere."

"I do."

"Practicing?" Val snickered.

I rolled my eyes at the cheesy joke. Getting engaged had turned us both into mush brains. "So, Miss Not-A-Morning-Person, what would you like to do today?" I grabbed her hand and kissed it. "Want to go shopping so I can put a proper rock on this finger? It was bad form for me to ask you to marry me before I had one."

"Hey, don't knock my accidental proposal," she said. "It was not bad form. It was perfect. Your heart spoke before your brain could stop it. It was actually very *you*."

That earned her another kiss. "Coffee maker's in the kitchen. Coffee should be right next to it. Why don't you get it started while I get dressed, and then I'll take you shopping. We'll get you a change of clothes while we're out too because I don't want to take you home first."

"Sounds like a plan."

Val smiled and wrapped her arms around me. After she kissed me again, I flashed her a wicked grin. "I get to pick out your underwear."

She smacked me playfully on the arm, but I noticed as she left the room that she hadn't said no to the idea.

Val was out on the deck with her cup of coffee when I found her. She stood at the balcony railing staring out at the ocean, still wearing nothing but my dress shirt. I took a moment to enjoy her mile-long legs, but that only made me desperate to touch them so I walked up behind her and did just that.

"You see, it really is meant to be," I said as I ran my hands over her hips and down her legs. "You already know the routine. I drink my coffee out here every morning."

She shivered again and leaned back into my chest. "It's such a gorgeous view."

"It's improved vastly as of late."

She smirked up at me. "Let me guess, because my just-rolled-out-of-bed look is sexy?"

"You know it is. And you know I have a weakness for these legs. You should wear nothing but this from now on," I said, making her kiss me again. I was never going to get tired of kissing her. Not even those quick little pecks. Fifty years from now, I was still going to make her kiss me every time I saw her.

We took our steaming mugs over to a patio couch and sat quietly for a moment, simply enjoying the peace between us. Val broke the silence first. "So," she said, "I was thinking about this whole getting married business."

"Cold feet already?" I teased. "You chicken."

She smiled but kept herself on track. She had something on her mind and she wasn't going to let me make her lose focus. "What's your take on weddings?"

Ugh. The wedding talk was starting already. I held back a groan and reminded myself that Val was worth it. "What do you mean?"

"Do you have a preference? Big, small, destination... theme?"

Theme? I shuddered and cut a glance at her. "I want whatever you want."

She snorted. "Spoken like a true man."

"No, spoken like a man who's known a few brides. A wedding is for the woman. It's your day, Val. We can do whatever you want."

We fell quiet again and I cast my gaze out to the ocean as I tried to figure out what kind of wedding Val would like. I didn't think she'd be as crazy as Adrianna was, but after watching her work the crowd with my mom yesterday, I could see some big political event-type wedding in my future with a high-profile wedding planner and my mom calling all the shots. Hell on Earth.

On the bright side, I'd be away on tour for most of the

planning, so hopefully I could just let them take over and I wouldn't have to do much.

Val pulled me from my nightmare thoughts. "What if I don't want one?"

I didn't know how to respond. What did she mean? I'd been teasing her before, but was she actually backing out? My pulse sped up at the thought. "What do you mean? You don't want to get married?"

When she laughed, my chest loosened up.

"I want to marry you," she said, "but what if we just skipped the wedding part? Would you be disappointed?"

No wedding? Just get married? Was she kidding? I was afraid to answer. "Is this a trick question? Some kind of girl test?"

She laughed again and shook her head. "It's not a test. I just know how much you hate all the fancy stuff, which I'm assuming includes weddings. Plus, you said you wanted to wake up with me every morning and it sounds like a good plan to me. Why not just make it happen?"

"Wait, are you saying we should elope?" There was no way in the world she really meant that. I am not that lucky.

Val shrugged. "Do you know what will happen if you and I announce our engagement? It will be a complete media circus. People would follow us around the entire time, wanting every detail and judging us on the decisions we make. They'd probably ask us to make our wedding a reality show. I want my wedding to be *mine*. I don't want to share it with the entire world."

Actually, I could totally see that happening. And Val had a point. She would hate all that attention.

"We could do something small," I said. "You don't have

to elope. If you want your family and friends to be there, I'm sure we could find a way to keep everything private."

Val shook her head and sipped her coffee again. "I'm *Virgin Val*, Kyle. Do you know what a marriage would mean to the world? It would mean the virgin is finally going to have sex. People will go crazy over that. Even if we managed to keep the wedding private, people would be in my face every second until the wedding day asking me all kinds of personal questions that I wouldn't want to answer. And then they'd find a way to stalk us after. The paparazzi would follow us to our hotel suite that night and camp out in the lobby in order to get the first interview with The Virgin post sex."

I sighed because she was right. I wished I could tell her we could keep that from happening, but I knew better. I'd been dealing with the paparazzi for way too long to be naïve about what they were capable of. I wouldn't be surprised if someone were able to figure out which room was ours and find a way to snap pictures of us in the act.

Val was going to be nervous enough about her wedding night. She didn't need that added stress. I wanted her to enjoy her first time, not dread having to face the world the morning after.

"I don't want that," she said. "I don't want the media to ruin the first time we make love."

My brain went completely haywire again. She said "we." She said the first time "we" make love. She was talking about us having sex, and suddenly I could think of nothing else. All I could do was sit there and picture exactly how that was going to go.

"I know they're going to ask," Val said. "I know I can't run from the press forever. I'm Virgin Val. I will have to talk about it at least a little. But if we just go get married and don't tell anyone, we could keep it a secret for a week or two. We could give ourselves some time to enjoy each other before the media circus starts."

She kept talking like she didn't realize she was preaching to the choir. She'd had me convinced way back at the "skip the wedding" comment.

Val set her mug down on the ground and turned to face me. She took my hands in hers and looked at me with so much intensity I could feel it. "When I give myself to you, I want you to be the only person in my head. I want to be able to think about nothing but you and me. Forget the world. This is about us. I may be a role model for a lot of people, but I saved myself for you, not them. I saved myself for *me*. This is what I want. As long as you're okay with it. As long as it's what you want, too."

I don't think I've ever cried. Not once in my whole adult life that I can remember. And I didn't cry now, but this was the closest I'd come to it. My throat felt as if it had closed up, my eyes burned, and my nose tingled. She was perfect. She was absolutely perfect, and she was mine. Or she would be, very, very soon.

I covered up the emotional attack with a laugh. "Val, you're asking me if I want to skip months of centerpiece crises, my fiancée becoming a bridezilla, my mother transforming into something a million times worse, and a party where I'd be forced to wear a tuxedo all day—all so that I can have you to myself and not have to share you with anyone. Are you crazy? I'm still waiting for the punch line."

Val thought for a minute, searching my eyes for any hint that I wasn't excited. She didn't find it. Once she finally believed I was on board, her lips quirked up into a wicked smirk. It was the kind of look I gave her on a regular basis, but I'd never seen it on her face and it got my blood pumping like crazy.

"How's this for a punch line," she whispered, wetting her lips as her gaze fell to my mouth. The action made me forget to breathe. "Marry me today, and I'll stay the night again tonight, only this time instead of asking you to stop, I'll beg you not to."

I sucked in a surprise breath and choked on my own spit. The way I grabbed her and devoured her in a kiss was downright animalistic, as primal as my need for her. My hands found her thighs, still beautifully bare, and I groaned.

"We'll never make it all the way to Las Vegas," I growled as I pulled her onto my lap.

"The county clerk's office can do it," Val gasped.

That sounded a lot closer. Closer was good. "Okay. Let's go there. Right now."

"It's Monday morning. You have rehearsals in a few hours."

"I'll call in sick. I believe I just came down with something that's going to take at least a week to recover from."

"I don't have anything to wear."

"We'll find a mall on the way. And now I really do get to pick the panties."

23

S IS FOR SEX!

WE DIDN'T WASTE ANY TIME. WE FILLED OUT THE MARRIAGE license application online and scheduled the first available appointment for the ceremony. It gave us just enough time to stop and buy an outfit for Val to wear. I'd tried to convince her to marry me wearing just my dress shirt, but was unsuccessful.

We stopped at Macy's and while Val was trying on a few different dresses, I bought out half of the lingerie section. There was just too much good stuff. All the lace and the silk was hard to say no to. Everything seemed like it would look good on Val.

Before we knew it, we were at the county clerk's office. My knee bounced as I sat in the waiting room, Val squirming in her chair next to me. "Nervous?" I asked curiously.

I was surprised by the irritated look I got in response. "Not nervous. I'm uncomfortable because I'm wearing a *thong*, Kyle," she grumbled as she shifted in her seat again.

"Mm," I agreed appreciatively. "A black, lacy one, I

know. I picked it out." I reached over to trail my fingers on her thigh. It was covered now, unfortunately, as Val had chosen a calf-length purple sundress to get married in today. "I can't wait to see it on you."

I got an eye roll for that, and she swatted my hand away when it got a little too close to the item of clothing in question. "For future reference, I'm not really a fan of the thong. They're a little too trashy and extremely uncomfortable."

I leaned over to murmur against her ear. "Then it's a good thing I plan to take it off of you very soon."

She hissed my name, embarrassed, but forgot her irritation when I kissed the sensitive spot on her neck just behind her ear. Her eyes fluttered shut and she sucked in a sharp breath. It drove me insane with desire. If one kiss could do that to her, I couldn't wait to see how she handled everything else I planned to do to her.

My thoughts turned once again to our post Get Married plans. I trailed my lips along her jaw and captured her mouth with mine. The way she kissed me back, I could tell she was as ready as I was. For a second, we both forgot we were in public.

We pulled apart at the sound of a cleared throat and sheepishly smiled up at the large woman in her mid-fifties frowning down at us. "I take it you two are the kids with the marriage appointment?"

And cue the dopey grins. "Yes, ma'am."

For some reason, the woman didn't seem as excited about that as I was. "You have your marriage license?"

I pulled the paper out of my pocket and proudly handed it over. "Fresh off the press."

She scanned the document and sighed. "Follow me."

It was a short trip to the room they set aside for weddings, but it felt like it took an eternity to get there. It was a small room that could hold up to thirty people tops, but considering it was just Val, me, and the county appointed official, it would do the job just fine. There a few rows of plastic chairs set up on either side of the room that created an aisle up the middle leading to a small podium. Behind the podium was a small lattice archway covered with fake flowers. It was the room's only decoration.

The man destined to marry us met us at the door. He was a short man with a full head of silver-gray hair wearing a crisp suit and a red power tie. So government, but at least he had a genuine smile for us. "Welcome! Come on in, don't be shy."

Val snickered at that. As if she thought the idea of me being shy about anything ever was funny.

The man greeted both of us with hearty handshakes. "I'm Gordon Pierce, and I'll have the pleasure of uniting you in holy matrimony today."

"Sounds good to me, Gordon," I said. "Thanks for seeing us on such short notice. Make it quick, and we'll throw a tip in there for you."

Gordon chuckled. "In a hurry, son?"

"More than you know. We've been waiting."

Gordon's brows pulled low over his eyes. "Waiting for what?"

I was going to let Val say it, but she blushed and looked away so I chucked my arm around her shoulder and explained. "We've waited for marriage to, uh, you know…"

I wriggled my eyebrows at Gordon and gave him a huge smile. His eyebrows flew toward the ceiling and he chuckled.

"I see. Well, good for you two."

"It's been a very long wait. Four *years*."

Gordon looked back and forth between us and laughed again. "Okay then, I guess you *are* in a hurry. We'll make it quick. Do you have anyone to witness?"

I'd forgotten about that. I turned around and smiled at the lovely woman who'd escorted us here and gave her my best smile. "Wanda?" I asked, glancing at her name tag. "Feel like being a bridesmaid today?"

I even batted my eyelashes for her and still no smile. Maybe she wasn't capable of one. "It's a thirty dollar fee for the county to provide a witness," she said.

I pulled some cash from my wallet. I handed over the thirty dollars, then held up an extra fifty and my phone. "Want to play videographer, too?"

She looked at the cash, then back at me. "You want me to tape your wedding on your cell phone for fifty bucks?"

"Is that a problem?"

She clearly thought I was crazy, but she snagged the cash out of my hands. She glanced across the room at Gordon, who had gone to the podium up front and was now messing around with the marriage paper Wanda had given him. In a low voice she muttered, "Sugar, for fifty bucks I'd kiss your fine-looking little white ass."

Val and I blinked and both burst into laughter. "She smiles!" I cheered when I saw Wanda's lips curve up. "You're a beautiful woman, Wanda. You should keep that smile on your face more often."

Wanda blushed and she shooed up toward the front of the room. "Go on, you crazy lovebirds. Go get married and get out of here before you make the whole building start smiling."

We didn't have to be told twice. We walked up the small aisle to the podium where Gordon was now waiting for us. Wanda walked around next to Gordon so she could get a clear shot of Val and me with my phone. I winked at her and she blew me a kiss.

"Should I step aside and let you the two of you have a go at this instead?" Val teased.

She started to step back, but I grabbed her and pulled her to me. "Don't even think about it. You're here, and you're finally mine, and you will say 'I do' today—even if I have to tickle torture it out of you."

Gordon laughed. "I suppose we should get to it, then."

"The short version," I reminded him. My hands on Val's waist were already starting to wander. "The Missus and I have plans after this." I squeezed her tighter. "Lots and lots and lots of hot, steamy, wild, sexy plans."

Both Val and Gordon blinked at me. "Sorry. Brain's a little preoccupied at the moment."

Gordon shook off his bewilderment and focused. "Okay, the extremely short version. Do either of you have vows you'd like to exchange?"

I looked at Val and she looked at me. "I do?" she offered.

I smiled. She'd told me before that she lacked creativity and was horrible with words, but those two, right then, were perfect. "I definitely do," I promised.

We both looked back at Gordon with expectant faces. "How was that?" I asked.

He gave us another baffled smile and chuckled. "Very… functional. Do you have rings?"

Oops. Val and I looked at each other again and I saw the

laughter in her eyes as she scrunched up her face. "We forgot about the rings."

I cut a glance to Gordon. "Are rings necessary to make it legal?"

For a second, I was afraid we were going to have to come back later. I'd have asked Wanda for some paper clips or tape or even a piece of gum—anything I could wrap around my finger. But then Gordon laughed again and shook his head. "They're just traditional."

I let out a breath of relief so big that even Wanda laughed at me. "Awesome. We'll get the rings later. What's next?"

Gordon smiled. "By the power vested in me by the state of California, I pronounce you man and wife. You may kiss the—okay, I see you already figured that much out."

Val and I laughed against each other's mouths, but we didn't break our kiss. I squeezed my arms around her and she jumped up, wrapping her legs around my waist. I spun her in circles once or twice, our kiss getting more and more heated until Wanda cleared her throat again. We turned our faces and smiled for the camera. "Congratulations, you crazy kids."

"Thanks, Wanda."

I kissed Val one more time for good measure and then set her back on her feet. It was time to get out of there.

"You're all set," Gordon promised. "You'll receive the official marriage certificate in the mail within two weeks. Congratulations; I think that was the shortest wedding I've ever performed."

"It was perfect," Val said.

The emotion in her voice caught me by surprise and a big lump formed in my throat when I looked over to see her eyes shiny with happy tears. "I love you," she whispered.

"I love you more," I promised and pulled her into my arms again, suddenly needing another kiss. "Let's get out of here."

For once, Val answered that request with a smile and a nod. "Let's."

"Good luck!" Gordon called as we left the room. He winked at Val and she turned bright red again. I gave her a wicked smile and said, "Luck will have nothing to do with it."

We got all the way back to our car before we found ourselves at another loss. There was one more part of this brilliant plan we hadn't thought of ahead of time. "Where do you want to go?" I asked as we buckled ourselves in. "I'll take you anywhere in the world you want to go…tomorrow. I need you sooner than that today. Marina Del Rey is close, or I know a great resort over the border in TJ."

Val grabbed my hand over the center console. "Why don't we just go back to your place?" she said. "Honestly, it's nicer than any hotel, the view is unbeatable, it's stocked with food, and the pool and hot tub are private."

I blinked at her, hardly able to believe such a perfect woman existed.

"And now that I have a lifetime supply of slutty underwear," she continued, "we shouldn't have to leave for days."

"It's *sexy* underwear," I corrected, "and you are brilliant. Home it is."

The drive back to Malibu felt longer than my last ten months of abstinence combined, but I knew it was worth it the minute I pulled into the driveway and realized that my house was no longer just my house. It was *our* house. Val gave me a questioning look when I didn't pull the car into the garage. "I have to do this right," I told her.

We walked to the front door, and as soon as it was unlocked I swept Val into my arms. "Welcome home, Mrs. Hamilton," I said as I carried her over the threshold.

The gesture made Val's eyes tear up again. I leaned in to kiss her, and the way she responded shocked me. She kissed me like she'd never kissed me before. Apparently, she'd always been holding back until now. She put everything she had into that kiss—lips, tongue, arms, legs, body, heart, mind, passion, and more lust than I knew she was capable of. She literally brought me to my knees and I almost took her right there on the entryway tile.

Then I remembered that this was her first time, and I was able to calm down. Yes, I wanted her, but this was about her. She'd saved herself for this moment, so I could do it right. I picked her up again and wordlessly carried her to the bedroom.

As I set her on the bed she looked a little nervous, so I kissed her very gently and laid down next to her. I propped myself up on my side and smiled down at her with what I hoped was more love than lust. "Are you ready for this?" I asked.

Her response surprised me. "I trust you."

It was exactly what I needed to hear.

I took my time with her, slowly introducing her to the world of lovemaking. It was easy not to think about my own needs when every touch, every kiss, every caress was a new experience for her. At first, she was shy and so completely vulnerable that it felt like a miracle she could trust me with her body.

I can't even begin to describe the emotions I experienced as we got to know each other in this new way. I'd been with so many women in my life—women I'd loved, women I'd only known for five minutes, women who knew a hundred different ways to please me, and even a few women I knew were virgins. But I'd never experienced the intimacy I achieved with Val.

In a way, it was almost as if I was experiencing something new right along with her. I'd had sex so many times I'd lost count years ago, but I'd never made love, not really, not with a woman I loved so much my heart literally ached with it.

It was during that time with Val that I finally understood why she'd wanted to wait. Because every time I looked at her, the only thing I could think about was that this beautiful angel was my *wife*. She'd already promised me the rest of her life. She'd taken my name and agreed to be my new family. There was no fear anywhere in my mind, no doubt at all that I loved her and she loved me.

In the end, I was glad we'd waited. Of course, I'd save that little confession for a day when I inevitably acted like a jackass and got myself in a lot of trouble. (It was bound to happen sometime: I am still *me*, after all.)

24

A IS FOR ANNOUNCEMENTS

VAL AND I DIDN'T LEAVE THE HOUSE FOR FOUR DAYS, BUT then life had to go on. There were final tour preparations and rehearsals to attend, a handful of media appearances to make, girly-smelling shampoos and soaps to buy because Val hated "smelling like a man," and there was family and friends to break the news to before the media found out and did it for us.

We told Cara, Shane, and Robin first. Cara squealed for ten minutes straight and then punched me for not inviting her. When I blamed the secrecy all on Val, she punched me again. She didn't calm down until we let her watch the wedding video. Oddly, though the whole thing was really quite comical, both Robin and Cara cried like babies through the entire video. (All three minutes of it.)

We visited Val's parents next, who were surprisingly relieved. They'd suspected an engagement was coming and were every bit as worried about a nationally covered wedding as Val had been. I'd gotten off on a really rocky start with

Val's parents, but they'd slowly warmed up to me after they realized I respected Val enough to wait for her. Now they were just happy to see Val so happy.

My parents were an entirely different story. They were pissed, but Val smoothed things over by promising that we would be home over Thanksgiving and asking my mom if she would throw us a reception. Since I was going to be busy on tour and she was going to be up to her eyeballs in homework, she gave my mother complete control over the event. It was a big mistake to let my mom be in charge, but it got her off my case about eloping, so I kept my mouth shut and would suffer through the nightmare party she was sure to throw.

After that, the only people left to tell was the rest of the world, and I knew exactly how I wanted to do it. Val would never have agreed, so I didn't tell her.

Flyin' Solo was the name of my debut solo album, and ever since Val and I got married I'd joked that I needed to change the name because I was never going to fly solo ever again.

The night of the first concert for the *Flyin' Solo* tour, it felt so good to be back onstage, but it was completely surreal. I was back at the Staples center—the same stadium where I kicked off the *S is for Sex* tour all those years ago, and, once again, I was buzzing with energy because I had a song to sing for Val.

The concert had been amazing. The crowd loved the new material and it seemed like they were as happy to have me back as I was to be back. Plus, between each song I got to look off to the side and see Val smiling at me from backstage. She and Cara stood there dancing and singing along the entire time, while Shane and I rocked our hearts out. It was all I'd ever wanted out of life.

Upcoming nightmare wedding reception notwithstanding, it was good to be me.

At the end of the show, I came running off the stage and into Val's waiting arms. After kissing her stupid, I looked down at her jeans and sighed. "The only thing missing tonight is Sassy."

"Sassy" was the killer miniskirt she'd been wearing the day I first laid eyes on her. It was also the skirt she'd been wearing the last time I'd dragged her out on stage with me. It felt wrong that I was going to make a spectacle of her again without my favorite feature—her legs—on display.

"I know it's disappointing," she teased me, "but I'm a little too old to be running around in miniskirts now."

"Oh, I beg to differ, Val."

"I'm sure you do." She laughed and kissed my cheek. "They're screaming your name, rock star. You'd better get back out there for the encore."

I listened to the crowd chant and grinned. I really did love that sound. With one last parting kiss she sent me back out on stage, slapping my butt as I went. It was so unlike her that I was lost in laughter when I met my audience again.

Once I regained my composure, I turned my smile on my audience. "I just want to thank you guys for being here tonight. It's been a few years, and it's great to be back."

The crowd agreed with me, roaring their applause. I waited for them to settle down and said, "How many of you guys were here with me four years ago for the *S is for Sex* tour?"

From the sound of it, most of them were. I was glad

for that. "You guys may remember back then I wrote a song about a girl, and wouldn't you know it, I've gone and done it again!"

The answering cheer I got was so energized that I had to laugh. "You guys like the new song?" Again, they went crazy. "Yeah," I said as soon as I could. "Val likes it, too. In fact, I think she's been waiting all night to hear this one song."

I turned to the side of the stage and found what I was looking for—who I was looking for. She blew me a kiss and I waved a hand at her. "Come on out here, Val. Come say hi to everybody."

Val gave me a dry look but it quickly morphed into a grudging smile. When she walked out on stage and took my hand, the crowd went absolutely insane. They started chanting her name just as they'd been shouting mine.

"Virgin-Val! Virgin-Val! Virgin-Val!"

"Who's the rock star now?" I teased as I held the microphone up to her. "Say hi, Val."

"Hello, everyone."

When that single polite greeting sent them into another tizzy, Val laughed.

"What do you say, Val?" I asked as a stagehand brought out a stool for Val. "Can I sing you a song? For old times' sake?"

Val, though she didn't always love the spotlight, had always been good with a crowd. She stepped away from me and brought a finger to her chin, pretending to think about it, then grabbed the mic out of my hands. "What do you say, ladies?" she asked the audience. "Should we let him serenade us one last time?"

"Sounds like a yes," she said when every female in the

audience screamed.

I held my hand out for the mic and she smiled at me. "What?" she asked. "You need this in order to sing?" She stepped away from me with a playful grin. "You'd better come get it, then," she said, placing it behind her back.

I was on her so fast I startled her. I pulled her into my arms and planted a movie-worthy kiss on her as I grabbed the mic from her hands. The crowed went insane and the music started. I didn't release Val's lips until the last possible second, and I almost missed the first line of the song.

Val sat on her stool and let me sing for her with a secret smile on her face that made me glad neither of us was leaving until tomorrow. I only had a few more hours with her before we'd be separated for a week or two at a time over the course of the next few months, and I wasn't going to waste them.

When the song was over, I took a bow and then pulled Val from her stool and made her take a bow, too. We stood there and let the crowd cheer for a minute, but then Val took a step to exit the stage. I clamped my hand over her wrist and pulled her back to me. "What are you doing?" she asked, confused.

"We're not done yet."

Val got that panicked look on her face that I loved so much that she gets when she knows I'm about to make a scene. "What are you up to?"

If ever there was a time to smirk, it was right then and there. "You said no live *proposals*," I told her, "but you didn't say anything about live *announcements*."

Her eyes popped as wide as saucers and she shook her head. "Kyle, no. Not right now. Not like this."

"Oh, yeah," I said, ignoring her protests. "There's a time

and a place for everything, Val, and right now, right here, is definitely the right time to let the world know the truth."

I ignored her further complaints and put the microphone back to my mouth. "Hey, everyone, hey, can I get you guys to quiet down for a minute? I've got something I want to say before you all leave."

It was amazing how quickly the entire stadium full of people settled down and gave me their full attention. With one last wink Val's direction, I gave the announcement I'd been dying to shout from the rooftops since the moment we became man and wife.

"Four years ago I kicked off the *S is for Sex* tour in this same stadium, and Val and I reconciled right in this very spot." I stamped my foot on the stage for emphasis. "She had me on my knees that night, and it only seems fitting that tonight I do it again."

I dropped to my knees in front of Val and then smiled at the crowd. "Well," I said, "maybe I only need to be on one knee this time."

When I adjusted my position so that I was kneeling on one knee for Val, the crowd thought I was going to propose and they went completely ballistic. They screamed and cheered so loudly that the entire building shook. I had to wait so long for them to calm down that my knee was starting to throb. "Val," I said, once I knew people could hear me again, "I've got something I'd like to ask you."

That, of course, set the audience off again and I had to wait some more. That was okay, though, because I was really enjoying the confused look on Val's face. She couldn't figure out where I was going with this.

"Val?" I said again when I got tired of waiting for the

crowd. They hushed down the second I started speaking. "What I want to ask you is…" I paused, and the entire stadium took a collective breath as they waited for the rest. I grinned again. This was going to be fun. "Can we finally tell the world that we got married last week? I'm tired of waiting to show off my wife."

It took a second for the crowd to understand. There was a moment of silence, and then thousands of gasps, and finally an eruption of cheers that rocked all of L.A. I got to my feet, kissed Val's hand, and then pushed her toward the crowd. "Everybody let me introduce you to my wife, Mrs. Valerie Hamilton!"

I'd screamed it as loud as I could. I think I might have even been more excited than the crowd. "I asked her to marry me last week, and she threw me in the car and dragged me to the courthouse. The woman just couldn't wait to finally get her hands on me," I told the crowd, earning an eye roll from Val. I winked at her.

Val had been worried about the sex thing, so I figured I might as well get it out there now, and on our own terms. "Needless to say, Virgin Val Jensen is no longer a virgin. I made sure of that. Many, many times."

The crowd hooted and hollered and cheered while Val turned pink and slapped my arm. But she was laughing along with me, being a good sport as always.

"So, Val, now that we've finally done it, there's only one thing left to do." I held out my hand and curled my fingers in a "give me" gesture. "Hand it over. I've earned it."

Val knew what I was talking about. She shook her head and laughed as she unclasped the infamous necklace from her neck. "Yes, I suppose you have earned this," she said into the mic as she placed the chain with that little white-gold *V* on it into my hand. In a dry voice she added, "Many, many, many times."

This time, I burst into laughter right along with the crowd. I undid my bracelet and held it up in front of me. "I definitely don't need to wear this anymore, either. I know it's yours, but it's been a good luck charm for me for so long that I'm going to hang on to it. However, I did get you something to replace your necklace. I slipped my bracelet into my pocket and pulled out the necklace I'd bought to replace Val's *V.* It was white gold just like her old necklace, but instead of a *V* charm it had a shiny little *K* dangling from it.

I held it up and watched Val's eyes gloss over. I guess I'd done well. She chewed on her bottom lip as I reached up to clasp it around her neck, and then brushed her hands over the charm when it fell against her chest. "It's beautiful," she said into the microphone, "but what does the *K* stand for?"

The crowed laughed and I pulled her against me. "Kiss me," I said.

I wasn't sure if it was an answer to her question or simply a command, but either way she said "Okay" and slid her arms around my neck.

I was still hyped up on a performance high, and this kiss was going to send me over the edge. It was time to finish this show and get busy enjoying the rest of my night. "I think we need to go out with a bang tonight!" I shouted to the crowd as soon as I broke our kiss. "Shane! We gotta do it, brother! Count it off!"

I glanced back at Shane and he gave me a huge smile, shouting, "One! Two! One, two, three, four!"

She's smokin' hearts with a burnin' flame
She's got a wild side without a name
And when she's riled it's a cryin' shame
Yeay! Yeah! Yeah! I've got it bad
Yeah! Yeah! Yeah! I'm goin' mad...

The audience went crazy when they recognized the intro to "Cryin' Shame." I hadn't performed this song for a crowd since the last time I was on this stage with Val. I'd cut it from my life when she'd cut herself from mine, and now that she was back, it didn't feel right not to sing it. I'd written "Worth Waiting For" for Val, but "Cryin' Shame" always was, and always will be, her song.

Judging by the state of the crowd as I sang, I was going to have to make this my show closer for the rest of the tour.

What can I say? It really is my best song.

CPSIA information can be obtained
at www.ICGtesting.com
Printed in the USA
LVHW04s2305100518
576816LV00001B/138/P

9 780991 457977